Tart of Darkness

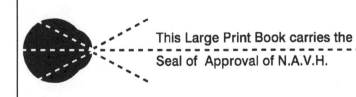

This Large Print Book carries the
Seal of Approval of N.A.V.H.

A CHEF-TO-GO MYSTERY

TART OF DARKNESS

DENISE SWANSON

WHEELER PUBLISHING
A part of Gale, a Cengage Company

GALE
A Cengage Company

Farmington Hills, Mich • San Francisco • New York • Waterville, Maine
Meriden, Conn • Mason, Ohio • Chicago

Copyright © 2018 by Denise Swanson Stybr.

All brand names and product names used in this book are trademarks, registered trademarks, or trade names of their respective holders. Sourcebooks, Inc., is not associated with any product or vendor in this book.

Wheeler Publishing, a part of Gale, a Cengage Company.

Wheeler Publishing Large Print Cozy Mystery.

The text of this Large Print edition is unabridged.

Other aspects of the book may vary from the original edition.

Set in 16 pt. Plantin.

LIBRARY OF CONGRESS CIP DATA ON FILE.
CATALOGUING IN PUBLICATION FOR THIS BOOK
IS AVAILABLE FROM THE LIBRARY OF CONGRESS

ISBN-13: 978-1-4328-5346-4 (softcover)

Published in 2018 by arrangement with Sourcebooks, Inc.

Printed in Mexico
1 2 3 4 5 6 7 22 21 20 19 18

To all the amateur chefs
who dream of opening
their own Chef-to-Go business.

CHAPTER 1

The tantalizing odor of pumpkin spice scented the air as Danielle Sloan watched her neighbor Ivy Drake stuff leftover Halloween cookies into her mouth. Dani had gone a little overboard trying out new recipes for the holiday, and as usual, Ivy had volunteered to handle the excess treats.

Dani was nearly a dozen years older than Ivy, who, having skipped two grades, was an eighteen-year-old junior at the local university. But over the past few months, the two of them had drifted into a sort of big sister/little sister relationship.

Ivy seemed to prefer hanging out with Dani to partying with friends closer to her own age. Most evenings, she ended up in Dani's apartment, chowing down on whatever Dani had cooked that day while they both watched *Cupcake Wars* or *Hell's Kitchen*.

Dani wasn't sure exactly why she enjoyed

having the girl around, but her old psychology professor would probably claim that it was because of Dani's deep-seated desire for siblings. She had begged her parents for brothers and sisters. But all they'd come up with to assuage her only-child loneliness had been a stupid goldfish named — *wait for it* — Goldie.

"What are these?" Ivy interrupted Dani's thoughts, gesturing with one hand to the cookie she was holding in the other.

"Mystic macaroons." Dani eyed the confections critically. "I'm not sure if I should have added the chopped candy corn or not."

"You definitely should. Candy corn is delish and corn's a vegetable, which makes these cookies good for you. It's a win-win," Ivy assured her, then licked her fingers and added, "I'm so glad you quit your job. My roomies and I were dying of starvation before you started cooking for us. The only time we ever got a decent meal was if Uncle Spence took us out to eat, and I was beginning to feel like we were mooching off him too often."

"I'm sure he enjoys the chance to spend time with you," Dani said, squirming until her back rested against the arm of her worn, plaid sofa. "So I hope you still go to supper with him."

She had never met Spencer Drake, but Ivy had mentioned that after retiring from a career in law enforcement in August, her uncle had taken a job as head of the university's security department. Dani pictured him as a lonely, old ex-cop watching reruns of *Law & Order* as he ate his solitary meal off a TV tray.

"Oh, we never turn down a free dinner." Ivy wrinkled her nose. "But your cooking is wicked."

"Thanks." Living in an apartment building full of college kids, Dani was fluent in the native lingo and interpreted Ivy's statement as a compliment. "I'm happy you like it because I'm thrilled to get the food out of my kitchen." She flicked a disapproving glance down at her curvy hips and belly pooch. "Otherwise, I'd eat it all myself." Her shoulders drooped. "It's not as if there's a guy in my life for me to feed."

"You were right to dump Dr. McCreepy." Ivy shot her a sympathetic glance. "You're nobody's side chick."

"Sadly, that's not correct. He might have told me I was his girlfriend, but I was just his fill-in." Dani massaged the back of her neck. Thinking about her ex, Dr. Kipp Newson, always made her tense. "It's hard to believe that I didn't realize he was engaged

9

to someone else. Who would have guessed he'd have two Facebook accounts?"

"Me." Ivy's expression was a mixture of pride and guilt. "I'm sorry I had to be the one to tell you, but I'm not sorry that I checked him out. I knew that loser was up to something when he claimed he worked *every* weekend."

"I figured as the newest doctor hired in the emergency room, he got the worst shifts." Dani defended herself knowing that wasn't the complete truth.

In reality, she had known something was off with her ex, but for once, her father had been proud of her and she didn't want to give up the guy who had finally won her dad's approval. He had been more impressed when she'd introduced him to Kipp than when she'd graduated from college summa cum laude. Her dad was delighted that Dani was dating such a handsome, successful man, and she hadn't wanted to acknowledge that there could possibly be anything wrong with their relationship.

However, in her heart, Dani always believed it was too good to be true. There was no way someone like Kipp Newson would really be interested in someone like her — a less than beautiful, less than thin, corporate drone whose greatest achievement was a perfectly risen soufflé. And all her fantasies about a future with him had shattered when Ivy exposed him as the selfish, heartless, egotistical ass that he was.

Dani had never been able to live up to her father's standards of beauty and charm. In her dad's eyes, she didn't come close to her mother's perfection. But living up to the memory of the gorgeous woman he'd loved and lost at such a young age was an impossible goal for his daughter to meet.

Breaking into Dani's depressing thoughts, Ivy said, "When Dr. Detestable threw such a fit when you posted a picture of the two of you, I knew he was hiding something."

"You're right." Dani swallowed the painful lump in her throat. "And working in human resources, I certainly should have thought to investigate his social media presence more thoroughly."

"Speaking of which . . ." Ivy popped a third, or maybe fourth, cookie in her mouth, then mumbled, "Last week, when you announced that you had turned in your resignation, you never said why you were bailing on your job."

"It's hard to explain." Dani paused, distracted by Ivy's moans of appreciation at the cookie's peanut butter and coconut flavor. Finally, Dani said, "I really didn't have much choice. I had to resign. I was turning into someone I hated."

She paused, thinking about the reason behind the reason — the one she couldn't share with Ivy. Even if she hadn't signed a nondisclosure agreement, she wouldn't have told her young friend about what she'd been forced to do. Although she'd resisted the CEO's directive to dissolve an entire department and sweep a scandal under the rug, in the end, she'd gone ahead and followed orders that she knew were morally wrong — something she'd never allow herself to do again.

"Oh?" Ivy tilted her head. "Who were you turning into that was so bad?"

"A sycophant." Dani spit out the words as if they were covered with slime.

"Huh?" Ivy's confused expression morphed into an accusing glare. "You just made that word up."

"I swear it's a real word." Dani hid her smile. Ivy was brilliant in the sciences, technology, and math, but her vocabulary lagged behind. Searching her mind for a relatable example, Dani said, "It means acting like someone's minion."

"Oh." Ivy nodded sagely. "But how did you know you'd been minionized?"

Dani chuckled, then explained, "It was

pretty damn clear that I was burned out. I mean, what kind of person hears that over the weekend their boss died of a heart attack and their first thought is, 'Gee, I guess we won't be having our usual Monday morning chew-out session after all'?"

"Yeah. Even if the guy was a hater, that was cold." Ivy used her tongue to rescue a crumb from the corner of her lips and frowned. "Which isn't like you at all."

"That's what worried me. At that moment, I knew that if I stayed, I'd only become more and more of a corporate zombie." Dani blew out a breath. "Originally, I'd thought by being in HR, I could make a difference in people's lives. Welcome new employees. Solve problems. Make the company stronger. But that didn't happen."

"Why?" Ivy played with one of the bright-pink wisps of hair scattered among her long, blond strands.

"Probably because I was working for the wrong firm," Dani confessed. "There's so much employee turnover, all I ever got to do was review résumés. After my inappropriate reaction to my boss's death, the more I thought about it, the more I realized that I couldn't stand to read one more stupid response on a job application."

"Like the one you told me about?" Ivy

giggled. "The guy who circled no to the 'Have you ever been arrested?' question, then felt the need to explain?"

"Exactly." Dani rolled her eyes. "He was doing so well until he got to the next question. Who knew a single word like 'why' would trip up someone so badly? If he would have just ignored it. But for some reason, he filled in the blank with 'Never been caught.' "

Both women laughed until they were gasping for air. They were still breathless when the doorbell rang.

"Do you think we were too loud?" Ivy asked, swallowing the last of her giggles. "Mrs. Edwards keeps reminding us of the 'no noise' clause in our lease."

"In an apartment building full of college students, I doubt the manager would consider us her biggest problem." Dani patted her friend on the shoulder, then headed down the hallway.

Dani looked out the peephole and saw a young man dressed in a dark uniform and wearing a baseball cap that read GUARDIAN DELIVERY SERVICE.

Raising her voice, she said, "May I help you?"

"I have a package for Danielle Sloan."

Ivy had followed Dani to the foyer, and

she snickered, "Have you been ordering kitchen stuff from the Food Channel again?"

Dani shook her head, unlocked the dead bolt, and opened the door a few inches.

"You need to sign for it, ma'am." The deliveryman thrust a digital clipboard through the gap.

Dani scrawled her signature, and the guy handed her an envelope with *Confidential* stamped on both sides. Thanking him, she locked up and returned to the sofa.

"What is it?" Ivy stood in front of her, bouncing like she was doing a Tigger imitation.

Having become used to Ivy's extreme nosiness, Dani didn't miss a beat as she answered, "It's from a local law firm."

"Aren't you going to look inside?" Ivy dropped down beside Dani.

"I guess so." Dani's heart was racing.

Was her ex-employer coming after her? She'd kept her part of the bargain. She hadn't said a word to anyone about the real basis for her resignation.

"Then do it before I die of curiosity," Ivy demanded.

Frowning, Dani slid her finger beneath the sealed flap and ripped it open. After a quick scan of the letter on top, she said, "It seems that I've inherited a house and the attorney for the deceased would like to meet with me at my earliest convenience."

Dani's pulse raced. *A house.* She now owned a house!

"What!" Ivy's shrill scream sounded like a teakettle boiling over. "From who?"

"Someone called Geraldine Cook." Dani crinkled her brow, searching her mind for any memory of that name.

"Where's the house at?"

Dani skimmed the next paragraph. "It says that it's in one of the older Normalton neighborhoods and fairly close to the university."

"Which one? Mine?"

"Got me." Dani twitched her shoulders. There was more than one college in Normalton, Illinois, and she was geographically challenged. North, south, east, and west didn't mean a lot to her.

"Why did this Geraldine person leave it to you?" Ivy narrowed her bright-blue eyes.

"I have no idea." Dani finished reading the attorney's letter, then turned to the handwritten note attached to the last page. "Here's a letter from Mrs. Cook."

"What does it say?"

Dani started reading aloud. " 'Dear Danielle: Your grandmother, Kathryn Sloan, and I were both members of Alpha Sigma Alpha sorority. We pledged together and became best friends.' "

"That's the grandma who died when you were really young, right?" Ivy asked.

"Uh-huh." Dani drew her legs up and hugged her knees. "I barely remember her. My parents never talked about her much because of some sort of feud between her and my mom."

"But your mom died nearly fifteen years ago." Ivy wrinkled her forehead. "Didn't your father talk about his mother then?"

"Nope. Dad's a world champion grudge holder and still refuses to discuss Grandma to this day." Dani's lips thinned. "I don't even have a picture of her." Dani's chest tightened. "Maybe I'll find some among Mrs. Cook's possessions."

Ivy got up and started heading for the kitchen, calling over her shoulder, "Why would your grandmother's friend leave you her house?" She came back a few seconds later with a can of Diet Coke in her hand.

Dani shrugged and continued reading from Geraldine Cook's note. " 'Kathryn and I made a promise to look after each other's families.' " Dani swallowed a lump in her throat. She wished Geraldine had contacted her while she was alive. It would have been nice to meet someone who knew her grandmother. " 'I was widowed several years ago and I didn't have children. My closest relative is a third cousin who I haven't heard from in the past ten years, so —.' "

"She left you her fortune!" Ivy screamed.

"I wouldn't go that far." Dani smiled ruefully. "According to the attorney's letter, the place is an old mansion that is currently undergoing an unfinished rehab."

"Why was an elderly lady without any family remodeling a big, old house?" Ivy sank down on the couch. "Was she planning to sell it?"

"The attorney says she was turning it into a bed-and-breakfast. But she got sick before it was completed." Dani picked up the lawyer's letter, then ran her finger down the page stopping when she found the description of the property. "It's a seventeen-room Italianate-style Victorian. Geraldine had completely renovated the top floor where she was living and was in the process of having the five bedrooms on the second level modernized for guests."

"What are you going to do with the place?" Ivy asked.

"Since I only just found out about it, I don't actually have a plan yet." Dani chuckled, then continued thoughtfully, "There are enough hotels and inns around here already. And besides, I'm not too keen on having strangers constantly checking in and out of my home." She blew out a long breath and added, "Plus, there's the taxes and everything. With my savings and investments, I have a fairly decent cushion to tide me over until I find another job, but not enough to support a mansion. Especially one that might take a lot of money to make operational as a B and B. I'll probably just sell it."

"What's left to do on the remodel?" Ivy finally popped open her can of soda and took a long swig.

"It looks as if three of the suites are completely finished. The kitchen has been totally gutted and remodeled and has passed inspection to prepare and serve food," Dani admitted. "That leaves two guest rooms partially renovated and the carriage house, which hasn't been touched."

"So you *could* move into the house and run it while you fix up the rest of it." Ivy pinned Dani with a hard stare.

"Probably."

"But?"

"But it would be a waste of my education." Dani chewed her lip, hearing her father's voice lecturing her about her foolish ideas.

"Have you sent out any résumés?" Ivy pressed.

"Not exactly." Dani didn't meet her friend's eyes. "I was going to do that this afternoon, but then I found this new recipe and . . ."

"And you got distracted," Ivy finished for her, then said, "Maybe, now that you're going to own a place with a fabulous kitchen, instead of looking for a new HR job, you could open your own catering business."

"I need a salary, not a boatload of debt." Dani doused the flicker of interest Ivy's suggestion had stirred up. "Besides, I'm probably not good enough to be a professional chef."

"You are too."

"Even if I have the skills, I'm not sure I'm interested in doing that sort of work."

"Seriously!" Ivy squealed. "You watch cooking shows like sports fans watch football."

"I do not." Dani's cheeks burned.

"You so do." Ivy poked Dani in the arm with her index finger. "You yell stuff like 'That's too much lemon juice, idiot' and 'Are you blind? Those scallops need two more minutes.' "

"I might have done that once." Dani

refused to meet Ivy's stare.

"Once?" Ivy raised a brow, but when Dani remained silent, she shrugged and said, "I better bounce. My homework isn't going to do itself." Grabbing another cookie, Ivy paused with her hand on the doorknob, then chided, "Anyway, I'm just saying that you're an awesome chef."

With Ivy gone, Dani turned on the television. After flipping through a couple hundred channels without finding anything that caught her interest, she shut it off. Staring at the blank screen, she considered her existence.

She closed her eyes and visualized what her life had been like a few months ago. She'd had a well-paying professional position, a handsome boyfriend, and a bright future. Levering herself off the sofa, she started to pace. She had vowed not to think of her ex or her resignation or the fact that she'd turned twenty-nine yesterday.

Thank goodness Ivy and her roommates didn't know about Dani's birthday. If they had, they would have wanted to throw her a party and Dani wasn't in a celebratory mood, especially since her father apparently had forgotten the day his only child was born. He hadn't even sent his usual impersonal greeting card. Or maybe he had remembered but was still angry at her for breaking up with Kipp. It couldn't be because she'd quit her job; she hadn't worked up the courage to tell him about that yet.

What would her dad say if, instead of finding a spot in a new HR department, Dani did as Ivy suggested and started her own company? Cooking had always been her first love. She'd wanted to go to culinary school, but her father had refused to pay for anything other than what he termed a "real degree."

In the silence, Dani heard the loud ticking of the vintage Gilbert wall clock hanging in the apartment's tiny foyer. Suddenly, it sounded as if it were counting off the seconds of her life.

Coming to a full stop, Dani stood frozen. She was twenty-nine freaking years old. It was past time to stop trying to please her father and start living for herself.

CHAPTER 2

Six months later

At the sound of gunfire, Spencer Drake exploded out of bed. Although he'd been out of the business for the past year, after being undercover for so long, his actions were automatic. Jerking open his nightstand drawer, he grabbed his Glock. Eyes scanning for any sign of an intruder, his gaze fell on his cell phone and he realized that the shots were coming from it — which, for some ungodly reason, was playing Pink Floyd's "The Final Cut."

Scooping up the annoying gadget, which he both loved and hated, he squinted at the screen. Why was Ivy calling him at three in the morning? And when had she programmed his phone with that annoying ringtone? She knew he was more of a country music buff than a psychedelic rock fan.

Spencer tapped his niece's picture, then

wedged the phone between his shoulder and ear and grunted, "Yeah?"

"Uncle Spence?" Ivy sounded as if she wasn't sure he was who she had intended to call, and he could hear the loud babble of several excited people talking in the background.

"Yep. Who were you expecting?" Spencer's pulse was still pounding from his rude awakening, but he finally succeeded in pulling on his pants. "You better not have butt dialed me."

"No." His niece's voice wobbled. "Can you . . . uh . . . come over to my apartment?"

"What's wrong?" Spencer's irritation turned to alarm, and he shoved his feet into a pair of motorcycle boots while plucking a T-shirt from the drawer.

"It's not my fault," Ivy said. "I'll explain when you get here."

"Just tell me." Spencer's patience wasn't great at the best of times, but after an evening spent arguing about the sale of their condo with his ex-wife, it was practically nonexistent.

When his ex had called, he knew the discussion wouldn't be pleasant. She'd started the conversation with the words *First of all,* which meant she'd done research,

24

made charts, and was prepared to destroy him.

Not that her viciousness was a surprise. Her wedding dress hadn't even come back from the cleaners before she'd drained their joint bank accounts and run off with his former best friend. Someone really should have warned him that marriage was the mourning after the knot before.

Ivy's cry broke into his thoughts. "Hurry!" A second later, the phone went dead.

Son of a —

Spencer snagged his keys and wallet, sprinted into the garage, and slammed his palm on the button to open the door. Hopping on his Harley, he headed toward Ivy's apartment.

The cloudy sky obscured the moon, but the bright streetlights guided his way down the deserted roads and the roar of his bike masked any other sounds. It was almost as if he were the only person on earth.

Although spring had officially arrived more than a week ago, the temperature hovered in the forties, and Spencer kicked himself for forgetting to grab his jacket. He wasn't used to being shocked awake in the middle of the night anymore, and his brain was still half-asleep.

He made the drive in a record three

minutes and hurried to the building's only elevator. The Up button didn't light when he tapped it, remaining dark even after several pushes. He swore and ran for the stairs. Ivy lived on the fifth floor, and he was panting by the time he burst into the hallway.

The sickly sweet stench of pot, stale beer, and idiocy surrounded him and his scalp prickled. Skidding to a stop, he rubbed his eyes.

In the bright, florescent light of the hallway, several college boys were lined up against the wall. The only things between them and an indecent exposure charge were the NU baseball caps covering their crotches. How the hats were staying in place, he didn't want to know.

Against the opposite wall stood four young women, including Ivy, who had tears streaming down her cheeks and was wringing her hands. Mercifully, the girls were fully clothed because Spencer could do without seeing his niece naked.

Spencer noticed that the corridor was littered with empty cans and discarded clothing. Closing his eyes, he counted to twenty. Ten was not enough in this situation.

When he felt calmer, Spencer opened his lids and spotted a fifty-something woman striding toward him. Her face was nearly purple, and the lines around her mouth were dug in deeper than the furrows in a freshly plowed field.

Meeting her halfway, Spencer identified himself as Ivy's uncle, then asked, "What's going on?"

"Your niece and her roommates' party has gotten out of hand." The woman used the sharp edge of her voice like a chisel. "Unlike those gigantic complexes that use management companies, I run a respectable apartment building."

"Of course you do." Spencer pasted a pleasant expression on his face. "That's why my brother and his wife allowed Ivy to live here." Turning to his niece, he said, "Your parents told you that you had three rules when they agreed to let you move out of the dorms: no drinking, drugs, or hooking up in your apartment."

"Uncle Spence," Ivy sobbed. "Tippi, Starr, and I were at the library studying for next week's finals, and when we got home, there was this gigantic party in our apartment. Kylie was locked in her bedroom with her boyfriend, and we tried to make everyone leave, but they were too drunk or high to listen to us. None of this is our fault."

"The library closes at two." Spencer

27

crossed his arms. "You called me at five after three."

"We thought we could handle it." Ivy scuffed the toe of her sneaker on the brown carpet, sliding a glance at Tippi, whose guilty expression revealed exactly who had been behind that idea. "Then when those guys tore off their clothes and started having dick races in the hall, I knocked on my friend Dani's door for help. But I forgot she'd moved away. Remember I told you about the house she inherited?"

"Uh-huh." Spencer held on to his patience with a firm hand. If he'd learned anything about dealing with his niece, it was that she'd get to the point only after she told the whole story.

"So with Dani gone . . ." Ivy sniffed back a tear.

Although Spencer had never met the woman, Ivy had been telling him about her neighbor Danielle Sloan for the past eight months. At first, he'd thought she was a college student like his niece, but then he realized that Dani had to be close to thirty. He'd wondered about their friendship, but Ivy had said that Dani was the big sister she never had and that she supplied Ivy and her roommates with baked goods and nourishing meals. In his mind, Spencer pictured her as the supporting character in a movie, someone who played the star's best friend.

"Anyway, with Dani gone . . ." Ivy sniffed again and glanced at her friends. Spencer noticed that they stepped backward. "Before we could decide what to do, Mrs. Edwards came running down the hall and threatened to call the police."

From the safety of the wall, Tippi muttered, "And she stopped the elevator so no one could leave."

Although a couple of years older than Ivy, Tippi looked about twelve. When Spencer first met her, he thought she resembled a tiny, dark-haired pixie, but he'd quickly learned that she was often the instigator when his niece and her friends got into any mischief.

"Probably a good thing." Spencer glared at the punks. "I doubt that bunch should be allowed to go anywhere on their own." Turning to the apartment manager, he said, "Mrs. Edwards, if my niece and her room-mates agree to shampoo the hall carpet, pay for any damages, and put a deposit down against any future problems, can we pass on involving the police?"

"Well . . ." Mrs. Edwards looked Spencer over and licked her glossed lips. Spencer briefly wondered if the landlady slept in her makeup, then refocused when she clasped his hand to her chest and said, "I suppose I could do you a personal favor and not call the cops." She turned toward the girls. "But no matter what, I'm terminating your lease and you have to be out of the building by Sunday."

Ivy gasped. "But that's only five days from now! And we have finals starting on Monday."

Mrs. Edwards smirked. "I guess you should have thought of that before you violated the morals clause in your lease."

CHAPTER 3

Probate had finally been settled yesterday morning, and Dani had officially moved into Geraldine Cook's mansion that afternoon. The sensation when the lawyer had handed over the keys was indescribable. She owned a home. As long as she paid the taxes, no one could throw her out. It was the first time she'd ever felt secure.

And today, she could finally examine her new kingdom in detail. With the exception of the two unfinished bedroom suites, the rest of the house was amazing. Dani fell in love with the arched doorways, the perfectly restored front parlor, and the stately library — a spot she planned to spend a lot of time in as she read though all the books on its packed shelves. And her suite on the third floor was the pièce de résistance: the cozy sitting room, spacious bedroom, and huge bathroom were almost too good to believe.

Finishing with the interior, Dani walked

outside. The exterior of the Italianate-style Victorian was in good shape — the tan clapboard and dark-brown, ornate trim freshly painted, the metal and cedar-shingle roof brand-new, and the cupola on top of the house tempting Dani to break out her telescope and star charts. She hadn't been stargazing in years, but her interest was still there.

Unfortunately, before she indulged in any hobbies, she needed to do something about the overgrown weeds and bushes that overwhelmed the front yard. A lawn service wasn't in her budget, but she wasn't sure she could hack through the enchanted forest growing around the mansion by herself. Besides, she was only willing to get sweaty for two activities: one was cooking, and the other certainly wasn't doing yardwork.

Moving on to inspect the carriage house, Dani was disappointed to see that it was pretty much just a huge, empty building. Maybe someday, she'd make the structure into apartments, but for now, she'd use it as her garage.

Suddenly, her stomach started growling, and she checked her cell. Seeing that it was after five o'clock, she let herself in the back door and headed for the refrigerator. She was contemplating what to make for dinner when the doorbell rang.

She hadn't expected to receive her first visitors so soon, but she wasn't too surprised when she opened the door to find Ivy and her posse on her front porch. The girls strolled inside, taking turns hugging Dani, who showed them into the front parlor.

The house's fancy Victorian furniture was a far cry from the comfy old couch and the pair of recliners in Dani's old apartment. The parlor's stiff settee and Eastlake chairs had been designed for a time when young ladies sat with their feet together and their backs straight. The three young women lasted less than five minutes perched on the uncomfortable furniture before sprawling on the brightly colored Persian rug covering the hardwood floor.

"So what brings you to see me instead of studying for finals?" Dani asked.

Ivy squirmed, then spilled the beans about the previous evening's party and the girls' looming eviction from their apartment building.

When Ivy stopped to draw in a breath, Starr said, "Which resulted in the fams freaking out and all getting together today at lunch to hold an 'intervention' with us." Her air quotes were exaggerated. "They told us no more apartments."

"But then I had an awesomely brilliant idea." Ivy flung out her arms. "You don't want to run this place as a B and B, but you need some way to pay the expenses of such a monster house. So you should let us live here."

"No." Dani shook her head vigorously at the girls as they lounged on various throw pillows they'd grabbed from the furniture and scattered on the floor.

"You can't just say no," Ivy whined. "Why not?"

"Yes and no are completely adequate answers to most requests." Dani stared at the weak light filtering through the grimy panes of the fan-shaped transom above the front casements. She really needed to get those washed. Refocusing, she added, "I'm not becoming your landlord."

"Just listen," Ivy pleaded. "If you don't agree to this, we have nowhere to live during finals and our parents will make us live in the dorm for summer school." Then, with disgust dripping from her voice, she added, "The only one with space doesn't have air-conditioning, and the cafeteria food is repulsive."

"Yeah." Tippi Epstein, the tiny brunette on Ivy's right, slumped. "All our parents are real hardcore about no more living on our own."

Three pairs of sad eyes gazed up imploringly at Dani, but she hardened her heart. "As well they should be." She crossed her arms. It took more than a sorrowful expression and some begging to change her mind. "What in the world were you thinking?"

"It was all Kylie's fault." Starr Fleming tossed her head, causing the beads woven into her multiple braids to click together. "When she moved in with us, we told her no booze, drugs, or guys."

"When you wallow with pigs, expect to get dirty." Dani wrinkled her nose. She sounded like an old woman. "Clearly, Kylie didn't listen, and now you all have to pay the price."

"But —" A gust of wind blew through the house, slamming the parlor door closed, and the girls jumped.

Spring had finally tiptoed into Normalton, and the temperature was a pleasant sixty-eight. It was a little cool for open windows, but Dani had been dying to air out her new home. The mansion had been sitting closed up and empty for more than six months, and the mustiness was killing her sinuses.

"But nothing." Dani shook her head. "Underage drinking. Weed. And naked guys chasing half-dressed girls down the hallway."

"Most of them were over twenty-one," Starr argued like the lawyer she hoped to become.

"And the guys had hats strapped over their junk." Ivy giggled.

"Besides, we weren't even home," Tippi added as a closing argument. "That is, not until near the very end."

"As soon as you walked in and saw what was happening, you should have left." Dani ignored their excuses. "You're lucky the apartment manager didn't call 911."

"That uptight, old bag only agreed not to contact the cops because Uncle Spence talked her out of it." Ivy's disapproval hummed like a swarm of bumblebees. "You should have seen her hitting on him."

"Yeah." Tippi frowned. "She was licking her lips like she couldn't wait to take a big bite of his a —"

"I get the picture." Dani's voice held a sharp edge.

"It's a good thing Ivy's uncle is head of campus security." Starr's dark-brown eyes sparkled. "Not to mention attractive, in a mature-man kind of way."

"I'm sure Mr. Drake was thrilled to step in." Dani pictured the poor old guy summoned from his bed at three in the morning.

"Spence was cool," Tippi said, then added, "Well, until he called our parents, that is, and got them so worked up they wanted to move us into a dorm."

Ivy elbowed her friend. "But then, once they heard my awesome idea, our parents all agreed that we could live here with you."

"Why would your parents agree to that?" Dani asked. Although she wasn't ready to admit it quite yet, Ivy had a good point. The upkeep on the mansion was beyond Dani's means, and she hated the idea of operating a B and B where people were continually checking in and out.

Ivy scooted over and laid her head on Dani's leg, crooning, "They said if you agreed to keep an eye on us, then it wou—"

"Whoa." Dani jerked away, causing Ivy's head to bounce off the settee's cushion. "I can't take that kind of responsibility."

"All you have to do is enforce the 'no booze, drugs, or guys upstairs' rule," Tippi wheedled. "And we are totally cool with that."

"We know you could use the money for your new business," Starr coaxed. "We could even pitch in as grunt labor when you needed us."

Starr was right. Dani could definitely use the cash. After turning down several offers for various HR positions, she had finally admitted to herself that she really didn't want to go back to doing that kind of work. And when she'd seen the mansion's restaurant-quality kitchen and found out that it had been remodeled specifically to pass all the inspections and gain the needed permits to prepare and serve food, it had almost seemed like a sign from above that she was meant to cook for a living.

Heck! Even her benefactor's name, Geraldine Cook, had been nudging her in that direction.

Once she had accepted that she wasn't going back to her old job, Dani had spent the months waiting for Mrs. Cook's estate to be settled drawing up a business plan and completing the necessary legal and financial documentation to establish her company. With the details taken care of, Chef-to-Go, a combination of personal chef services, catering, and ready-to-pick-up lunches, had been born.

Now, she gazed speculatively at the three young women waiting for her to speak. Having in-house helpers would be a huge bonus to her fledgling enterprise. She certainly couldn't afford full-time employees. And according to the online courses she'd taken, the availability of reliable workers could make or break a company.

"Come on," Ivy said in a soft, singsong tone. "Our plan is totally solid."

Dani narrowed her eyes. "Exactly how would this work?"

"Mrs. Edwards says we have to be out of our apartment by Sunday, and we're all enrolled in the summer session at school, which starts the week after finals. Which, by the way, we currently have no place to live while we take them," Ivy said. "If you give the okay, our parents will meet with you, then we'll all sign some sort of agreement as to the rules and rent."

"Hmm." Dani thought it over, then said, "I'd also want a clause guaranteeing me a certain number of hours that you all would work for me."

"Bring it on." Starr motioned with her fingers.

"Totally," Tippi agreed.

"No problem," Ivy chimed in, then paused and added, "Oh, I almost forgot. Our parents also want Uncle Spence to check with you every week to see how we're behaving."

Tippi snorted. "Yeah. Can you believe we're almost twenty-one and they think we need not one, but two babysitters?"

"Contrary to popular belief, no one owes you anything. Even your folks have met their obligations once you reach eighteen," Dani pointed out. "You could always refuse."

"Not really." Red flooded Starr's face. "We have three choices. The dorm. You and Spence. Or no more money from our parents."

"Yep." Ivy snickered. "They have us by the checkbook." She shot Tippi a dirty look and added, "And not all of us are close to twenty-one."

"All of us who aren't geniuses," retorted Tippi.

"Whatever." Ivy stuck out her tongue at Tippi, then turned to Dani and said, "But we'd all be thrilled to stay here. We think it would be even better than the apartment."

"My bad." Tippi dipped her chin apologetically. "I'd love to live with you, Dani. I'm just ticked that my parents don't trust me."

"I understand." Dani turned her face to hide her smile. These young women hadn't yet learned that trust had to be earned. "However, I will need to look into the legalities and do some cost analysis to figure out how much rent to charge you."

"At least as much as the dorms." Ivy winked.

"Absolutely." Dani grinned.

She was beginning to get on board with the idea. She already felt like the girls' older sister. She could easily give them their freedom but with the security of rules to keep them safe. And with the added bonus of filling the three finished guest suites on the second floor without resorting to renting them out to strangers.

"You'll give me your words that you'll obey the rules and not sneak around behind my back?" Dani met each girl's eyes.

"APAF!" the trio shouted in unison.

"Huh?" Dani blinked. *What in the heck is an APAF?*

Ivy snickered, then explained, "Absolute promise as friends."

Dani chuckled. "Got it."

Shaking her head, Dani hoped her dealings with Spencer Drake wouldn't be too challenging. From some of Ivy's comments, she thought that the old cop might be a bit of a curmudgeon.

Hmm. Would her new recipe for apple cider crullers win him over? Cops were supposed to love doughnuts, and she'd bet that applied to retired ones too.

Once Dani agreed, the girls immediately called their parents. To seal the deal, Dani made them her newest recipe creation, bruschetta pizza. The whole-wheat crust and balsamic vinegar–infused sauce was a big hit, and as they all worked cleaning up the kitchen, Dani's heart warmed.

Having her young friends live with her was a good idea. It would be too easy to withdraw into this huge mansion. And the last thing Dani wanted was to turn into a bitter recluse like her father, who only left his house for work.

Less than a week later, after meeting with the girls' parents and getting the rules and rent agreements signed, Ivy, Tippi, and Starr had moved in. The young women each had a private suite, which included a bedroom, a sitting area with space for a desk, and a bathroom.

Unfortunately, one of the three finished rooms had a pair of twin beds instead of the kings in the other two, and Tippi had drawn the short straw. This had caused a bit of a rift among the three friends, and Dani hoped Tippi would get over her disappointment before it hurt the girls' friendship.

The girls were allowed full use of the first floor, but unless invited, they were forbidden from entering the third story, which contained Dani's personal living quarters. All meals were provided, and each girl agreed to work up to ten hours a week for Chef-to-Go as part of the rent. Their parents had particularly liked that clause in the contract. And Ivy's mother, who had been a master sergeant in the air force, had announced that KP would straighten out the girls and make them "fly right."

While getting the mansion ready for Ivy, Starr, and Tippi to take up residence, Dani had begun an advertising campaign for her business. She'd already acquired quite a few steady customers for her sack lunches, as well as one couple who had begun hiring her as their personal chef a couple of nights a week. Now, she just needed to get the catering arm of her company off the ground.

A week after her tenants settled in, instead of a visit, Dani received a text from Spencer Drake. He apologized for being unable to stop by to see how the girls were doing and explained that he had been called out of town to testify on a former case. He requested that Dani contact him immediately if she had any concerns regarding Ivy or the other young women.

Dani grinned, then quickly sent him a reply assuring him that she had everything under control. The girls were doing great, and everyone was safe and sound. She wished him good luck in court and crossed her fingers that all their interactions could be conducted quickly and efficiently via text. As long as her boarders remained on the straight and narrow, maybe she wouldn't ever need to have a face-to-face with the ex-cop.

CHAPTER 4

Although it was barely 10:00 a.m., the scent of sautéed peppers and onions drifted through the air. Dani inhaled the tantalizing aroma as she hummed along to "Come Rain or Come Shine," which was playing softly on the kitchen's sound system.

"You'll never guess who is in my differential equations section." Without waiting for Dani to respond, Ivy continued. "Regina Bourne. And she asked me to be in her study group." Ivy beamed as she assembled the Grill Murrays, beef tenderloin sandwiches, destined for the lunch-to-go sacks. "She's the first girl in the history of the Normalton University to be elected homecoming queen three years running."

"Impressive." Dani finished tossing a huge bowl of broccoli-and-cashew salad. "But is she good at math?"

Dani turned toward the enormous pan of seven layer bars and began to cut them into squares. She was glad that Ivy couldn't see her concerned expression. The girl was a brilliant student, double majoring in economics and mathematics, but because she was always the youngest person in her class, she tended to be a tad naive. And Dani had a bad feeling that Regina might be taking advantage of her.

"Hmm. Hard to say," Ivy mumbled around the handful of nuts she'd just thrown into her mouth. "Monday was the first day of class."

"You might want to wait a bit to commit to a study group," Dani cautioned as she finished with the dessert and started packing the lunches in her specially designed red-and-white bags. She offered two lunch choices per day — one indulgent and one healthy. The Grill Murray was the former. "You know, see who might be able to help you as much as you could help them."

"But that's the thing." Ivy crossed to the sink and ran her hands under the tap. "I don't need help with my studies. I need help with my social life, and that's where Regina shines."

"I see." Dani nodded, impressed with her young friend's perceptiveness. She was silent as she packaged the fresh fruit cups and oatmeal carmelitas, then said, "I guess as long as you're both getting something from the relationship, there's no need to worry. But remember that when you follow the masses, sometimes the *m* ends up being silent."

"You are *so* not funny." Ivy threw a broccoli stalk at Dani, then shook out a paper sack before placing the Fowling for U sandwich, a turkey sub with lemon basil hummus and balsamic onions, inside. "How many of each are we making?"

"Twenty-five healthy and forty indulgent." Dani stifled a yawn. They'd started cooking at 6:00 a.m. She checked the time. Fifteen more minutes and the customers would start stopping by for the to-go lunches. "I've noticed that we run nearly two to one."

"Not that your cooking isn't totally worth it, but I'm a little shocked that students are willing to pay ten ninety-five," Ivy commented.

"A fast-food lunch costs seven or eight bucks." Dani opened the massive refrigerator and added the final batch of filled lunch sacks to the shelves. "And even my indulgent selection is way better for you than greasy fries and burgers."

"Definitely." Ivy nodded vigorously. "It's awesome that you have the perfect location here. The house is midway between most of the student apartments and the NU campus."

"And your idea to distribute flyers in those apartments was brilliant." Dani grinned. "Especially since I had three serfs, I mean employees, to slide them under each and every door."

Ivy hopped off her stool and stretched. "I'd better get into the shower if I'm going to make my noon AMALI class."

"Amali?" Dani asked. The summer session had only started yesterday and she wasn't familiar with all the girls' courses yet.

"Asian, Middle Eastern, African, Latin American, or Indigenous cultures," Ivy explained. "NU's attempt at providing a politically correct, diverse education. Three hours are required for graduation."

"What did you pick?" Dani tilted her head. Ivy wasn't fond of studying anything that wasn't related to math or business and usually tried to wiggle out of what she called "breathing for credit" courses.

"The only one that seemed even a tiny bit relevant to my future career was Japanese communicative strategies, so I took that."

"Sounds fun," Dani teased.

"I'm sure it'll be fascinating," Ivy said dryly. "But on the bright side, the professors who teach stuff like this are so afraid of hurting our itty-bitty self-concepts that they grade really easy and no one gets below a C. Which means as long as I sit in back, I can catch a nap if it gets too boring." Ivy wiggled her fingers in farewell and dashed out of the kitchen.

Dani smiled and shook her head. Having Ivy, Tippi, and Starr as boarders wasn't anywhere near as problematic as she'd feared. The three college girls were good kids, and she had to admit their rent eased a lot of her worry about starting a business versus taking one of the HR jobs that she'd been offered.

Between inheriting Mrs. Cook's property and the girl's payments, the amount she'd needed to borrow to start the company had been cut in half. She truly was fortunate.

Dani had found a picture of Geraldine Cook that appeared to have been taken ten or fifteen years prior to her death. In the photo, the seventyish woman was seated in the sidecar of a red motorcycle wearing a bright-pink helmet tied on with a black, fringed silk scarf and clutching a huge tapestry bag in her lap. Although not exactly Dani's image of a person who would create a chef's dream of a kitchen, Mrs. Cook did seem like the kind of person who fully embraced life.

Running her hand lovingly across the four-sided stainless island that contained two commercial stoves, a griddle, a broiler, a salamander, sink, pot filler, and a built-in ice container all integrated in the counter-top, she still wondered why Mrs. Cook had thought she needed such a lavish setup to serve breakfasts. Oh well. She wasn't about to look a gift benefactress in the mouth.

Dani patted the island affectionately. She was so lucky to have a space versatile enough to use for all three parts of her company. Simultaneously handling the trio of businesses was going to be tough, but the mansion's setup made it a lot less stressful.

The kitchen was spacious enough to prep all the food she would need for her catering gigs, and with the addition of the pass-through window that she'd had installed near the back door, it made selling the sack lunches a snap.

And the restaurant-sized refrigerator was a dream come true for storing the perishables she needed for her personal chef services.

Dani hummed her satisfaction as she began to clean up the mess she and Ivy had left behind in their haste to get the lunches ready. She was placing the last dirty bowl into the dishwasher when a bell chimed to indicate that her first customer had arrived.

Sliding open the window, Dani smiled at one of her regulars and said, "Good morning, Abby. Today, we have the Fowling for U, a turkey sub, fresh fruit, and an oatmeal carmelita."

Abby Goodman had told Dani that she was finishing her sophomore year at NU and struggled to find healthy eating options on campus. From her unhappy manner, it seemed she was struggling with more than her quest to find nutritious food.

"Sounds yummy." Abby's mouth tilted up briefly, then she wrinkled her brow and asked, "How many carbs in the dessert?"

Dani glanced at the printed list taped to the wall and said, "About thirty grams."

"Sugar?"

"Close to eleven grams."

Initially, Dani had been surprised at the questions her patrons had asked her about carbs, calories, and fats, but now she was prepared.

"That's acceptable." Abby tapped her credit card on the machine attached to the narrow shelf. Taking the red-and-white-striped paper sack, she waved and said, "See you tomorrow."

Marveling at the girl's willpower, Dani

51

watched the young woman hop onto her bike and head toward the university. Abby routinely refused any part of the meal that didn't meet her nutritional goals. The gorgeous college coed was already model-thin. Apparently, she intended to stay that way.

When the serving window swished open next, Dani's eyes watered and she blinked back tears. It was another of her frequent flyers, a guy that Dani had nicknamed Smokey. He always stank of cigarettes, stale sweat, and beer. Dani hadn't been surprised that he ordered the indulgent meals versus the nutritious ones. Healthy habits didn't seem to be high on this student's priority list.

It was a little after two by the time Dani sold the last lunch-to-go and finished prepping for the following day. Her boarders' supper was in the slow cooker, and she didn't have to be at the Karneses' until six o'clock to begin her personal chef duties. The university professor and his plastic surgeon wife liked to eat at seven thirty, and even with the two additional guests they'd added at the last minute, it wouldn't take her more than ninety minutes to cook their dinner.

Because the university's summer classes were three to four hours long and each course required more study time than a semester-long class, Ivy, Tippi, and Starr were gone most of the day. This meant that the house was empty, and she intended to enjoy the solitude.

Yawning, Dani rubbed her tired eyes. This past month, she'd really been pushing herself and she was bone tired. But she couldn't let up now. Not when the business was still in its infancy. She just needed a long bubble bath and maybe a power nap. Then she'd get her second wind and be ready to feed the picky professor and his snooty wife.

Climbing the stairs to the third floor, Dani admired Mrs. Cook's taste. Her grandmother's friend had possessed an excellent eye for both form and function. Unlike the antiques in the first-floor rooms, the well-appointed owner's quarters contained beautiful yet comfortable furniture. And the spa-like bathroom was straight out of HGTV.

While the claw-foot tub filled, Dani grabbed her MP3 player from the bedside table and Mrs. Cook's journal, then stripped off her clothes. Sinking into the hot water, she felt her muscles relax.

The first time Dani had met with Mrs. Cook's lawyer, he had handed her a stack of books. There was a note rubber banded to the covers, and in beautiful copperplate handwriting, Mrs. Cook had asked Dani to read her diaries. Mrs. Cook had started journaling when she entered college, and Dani's grandmother Kathryn was mentioned on nearly every page.

Dani had been going through the books for the past six months and was currently reading the year in which her mother and father had gotten married. Evidently, Dani's mother and grandmother had been at odds from the very beginning.

Mrs. Cook had recorded a conversation she'd had with Dani's grandmother. Apparently, Kathryn had found the perfect dress and showed it to Dani's mom, Jenna. A week later, Jenna had called Kathryn and told her that she couldn't wear the dress because her own mother was wearing one just like it.

Mrs. Cook had been surprised that Kathryn didn't argue and readily agreed to get a new gown. Mrs. Cook had asked her friend if she was returning the original dress since she wouldn't have any other occasion to wear something that fancy, but Kathryn had laughed and said of course not, I'm wearing it to the rehearsal dinner.

It had taken Mrs. Cook a moment to realize that the dinner was the night before the wedding, which meant Jenna's mother would be wearing the same dress the day after Kathryn had already been seen in it.

Putting aside the diary, Dani laid her head back and laughed. How she wished the unsinkable Kathryn Sloan was still around.

Sometime later, Dani blinked awake. Shivering, she jumped out of the tub. The water was ice cold. How long had she been sleeping? She quickly dried off, dashed into the bedroom, and grabbed her watch from the dresser.

Shit! She'd been in the bathtub for nearly three hours. No wonder she was chilled, not to mention her skin was as wrinkled as the used tissue paper from the bottom of a gift bag. It was a miracle she hadn't slid below the surface and drowned.

She could see the headline now. *Chef-to-Go owner commits suicide. Details at ten.* Wouldn't that be a great way for her father to find out she was no longer gainfully employed at Homestead Insurance?

As Dani hurried to get ready for the Karneses' dinner party, she thought about her dad. She really needed to update him on her current situation. During her Thanksgiving visit home, she'd tried to tell him about the mansion and her idea to open her own company, but when she brought

55

up her grandmother, he'd shut her down.

She'd planned to explain everything at Christmas, but he'd texted her December 23 to say he was flying to China on business and would try to see her at Easter. He'd avoided spending that holiday with her as well. She wanted to give him her news face-to-face, but at this rate, she should probably just send him an email.

Pulling on black chef pants and her signature red chef coat, Dani slid her feet into comfortable nonslip shoes and ran into the bathroom. Leaning close to the oval mirror on the wall above the vanity, she flashed a quick glance at her long, dark-blond hair, then twisted it into a high bun and used gel to make sure the sides were smooth with no threat of flyaway strands getting into the food.

Dani glanced at the watch she'd attached to her belt loop. Five thirty. No time for makeup. Barely time to load the supplies in her van and make it to the Karneses' before her clients started texting her.

Fortunately, Dr. and Dr. Karnes only lived a few miles away. Dani sped through the busy side streets, then drove into an affluent neighborhood filled with large houses on lushly landscaped lots. A couple more turns and she passed through an open gate into a secluded cul-de-sac. Suddenly the homes went from upscale to lavish. Three-car garages turned into four or five. Properties doubled and tripled in size. And square footage quadrupled.

Dani pulled into the first driveway on the right and glanced at the dashboard clock. It was six on the dot. She gathered up as much food and equipment as she could carry, followed the sidewalk to the rear of the faux castle, and rang the bell.

Several minutes later, Chelsea Karnes, dressed in a thick terry robe and wearing a towel around her head, flung open the back door and announced, "Our guests need to catch an early fight tomorrow morning, so you'll have to serve dinner at seven instead of seven thirty."

Without waiting for a response, the slender woman led Dani through a mudroom lined with shelves, cubbies, and a long bench that stretched across the entire back wall. As Dani followed her employer, she quickly reviewed the menu, hoping that she would be able to make the new deadline.

The asparagus and parmesan puff appetizers were ready to pop in the oven. The cantaloupe, prosciutto, and arugula salad just needed a drizzle of olive oil, salt, and pepper. And she could whip up the halibut bourguignon with minted new potatoes in less than forty-five minutes.

Dessert was the tricky part. Because the chestnut tart was best served right out of the oven, the only thing Dani had prepped for it was the side of ginger ice cream. She would need to work on it quickly while her clients were eating and pray it would be done in time.

Entering the kitchen, Chelsea glanced over her shoulder and said, "I have to get dressed. The Bournes will be here in thirty minutes. We'll have drinks on the patio first, but appetizers need to be on the table in less than an hour."

"Then I better get cracking." Dani remained expressionless as the woman marched away, then scowled and hurried back out to the van to carry in the rest of the supplies. She needed to get a couple of carts so she could load the whole shebang onto them at once and avoid multiple trips.

When Dani had her supplies inside, she turned on the double ovens to preheat, then stowed the perishables in the huge stainless steel refrigerator. Checking the walk-in pantry, Dani was happy to see that the Karneses had followed her request and stocked the shelves with the staples she needed.

With the exception of the Keurig and the microwave, neither the professor nor the doctor appeared to use anything in the gourmet kitchen, and the first time Dani had cooked for them, the pantry was as bare as Mother Hubbard's cupboard. At least now they had the basics — flour, sugar, vinegar, oil, chicken broth, rice, pasta, and some canned goods.

Although Dani couldn't understand how people like Chelsea and Trent Karnes could live without acquiring the basic skills necessary to feed themselves, she was grateful they did because that meant more clients for her. Shaking her head, she started making the crust for the chestnut tarte.

Twenty minutes later, the doorbell played the first few bars of Beethoven's fifth symphony and Dani heard Chelsea and Trent greet their guests. The first time Dani had cooked for the Karneses, Trent had just acquired his new toy and had explained to her how the programmable chime worked. Now, with each subsequent visit, she tried to guess which song would be playing. So far, she had a perfect score of zero.

After some initial chitchat, there was the clink of ice cubes. Seconds later, the sound of the patio door opening preceded their voices fading as they stepped outside.

Setting the timer, Dani slid the asparagus and parmesan puffs into the oven, and at precisely 6:58 p.m., she removed the baking sheet. She arranged three of the steaming appetizers on each of four small glass dishes and carried them into the dining room.

The Karneses and their guests were just sitting down as she approached the imposing dark-maple table with its shiny chrome pedestal base. The two couples barely glanced at her as she slid their plates in front of them.

Dani served course after course, her rubber-soled shoes silent on the travertine floors. Beyond an occasional thank-you, no one spoke to her. Feeling almost invisible, she overheard snatches of conversation and from what she could piece together, the Karneses' guests, Anson and Honoria Bourne, were leaving for their annual ten-week cruise. Throughout dinner, the two couples discussed the various ports and traded travel stories.

At eight thirty, when Dani entered the dining room with the chestnut tart, Chelsea leaned toward Honoria and said, "Of course, we would be happy to look in from time to time on Regina." Chelsea raised an elegant brow at her husband, then continued, "Wouldn't we, darling?"

"Certainly." Trent bared his teeth in what was probably supposed to be a smile.

Trent Karnes was an attractive man in his midforties. He was tall and slender, with aristocratic features and a perfectly groomed beard and mustache.

"It's a shame she isn't in any of your classes this session." Honoria stirred cream into her coffee. She had the sleek, well-bred appearance of a greyhound. "If she had one of your courses, you'd see her several times a week."

"My baby girl loved the class she took from you last semester." Anson's voice was a bit loud, and Dani noticed his nose was red and the buttons on his Armani dress shirt gaped open over his paunch.

"Yes." Trent's expression was frozen. "It's too bad the timing is off."

"I'm sure she'll want to take another with you." Honoria continued to stir her coffee.

"Well." Trent drained his wineglass. "Regina may not have room in her schedule with all the required courses. For her, mine are electives."

Dani wrinkled her brow. The whole exchange sounded off in some way. Like their words had an entirely different meaning than what she was hearing. And why did the name *Regina* sound familiar?

After serving the tart, Dani asked if they needed anything else. No one had any requests, so she retreated to the kitchen. While she packed her equipment, she repeated the name *Regina* over and over again. Finally, it came to her. Regina Bourne was the girl who had invited Ivy to join her study group. Apparently, as well as being beautiful and popular, she also had extremely wealthy parents. Was Ivy prepared to become a part of that type of crowd?

Shrugging off her concern, Dani began to clean up the mess. An hour later, Dani was putting away the last pan when she heard the Bournes leave. She gave the counter one final wipe, then went in search of the Karneses.

Dani found them drinking brandy in the professor's study. She knocked on the partially opened door and said, "I hope dinner was okay."

"Come on in." Trent smiled. "The food was delicious as always. Thank you for serving it earlier than we'd scheduled."

"Glad I could do it." Dani entered the room, pulled her phone from her pants pocket, and held it out. "Everything is spic and span, so if you'd like to settle the bill, I'll take off."

Trent reached into his pocket, pulled out

his wallet, flipped it open, and scowled. "Hell! I forgot. My new credit cards haven't arrived yet."

"Good thing I have separate charge accounts. I'll get my purse." Chelsea got up. "Be right back."

"What happened?" Dani frowned at Trent. "Did you lose your wallet?"

"No. I was the victim of identity theft."

"How did you find out about it?" Dani asked.

"My bank called because our checking account was overdrawn." Trent sighed. "But it should have contained several thousand dollars. When we looked into it, we found the trail."

Before Dani could inquire further, Chelsea returned and handed over her American Express. Once the transaction was completed, Dani wished the couple good night and headed home.

As she drove down the dark streets, she thought about the Karneses. The idea of someone stealing her identity was terrifying. Maybe she should find out how much a protection service would cost. The last thing she needed was that kind of trouble.

CHAPTER 5

The rest of the week and weekend flew by, and the text from Spencer Drake on Monday caught Dani by surprise. Once again, he apologized for being unable to stop by in person to check on Ivy and the other girls. His ex-wife had finally agreed to sell their condo, so he needed to travel to Chicago and sign some papers before she changed her mind.

Dani sent Spencer a message assuring him that Ivy, Tippi, and Starr were all behaving, wished him luck on the real estate deal, and returned to her latest project. A gardening club had asked her to provide a trio of desserts for their annual flower walk at the end of July. Today she was experimenting with a new recipe for that event, a chocolate-espresso dacquoise.

The cake — made with layers of almond and hazelnut meringue, buttercream, and ganache — was exceedingly complicated and labor intensive, but Dani hoped that if she impressed the club members, the ladies would keep her in mind for their personal catering needs as well.

Dani was grinding almonds, hazelnuts, cornstarch, and salt together in the food processor when the back door banged opened. She jumped back, fearing that a gang of culinary thieves was breaking in to steal her beloved Henckels knives, but before she could grab the pepper spray from her purse, Ivy burst into the kitchen.

Gasping for breath, she said, "Regina wants to talk to you."

"Okay." Dani stretched out the word, waiting for her heart to return to its normal rhythm. "But I have to warn you both: math wasn't my best subject."

Smacking Dani's shoulder, Ivy said, "Don't tease." She glanced at the dirty bowls and pans covering the stainless steel island and added, "She'll be here any minute."

Ivy had been peppering Dani with stories about her new BFF, Regina Bourne. According to Ivy, Regina was nothing less than a combination of Gisele Bündchen, Mother Teresa, and Albert Einstein (although admittedly without much of his mathematical talent). However, much to Ivy's dismay, the supermodel/saint/genius hadn't seemed interested in a relationship beyond their study group. Maybe now that was about to change.

"I'm in the middle of a complicated dessert that I'm trying out for the garden club event." Dani added a half cup of sugar to the nut mixture and hit the Pulse button on the food processor. "We'll have to chat while I work."

"I don't know why you try out recipes and waste your time and the ingredients before you make them for your clients," Ivy said.

"Because recipes and the people on internet dating sites have a lot in common." Dani grinned. "They never end up looking quite like their posted pictures."

Ivy made a face, then said, "Maybe you should clean up a little."

"Princess Regina will have to take it or leave it if she wants to talk to me today."

"At least put on your chef jacket," Ivy begged, twisting her hands.

"Absolutely not." Dani wiped the sweat from her face with a paper towel and threw it into the trash. It might be pleasantly warm outside, but inside the kitchen, with the ovens going, it was hot as Hades. "The laundry charges me three bucks to wash and starch each one of those suckers."

"How about fixing your hair?" Ivy pleaded. "You look like you're trying out for the role of Jane Eyre."

"My hair is fine." Dani caught a glimpse of herself in the window of the microwave. "*Glamour* put tight buns on their 'do' list this year."

"They also said that cat-ear headbands were in style." Ivy blew a raspberry at her. "You going to wear those too?"

As Dani opened her mouth to defend her style choices, there were several sharp raps on the door. A second round of knocking instantly followed the first volley.

Ivy squeaked, then hurried over, flung open the door, and fawned. "Regina, come on in. Did you have any trouble finding the place?"

"Duh, no," a feminine voice mocked. "My Jag does have a GPS."

"Right. Sure. Of course." Ivy's giggle was forced. "Anyway. Regina, this is my friend Dani Sloan."

Dani finished adding cream of tartar to the egg whites in the mixing bowl, then turned to greet Ivy's friend and was struck speechless. The rest of the room faded away as the stunning young woman stood illuminated in the bright sunlight spilling in the window. Even with a sneer on her face, the girl was absolutely gorgeous.

If Dani had seen her image in a photograph, she would have sworn it was airbrushed. Regina's long hair was so blond it was nearly silver. Her incredible eyes were so blue Dani wondered if they were colored contacts. And her sun-kissed skin was so creamy it appeared to be flawless. Either the girl had the best hair stylist, optometrist, and makeup artist in the world, or she was just that exquisite.

Wiping her hands on her apron, Dani schooled her expression and said, "Hello. I understand you want to speak to me. I'm afraid that I can't stop what I'm doing, but if you don't mind talking while I cook, have a seat and go ahead." Dani gestured to the stools lining the island. "Would you like something to drink?"

"An iced skinny mocha, no whip." Regina perched her tiny, designer-jean-covered derriere on the stool, opened her bubblegum-pink Hermès Birkin purse, and dug out a tube of Dior lipstick.

Dani opened her mouth to limit her beverage offer to water or soda, but Ivy scurried over to the coffeemaker and said, "It'll be ready in a sec."

Did her new Ninja Coffee Bar make those kinds of drinks? The machine had been a housewarming gift from her boarders' parents, and Dani hadn't had time to explore all its capabilities yet.

The only sound in the kitchen as Dani added sugar to the eggs and cream of tartar was the hiss of the coffeemaker. Pushing the mixer's speed control lever to high, she kept an eye on the bowl's contents as she turned to Regina and waited.

After a few moments of trying to stare down Dani, Regina finished applying her lipstick, inhaled, and said, "Do I smell hazelnut?"

"And almond." Dani smiled. "I'm making a chocolate-espresso dacquoise."

"Ah." Regina adjusted the engagement ring on her left hand, making sure Dani got a good look at the huge diamond, and said, "I had that in Dax, when my parents and I were touring the south of France." She lifted a perfectly groomed eyebrow. "Of course, an American chef could never hope to meet that type of standard, but I must say yours smells divine."

"Thank you." Dani managed to resist the urge to roll her eyes at the girl's pretentiousness.

"Ivy tells me you're a caterer."

"That's one part of my Chef-to-Go business." Dani nodded. "Are you planning a party?"

"My annual SummerPalooza bash." Regina curled her lip. "My regular caterer canceled on me at the last minute and it's this coming Saturday." Her voice was heavy with importance. "Otherwise, I wouldn't dream of using someone without references."

"I see." Dani hid her amusement at the young woman's patronizing attitude. "I'm flattered you're willing to give me a chance, but four days is too short notice even for a nobody like me."

"Dani!" Ivy yelped, abandoning her barista duties to dart over and tug on Dani's hand. "Can I speak to you in private for a moment?"

The panic in Ivy's eyes was the only thing that kept Dani from refusing and kicking Regina out of her kitchen. Turning off the mixer, she followed the girl out into the hallway and crossed her arms. "What?"

"Please, please, please cater Regina's bash." Ivy's hands were clasped as if in prayer. "If you do it, she says that I can go."

"Do you really want to attend a party where you aren't truly welcome?"

"Hell yes!" Ivy screamed, then slapped her palm over her mouth. "An invitation to one of Regina's events is like a golden ticket to Willy Wonka's chocolate factory. I'll meet all the right people. Maybe even get to network myself into a good internship."

"I doubt that the CEOs of the companies you're interested in will be at something called SummerPalooza."

"Maybe not," Ivy said. "But their sons and daughters will be."

"Do you know how many are on the guest list?" Dani asked, weakening.

"Regina likes to keep it intimate, so she limits it to a hundred."

"A hundred guests are an intimate gathering?" Dani snorted. "What kind of menu is she thinking about? I'm guessing something complicated?"

"Not really." Ivy stared at her feet. "It's a Polynesian theme."

"I'm not roasting a whole pig in the ground." Dani crossed her arms again.

"That's fine."

"The only way I could do it is if you, Tippi, and Starr give me a lot of time this coming week," Dani warned. "Like double your normal hours. Will Tippi and Starr be on board with that?"

"Absolutely. Regina said they could come too." Ivy threw her arms around Dani and squeezed. "Thank you! Thank you! Thank you!"

"Don't thank me yet." A shiver of dread ran up Dani's spine as she imagined working for an entitled, patronizing girl like Regina. "There's a lot that could go wrong. And if it does, I bet Regina won't be pleased."

"I know you." Ivy tugged her back into the kitchen. "It'll be perfect."

Planning the luau menu had been more fun than Dani wanted to admit, although Regina's constant micromanaging had been a challenge. The girl reminded her of star fruit. It looked pretty, but it didn't bring much else to the platter.

However, with the countdown to the party dwindling, Dani had the upper hand and, for the most part, Regina grudgingly backed off from most of her demands. Dani had refused to wear a hula skirt or a muumuu but had agreed to Hawaiian shirts for her staff. Tippi, Starr, and Ivy would serve appetizers for the first hour, but once the buffet opened, they would change out of the garish floral blouses into their own tops and could mingle with the other guests.

Now that the big day had arrived and Dani steered her van between two brick columns and onto the private road leading to Regina Bourne's home, her stomach fluttered. She ignored the excited chattering of Tippi, Ivy, and Starr, instead running the pre-party to-do list through her head. This event was her first big catering gig and could very well make or break that part of her business. At least, make it or break it with the high-end consumers in this part of town.

Following Regina's instructions, Dani turned onto an offshoot of the main driveway that led toward the rear entrance of the imposing brick house. Ivy was the first one out of the van, and she ran up to the back steps while the rest of them were still exiting the vehicle.

Before she could ring the bell, the door swung open and a sweet-faced woman in her late sixties or early seventies skimmed Ivy's bright-turquoise-and-yellow flowered shirt and said, "Hello. You must be with the catering company." She glanced over Ivy's shoulder and beamed at Dani and the others. "Oh my. You all are right on time. My name's Mrs. Carnet and I keep house for the Bournes. Can I help you carry anything?"

Dani walked up beside Ivy and introduced herself, then said, "Thank you, but if you could just direct us to the kitchen, we're good."

They loaded supplies onto the four rolling carts Dani had purchased a few days ago, then followed the housekeeper down a hall and into a huge kitchen. As Regina had promised, the massive Sub-Zero refrigerator was empty, and Dani's crew quickly stowed the perishables on the waiting shelves, then made several more trips for all the other food and equipment.

Once they had everything inside, and Dani had tucked away the tray of desserts that Regina had requested be reserved for her private consumption, she turned to Mrs. Carnet, gestured to a pair of French doors, and said, "I take it those lead to the backyard."

"Yes." The housekeeper twisted her fingers in her apron and added, "Miss Regina is out there with the men putting out the tables and chairs."

A local party rental company was handling the setup, and Dani was anxious to see how things were arranged and to make any necessary tweaks. Instructing her crew to start prepping the appetizers, Dani rushed outside.

Dani took a few hurried steps onto the tiled patio and came to an abrupt halt. The stunning view of Hawthorne Lake was mesmerizing and she had to tear her gaze away from the dock bobbing on the beautiful blue water. Looking around, she realized that the Bournes' enormous property was more like a resort than a backyard.

There was an in-ground pool, a fire pit surrounded by gorgeous slate tile, and a multilevel deck that meandered around the house, garage, and hot tub. As Dani finished gaping at the luxurious surroundings, she noticed the luau decorations and rolled her eyes.

Regina must have purchased or rented every inflatable palm tree, thatched umbrella cover, and tiki hut bar in Normalton's city limits. There was enough netting, fake starfish, and plastic parrots to furnish a Hawaiian village. Not to mention the dozens and dozens of bamboo tiki torches scattered throughout the party area.

Although Dani thought the decor was way overdone, it wasn't her problem. She had been hired to provide the food, not the atmosphere. Glancing to her right, she saw Regina supervising two men attaching raffia skirts to several long tables set end to end in the middle of the open area. Dani shaded her eyes and mentally calculated the number of chafing dishes and bowls that the buffet could hold.

Regina spotted Dani and waved her over. "Are you all ready to go?"

"Yes." Dani nodded, then added, "As I mentioned, my servers aren't old enough to handle liquor. But as per your request, I made two hundred lime, coconut, and rum Jell-O shots this morning. If you'll come with me, I'd like to deliver them to you. And we'll need a witness."

Yesterday, when Regina had stopped by Dani's house to add the shots to the catering contract, Dani had checked her identification. Once she'd been assured that the girl was twenty-one, Dani had outlined her conditions for making the drinks, which would ensure that she would not be held responsible if underage kids happened to get ahold of some of them.

"Fine." Regina tossed her long, blond hair and trailed Dani through the kitchen, where she ordered Mrs. Carnet to follow them. The three women marched out the door to where the Chef-to-Go van was parked.

After placing four insulated chests containing ice and fifty shots each on a wheeled cart, Dani handed Regina an agreement stating that the client would assume responsibility and serve the drinks only to guests over twenty-one.

Regina scribbled her name, thrust the sheet of paper at Mrs. Carnet to add her signature as a witness, then tossed it at Dani, who carefully attached the rider to the original contract. As Dani locked the file in the glove compartment, Regina instructed Mrs. Carnet to take the boxes into the pool house and store them in that refrigerator.

Once the housekeeper had hurried away, Regina walked with Dani into the kitchen and, after looking at the wall clock, said, "The bartenders should be here any second. Mrs. C will take care of them. I'm heading upstairs to change. When my guests begin showing up, I expect you and your crew all to be out there serving the appetizers."

"Certainly." Dani turned to Ivy, Starr, and Tippi. "Okay, girls. Let's get ready for battle."

At first, people drifted in twos and threes, each selecting a lei from a table strategically stationed near the backyard's gated entrance. But soon, larger and larger groups arrived and the flowered garlands began to be tossed out into the crowd like beads at Mardi Gras.

By the time the appetizers of grilled sweet potato fingers with curry dip, mini Polynesian chicken salad sandwiches, and shrimp-

and-coconut nachos were eaten, and Dani opened the buffet, the place was full of people. Dani sent Ivy, Tippi, and Starr to change out of their work clothes and prepared to handle the hungry hoards by herself.

Between the conversations and the Hawaiian music, the noise level was earsplitting. Dani had asked Regina if there would be any problems with the neighbors and Regina had said that most of the owners of the houses nearest to the Bournes were away on vacation. Dani had briefly wondered if Regina chose the SummerPalooza date because of their absence, or if the neighbors booked their trips in anticipation of her party.

As the first few waves of people hit the buffet line, Dani kept a close eye on the food. She saw that the side dishes and the sweet-and-sour pork were holding up well, but the barbecued steak was disappearing much faster than she'd estimated. Good thing she had another fifty rib eyes marinating inside.

Dani hurried into the kitchen to grab the plastic bins of meat from the refrigerator. After putting the steaks on the nearby grills, she returned to her spot behind the buffet.

It seemed as if most of the party's attendees were more acquaintances of Regina than real friends. However, every single guest approached Regina to pay their respects. It was almost like a scene from a *Godfather* movie. The young men and women did everything but kiss the large engagement ring on their hostess's left hand.

When the feeding frenzy finally died down, Dani had a chance to study the guests, recognizing a few of her lunch-to-go regulars. Some attendees looked as if they weren't sure if they were thrilled or scared out of their mind to be there.

One of Dani's customers, a muscular young man who had informed her he was the star pitcher on the college's baseball team, had his arm around a cute brunette wearing a bright-pink bikini top. He shouted over the music to a guy busy pawing his own date, "Damn straight, I'm good in bed."

His buddy snorted and roared, "Yeah. You can stay there all day."

The girls both giggled and Dani turned her attention to Regina's inner circle. For the past week, Ivy had been chattering about them, and Dani was curious to see them for herself.

Regina's clique had claimed the table nearest the buffet and thanks to Ivy's briefing, Dani could identify them all. The young man Dani understood to be Regina's fiancé, Laz Hunter, was tall, dark, and drunk. He'd turned his handsome nose up at Dani's carefully prepared cuisine and had been silently pounding Jell-O shots since he sat down.

Bliss Armstrong, a tiny redhead with a dusting of cute freckles across her nose, was Regina's BFF. She picked at her food and seemed bored. Bliss's boyfriend, Vance King, was one of NU's starting football players. According to Ivy, rumor had it that he was hoping to make the NFL draft but probably wasn't quite good enough. Although Vance had filled his plate three times, he was also knocking back bottles of beer as if he owned stock in Anheuser-Busch.

Dani wrinkled her brow as she observed Vance's repeated attempts to pull Regina away from the group. Granted, the girl was beyond beautiful and only wearing a coconut shell bra and bikini bottom covered by a short grass skirt, but had Dani misunderstood Ivy as to who was dating whom?

Shrugging, Dani turned her attention to clearing the empty chafing dishes and bowls. The college crowd's love life wasn't her problem; the party's desserts were.

After a few trips back and forth to the

kitchen, Dani was putting down the last trays of banana-coconut upside-down cake and dark chocolate truffle tarts when Vance spotted the sweets. He and Regina had been whispering a few feet away, but he grabbed her hand and pulled her toward the food.

As he lumbered drunkenly toward the cake, he stumbled against one of the bamboo torches that Regina had insisted bracket the buffet. The torch snapped in half and fell across the tabletop. The fuel canister's lit wick touched the raffia skirt, which burst into flames.

Dani's pulse raced, and for an instant, she froze as the dried grass fiber blazed. Then instinct kicked in and she dropped to her knees. Searching under the table for the fire extinguisher she kept handy anytime she used Sterno to keep the food in her chafing dishes warm, she nearly cried in relief when her fingers brushed the metal canister.

Yelling for everyone to stay back, Dani held her breath and sprayed the flames until the foam ran out. Shakily, she put the extinguisher down and sucked air into her starving lungs.

Before she could catch her breath, Regina marched up to her and demanded, "Clear off this table, and get new trays of desserts out here right now."

Dani blinked. She'd been expecting Regina to thank her, not issue impossible orders. "I beg your pardon?" Drawing on her HR experience to help keep her cool, she calmly said, "I can bring out the selection that you asked me to put aside for you."

"Absolutely not."

"All the other desserts were on the buffet. There are no more."

"You don't have any backups?" Regina screeched. "What kind of incompetent moron are you?"

"The kind who just saved your party from going up in an inferno."

"You . . . you . . ." Regina waved her hands in the air as if she were signaling a jet to land.

One of the bartenders passing by with a tray of Jell-O shots stepped up to Regina and asked, "Are you okay, miss?"

"Of course I'm not okay, you idiot." Regina snatched the tray from his hands and dumped the contents over Dani's head.

Shocked, Dani stiffened, then grabbed a napkin and wiped her face. Turning back to Regina, she said, "That does it. I'm out of here."

Regina stomped her foot and screamed, "If you don't come up with a hundred servings of dessert, I'll ruin you. You'll never get another catering gig."

Ivy, Tippi, and Starr rushed to Dani's side and began to help load equipment onto a cart.

Regina jerked her away from the others and said, "I should have known that a loser like you would hook me up with a worthless company." Regina sneered, "Stick to math, because you certainly will never be anything but a nerd who the popular girls use to pass their courses."

"But . . ." Tears pooled in Ivy's eyes. "I thought we were friends."

"In your dreams."

Ivy swallowed a sob and ran for the exit. Tippi, Starr, and Dani quickly followed. The last thing Dani heard as she shut the van's door and drove away was Elvis singing "Blue Hawaii."

CHAPTER 6

After the horrible way her first big catering gig had ended, Dani took Sunday off, attending church and going to brunch with some of the other parishioners. And by Monday, she was almost able to put the SummerPalooza disaster behind her.

Still, Dani had been tempted to skip making the lunch-to-go sacks. But she knew her regulars had already started depending on her for a nutritious midday meal and the idea of letting them down had forced Dani out of bed.

Chatting with her satisfied lunch customers had lifted Dani's spirits. Several of her clients who had been at the luau told Dani that her food had been the best part of the party, and by the afternoon, her usual optimistic mood had returned and she resumed her quest to find the perfect trio of desserts for the garden club's event.

Now, stepping back from the stainless

steel countertop, she sighed contentedly. After spending seven years working in a career to please her father, she was finally doing what she wanted to do, cook. No more routine. No more mountains of useless documents. No more suits and heels.

Yes, she had to keep records of expenses, have clients sign contracts, and complete various tax forms. However, all of that was for her own business — not simply to comply with a busywork mandate from a faceless CEO.

Smiling, Dani refocused on her next project and picked up the recipe for her latest culinary experiment. With her boarders sprawled around the kitchen table doing homework, she was about to try her hand at a croquembouche. The tower entirely constructed of cream-filled puff pastries and decorated with caramel and spun sugar was complicated to construct but would evoke a sense of elegance and sophistication.

The chocolate-espresso dacquoise that she'd already put on the menu represented decadence and guilty pleasures. If the croquembouche was a success, she'd have to find a third dish that epitomized sunshine and innocent delights. However, the trick was that it couldn't be something so down-to-earth and easy to make that the club members would feel like they could bake it themselves.

As Dani waited for the water, butter, salt, and sugar to come to a rolling boil, she pondered the possibilities for the remaining dessert of the threesome. Maybe a selection of tea cakes. No! Macarons. Their perfectly smooth and shiny shell was bright and inviting, but the cookies were anything but simple to produce. She vowed to spend the evening browsing the internet for the ultimate recipe.

Refocusing on her current project, Dani spent the next hour working on the dough for the croquembouche. She had finished piping the *pâte à choux* onto the parchment-lined baking sheets and was brushing the pastry puffs with egg wash when the kitchen's silence was interrupted by the doorbell's clamorous ring.

Unable to stop what she was doing, Dani glanced at Ivy, Tippi, and Starr and called out, "Can one of you see who that is?" All three girls were engrossed in their textbooks, and when the bell rang three more times in rapid succession, none of them even looked up. Dani raised her voice and repeated, "Can someone get that?"

"What?" Ivy frowned, then when the bell rang again, she said, "Oh, sure." Jumping to her feet, she darted into the hall, calling over her shoulder, "Maybe it's Uncle Spence. He said he'd try to stop by this afternoon or evening."

Dani had just popped the completed trays in the oven when a sour-looking middle-age man entered the kitchen with Ivy hard on his heels.

"Sir." Ivy tried to grab his arm, but he flicked off her hand as if it were a piece of lint. Her face reddened and she said, "I asked you to wait in the parlor. No one is allowed back here."

The man's unblinking, cold, gray eyes skimmed the messy counter, and his lips pressed together in a disapproving, thin, white line.

"Ivy, get back." Dani hastily snatched a rolling pin from the counter, moved around the island to block the intruder's path, and said, "Who are you and what do you want?"

"Danielle Sloan?" the man barked, seemingly unimpressed with her weapon.

"Yes." Dani wasn't sure why she answered instead of smacking him upside the head. "If you're here on business, please call for an appointment."

The guy grunted and pointed to the seated girls. "Tippi Epstein and Starr Fleming." When they nodded, he turned toward Ivy and said, "Ivy Drake I presume?"

He skirted around Dani and headed to the table, walking as if each step was preordained and nothing short of Armageddon would stop him from reaching his intended goal. With his emaciated torso, jerky movements, and cruel expression, the man resembled a Halloween skeleton. Was he some mentally ill homeless guy who had wandered up to the house by accident? But he was awfully clean and dressed really nice for someone living on the streets. And if he were here by chance, how did he know their names?

"You need to get out of here right now or I'll call the police." Dani motioned with her chin to Tippi and Starr, signaling them to keep their distance from the man. He was starting to frighten her. She gestured to the back door. "Leave."

The man ignored Dani and pinned Tippi and Starr with his gaze. "You two stay put."

Alarmed, Dani glanced back at Ivy. She seemed frozen, and Dani said sharply, "Call 911."

As Ivy frantically patted her pockets looking for her cell phone, the man declared, "You were all at the Bourne party yesterday."

When he scowled, for just a half second,

his features seemed familiar, but Dani couldn't place him. Had she met this guy before?

When no one responded, a sneer twisted his gaunt features, and he enunciated each word, "You. Were. All. At. The. Bourne. Party. Yesterday. Correct?"

"Yes." What in the world did this creep want? To cover her panic, Dani put on her best don't-mess-with-me expression, the one she'd perfected working in HR, and asked, "What's it to you?"

"I'm Detective Mikeloff."

That would explain the suit and tie, but not his bad attitude.

"May I see some identification, please?" Dani asked, not sure she believed him.

Mikeloff reached into the inside pocket of his jacket and retrieved a shiny leather wallet. He flipped it open, displaying a police ID card on one side and a gold badge on the other.

Ivy stopped searching for her phone and peered over the man's shoulder. She gazed at the identification, then shot a worried glance at Dani. What had they done to merit a visit from Normalton's finest? Were they in some kind of trouble?

"Satisfied?" Detective Mikeloff said, a challenge in his voice. When Dani nodded, he closed the leather folder, returned it to his pocket, and stated, "I understand your company" — he pulled out a notebook and consulted it — "Chef-to-Go, catered Regina Bourne's party on Saturday."

"That's correct," Dani answered carefully. Had Regina accused them of something?

"How well do you know Ms. Bourne?"

"Not very." Dani shrugged. "I met her for the first time when she hired me. Why?"

Detective Mikeloff ignored Dani's question. "But you did work with her closely this past week? And had several arguments with her?"

"Regina had some requests that weren't possible to fulfill on such short notice." Dani's stomach clenched. Had one of the guests got caught drinking underage? Knowing Regina, she'd point the finger at Dani's Jell-O shots. "Why are you asking me about her? Did something happen after we left her party?"

"What would make you think that?" Detective Mikeloff's tone implied that Dani was guilty of something. "Do you have a reason to think there would be a problem?"

"Well." Dani figured he already knew about the fire. No doubt someone who had been at the luau had been happy to tell Detective Mikeloff all about the incident.

"There was an accident with the tiki torches earlier."

"At which time" — he consulted his notepad — "you saved the day using a fire extinguisher that you just *happened* to have handy." Mikeloff looked like a malevolent raven, particularly when he tipped his head and narrowed his beady eyes. "But Miss Bourne wasn't as grateful as you expected, was she?"

"Are you implying that I somehow conspired with the young man who tripped?" Dani's head had begun to pound. "Why would I do that?"

"Perhaps to look like everyone's savior?" Mikeloff's expression reminded Dani of the Big Bad Wolf after he ate Red Riding Hood's grandmother. "It had to be infuriating that instead of fawning over you, Miss Bourne demanded you produce another round of desserts."

"That's ridiculous." Dani smoothed her apron, wishing she was dressed for her previous job rather than her current one. Although she hadn't enjoyed wearing them every day, there was just something about a suit and heels that commanded respect. "I would never endanger people's lives like that. And it's absolutely normal protocol for caterers to carry a fire extinguisher when open flames are involved. I'd be violating my insurance policy if I didn't have one with me." She shoved her hands into her jeans pockets so the detective wouldn't see them shaking. "Why would I care about appearing to be a hero?"

"Let's see." Detective Mikeloff tapped his lantern-like jaw with a bony finger. "Perhaps because you lost your high-paying job. And instead of getting a new one, you went into debt in order to open some weird hybrid business. Seems to me you were seeking a benefactor. Someone who would recommend you to all her rich friends."

"First," Dani said, in her stop-screwing-around-with-me voice, "I did not lose my job. I made a decision to leave and tendered my resignation. Second, Chef-to-Go isn't weird, it's creative."

"But you *are* in debt."

Dani opened her mouth to defend her business plan, then crossed her arms. If she had learned anything from her last job, it was never to miss a good opportunity to shut the heck up.

"Nothing to say?" Mikeloff gloated.

"I'm finished talking until you tell me what this is all about."

"We can do this at the police station if you prefer." Detective Mikeloff glared at her, then added, "And I mean all four of you."

"Fine." Dani refused to back down. "I'll call my attorney and have her meet us there."

"And I'll call my uncle." Ivy moved so that she was shoulder to shoulder with Dani. "He's the head of campus security."

"Guess I better call my mom." Tippi joined them. "She's a judge."

"Well, shoot." Starr stood up. "My father's only the thoracic surgeon that saved the mayor's life, but he'll want to know what's going on too."

Minutes went by as Detective Mikeloff stared at the four women, and when they didn't break the growing silence, he blew out an angry breath. "Regina Bourne was found dead yesterday afternoon."

"No!" Dani had been prepared for something bad, but not that.

As she tried to come to terms with the fact that someone she had spoken to less than twenty-four hours ago was no longer alive, Mikeloff turned to Ivy and dropped another bombshell. "I understand Miss Bourne said some nasty things to you before you left her party. What were you doing back at her house later that night?"

"What?" Dani gaped at her friend. "You

told me you were going to the library."

"I went there, but as I was studying, I reached for my locket, and when it wasn't around my neck, I remembered that I had left it in Regina's kitchen," Ivy explained. "The chain broke while we were prepping the appetizers and I put it on the windowsill. I went back to get it."

"At one in the morning?" Detective Mikeloff jeered. "Why not just text Miss Bourne and ask her to bring the thing to class?"

"I didn't want to take a chance on it getting lost." Ivy's cheeks reddened. "My first boyfriend gave it to me and he died in a car crash our senior year."

"So when Miss Bourne refused to let you in the house, you must have been angry." Detective Mikeloff checked his notebook. "I understand she had Lazarus Hunter escort you off her property."

"Yes, I was sort of mad." Ivy put her hands on her hips. "But when Laz walked me to my car, he promised to find the necklace and bring it to me. He said he'd text me to get a time that we could meet up."

"Really?" Detective Mikeloff's eyebrows rose. "Funny he didn't mention that."

"That's —" Ivy started, but Tippi clamped her hand across Ivy's mouth.

"She won't be making any further statements without an attorney present."

"Which is your right." Detective Mikeloff jotted something on his pad. "But don't think this is finished. You're on my radar."

Dani took a relieved breath. She really should have had Ivy phone her uncle as soon as she heard Regina was dead. Thank goodness Tippi was prelaw and came from a family full of lawyers.

Still berating herself for her lack of judgment, Dani startled when the detective whirled on her and said, "You used to work at Homestead Insurance."

"Yes." Dani already knew he'd been checking up on her, but why was he bringing up her previous employer? "As I mentioned, I quit many, many months ago."

"But not before you figured out a way to ruin someone's life?" His nostrils flared. "Or did you get the cash you saved the company under the table?"

Suddenly Dani was even more worried than she had been when she thought Mikeloff was mentally ill. Was the detective referring to the incident that had been the tipping point in her decision to quit? She'd eliminated an entire division specializing in the most difficult claims.

A woman involved in a particularly complicated case had come forward with proof that the three men working in that department had been threatening her with sexual assault to get her to drop her appeal. They hadn't touched her but had been calling at all times of the day and night, taken pictures of her through her bedroom window, and put a profile featuring her on an online hookup site.

Homestead's CEO was so anxious to cover up what had happened, he had offered the victim twice the total amount of her already substantial claim and promised to fire the men without severance. All she had to do was agree to let the matter drop without bringing in the authorities.

Dani had been assigned to handle the dismissals. Everyone involved, including Dani, had signed a confidentiality agreement. The lack of explanation had made it appear that Dani was a coldhearted witch who, without any justification, had demolished an entire department, depriving the employees of any compensation.

Still, she was surprised at the detective's acrimony and hurriedly said, "I assure you that I didn't receive any money for any of my actions on behalf of Homestead."

"Are you telling me that you quit a high-paying job to cook for people for no good reason?" Detective Mikeloff's pupils dilated.

"I've learned that money is a crummy way of keeping score, and I did have a good reason." Dani stepped back. When had the detective moved so close? "Although it might not be one you would understand."

"Are you suggesting that I'm stupid?" His fist came down hard on the stainless steel surface of the island, and a large bottle of vanilla extract fell over and broke.

Dani jumped as the dark liquid splashed on the front of her T-shirt. "No. It's just difficult to explain why I quit." She hurried to clean up the broken glass and oozing liquid. "Heck. I haven't even told my father yet. But cooking makes me happy. My HR job, not so much."

"I see." Detective Mikeloff seemed to be appeased by Dani's apprehension and he squared his shoulders. "You're just a Martha Stewart wannabe."

"It took me a while to see that a high salary and corporate success aren't everything." Dani knew it sounded corny, but it was the truth. "Providing nourishment for people's stomachs and their souls is a lot more important. Food doesn't ask you to make difficult decisions between right and wrong. It just asks you to enjoy."

Detective Mikeloff snorted, then lobbed another grenade. "Is that why you killed Regina Bourne? She got in the way of your plans to feed the world?"

"No!" Dani yelped, her knees started shaking. "You're saying Regina was murdered?"

"Don't act so surprised." His tone was harsh. "Why else would I be here?"

"But how —" Dani controlled her voice with an effort. "I mean . . ."

Tippi released Ivy and clamped her hand across Dani's mouth. "Either you tell us the whole story, or Dani's not saying another word until she speaks to her lawyer."

"You're going to hide behind the skirts of a college girl?" Detective Mikeloff's stare frosted with resentment. When Dani nodded, he unclenched his teeth and said, "I'm sure the old biddy who called the ambulance for the vic has already talked to the newspapers . . ." The detective trailed off, then as if some switch had been thrown in his brain, his eyes took on a disturbing gleam, and with an air of professionalism that had been absent up until now, he stated, "Miss Bourne was found in a lounge chair by her pool. It appears that sometime between noon and one on Sunday, she'd had an orgy with the leftovers from her party, as well as several boxes of snack cakes, then passed out. When the housekeeper couldn't revive

Miss Bourne, she called 911, and Miss Bourne was pronounced dead shortly after her arrival at the hospital."

"Although that's awful, how do you know it was murder?" Dani bit her lip. "Couldn't it have been natural causes?"

"Anytime someone as young as Miss Bourne dies without being under a doctor's care, an autopsy is performed," Detective Mikeloff snapped.

"Oh." Dani blinked.

"Especially since while the housekeeper was waiting for the ambulance, she found a syringe on the driveway. She gave it to one of the paramedics and traces of insulin were found. With that information, and the assurance of the housekeeper that Miss Bourne was not diabetic, the medical examiner was asked to make Miss Bourne's autopsy a priority." He flipped several pages in his notebook, and when he found what he was looking for, he read, "The ME performed a serum C-peptide analysis that showed an inappropriate ratio of insulin and C-peptide molecule concentration. When there is a large disparity between serum insulin versus C-peptide concentration, insulin OD is suspected unless another physiological pathology like an insulin-producing tumor is found. There was no such pathology, which led the ME to the conclusion that nothing except a deliberate act could have resulted in such an extraordinarily high insulin level."

"Oh," Dani murmured again. She was surprised that after the detective's initial reluctance to share information he was telling her so much, but she was happy for the change. Still, her last hope that this was all a mistake was fading when she suddenly realized that there might be a way of clearing herself and the girls. She brightened and said, "If you have the syringe, you can take our fingerprints, and when they don't match, you'll realize we're innocent."

"When the housekeeper found the syringe, it was dirty. She wiped it clean before handing it over." Mikeloff gritted his teeth. "The only prints on it were the paramedic's."

"Crap!" Dani groaned.

"So" — Detective Mikeloff glanced from Dani to Ivy — "which one of you shot Miss Bourne full of insulin?" His predatory eyes studied each of them for another long moment. And when neither of them spoke, he threatened, "It will be easy to discover if either of you are diabetic or has a close association with someone who is."

"That really doesn't matter." Starr put her hands on her hips. "You don't need a prescription for insulin or syringes, so everyone has access."

"Did your daddy the doctor tell you that?" The detective's pasty complexion turned an ugly purple.

Dani wrinkled her brow. What was up with this guy? It was almost as if he wanted her or Ivy to be the guilty party.

"I worked in a pharmacy when I was in high school," Starr answered calmly.

Beads of sweat formed on Dani's upper lip as she struggled not to show her panic. Mrs. Cook had been diabetic and when her possessions had been turned over to Dani, she disposed of several vials of insulin and packages of needles. If the detective found out, would that make Dani the prime suspect?

A flashback of her one and only visit to a police station nearly paralyzed her. She'd been seventeen, hanging out in the park with a bunch of friends when several of the guys had gotten into a fight. The police had arrived and hauled them all to the station to sort things out. Her father refused to come to the station, and with too much imagination for her own good, Dani had been terrified that the cops would never let her leave. What if Detective Mikeloff made that nightmare come true?

Ignoring the sharp pain behind her right eye, Dani lifted her chin and, with as much conviction as she could muster, said, "Neither Ivy nor I have any reason for wanting Regina dead. I barely knew the girl, and Ivy certainly wouldn't kill over a few nasty words or an inexpensive necklace."

"I've seen murder committed for a lot less," Detective Mikeloff sneered.

"Do you know when the insulin was given to her?" Dani asked.

"Not at this time." Something flickered in the detective's eyes and Dani wondered what he wasn't saying.

"Fu—" she stopped herself. She had given up using the f-bomb when she'd agreed to have the girls live with her. "Crap!" Dani substituted the lesser curse for her expletive of choice. She'd been hoping she and Ivy could provide him with an alibi. On to plan B. If only she had one.

"Look, let's make this easy for all of us. You don't want your friend to get in trouble because of something you did." He looked between Ivy and Dani. "Just tell me what happened." Sincerity oozed from his voice. "Juries are suckers for crimes of passion. With a good lawyer, you'll probably only get a few years in minimum security."

Dani forced herself to quit hyperventilating and think. If Mikeloff could make a case against either of them, he would have already taken her or Ivy into custody. He was trying to trick them into confessing, but he really didn't have any bait to put in his trap.

"The scenario you paint would be great, if either of us were guilty, but we didn't do it." Dani crossed her arms and leaned a hip nonchalantly against the island. "So, unless you're ready to arrest either of us, get out of my kitchen."

"Who do you think you are?" Detective Mikeloff's expression darkened. "You can't order me around."

"I apologize. I didn't mean it that way." Dani backed up, putting more space between them. She was increasingly convinced that something wasn't right with the man. His slinky was definitely kinked and that made him dangerous. Frightened, she asked, "Uh, don't police officers usually travel in pairs? Where's your partner?"

"I sent him on an errand." Mikeloff moved toward her. "I wanted to do this by myself."

His smile sent a chill up her back, and she was about to grab the girls and make a run for it when she heard someone ringing the bell and beating on the front door.

When Starr took a step toward the hall,

Detective Mikeloff threw out his arms and growled, "Ignore that. No one is interfering with this investigation."

"Too late." Ivy tossed her hair. "I texted my uncle Spence that you're harassing us. That's probably him at the door. And when he finds out you've been mean to us, he'll kick your butt so far into the stratosphere even Google won't be able to find it."

For a long moment, Mikeloff stared at Dani, his eyes glittering with malevolence, then he snarled, "You haven't heard the last of this. This time, you'll pay for your sins." He whirled around and marched to the back door, muttering as he went, "You may have had all the power at Homestead, but now I'm in charge."

As soon as he stepped out the door, Tippi ran over and locked it behind him. They all took huge gulps of air, breathing as though they'd been deprived of oxygen for a week. The banging from the front of the house continued, but Dani and the others sank to the floor, unable to move.

Ivy gasped, "I should see if that's Uncle Spence." But when she tried to stand, her legs wouldn't support her.

Dani said, "We'll go get him in a minute. Just concentrate on breathing for a few seconds."

During Dani's years working in HR, she'd developed a way of compartmentalizing her feelings. It had been such an emotionally charged atmosphere that the defense mechanism was the only way to survive situations in which her actions — actions she didn't always agree with — affected so many people's lives.

It had been tough at first, but with practice, she'd learned to box off her feelings quickly, and now, within a few moments, Dani's mind cleared.

What had Mikeloff meant about paying for her sins and having all the power? Did it have anything to do with why his features seemed familiar? But who did he resemble? It had to be someone from Homestead.

Mentally, she flipped through her coworkers and all the personnel and potential employees with whom she'd interacted. Most were in their twenties or thirties, so she tried to imagine a younger Mikeloff, but there was still only the slightest flicker of recognition.

Did the detective have a relative who worked at Homestead or had applied for a position there? Had Dani done something that caused that person to lose their job or not be hired? If so, she, and maybe Ivy by her association with her, could be in big trouble.

The clearly unhinged detective would need no other reason than payback for concentrating all his efforts in trying to prove Dani had murdered Regina.

CHAPTER 7

Spencer had spent most of the day with his boss, the university vice president in charge of safety and security. It had taken them all morning and into the afternoon, but they had finalized the campus's new severe weather response strategy. After the tornadoes that had ripped through Illinois last August, the college administration had been determined to update their old plan.

Once he had checked in via phone with his on-duty security officers and been assured that the campus was quiet, Spencer had shed his suit jacket and decided to walk over to see his niece. The Cook Mansion was less than two miles from the vice president's office and the early June temperature was an ideal seventy-eight degrees. Central Illinois wasn't blessed with enough perfect weather days to waste this one inside the cab of a truck, and his motorcycle was in the shop for a tune-up.

Spencer had been strolling down the narrow sidewalk a couple of blocks from the mansion enjoying the warm breeze whispering through the leaves of the hedge maple trees when he'd gotten Ivy's text: Crazy cop harassing us. He's scary. Help!

Wishing he had on his sneakers rather than his dress shoes, Spencer had broken into a dead run. He'd kept a careful eye out for cracked paving slabs, leaping over the buckled concrete. The last thing he needed was to fall. He'd had a bad feeling that seconds mattered.

His niece's message had screamed in his head as he ran, and by the time he reached the mansion's front step, adrenaline was surging through his veins. His heart thudded louder and louder as he pounded on the door and rang the bell. All the while, hundreds of possible scenarios raced through his mind, none of them reassuring.

Several long minutes went by, and when no one answered, Spencer tried the knob. Finding the dead bolt engaged, he resumed hammering on the heavy oak door. Given enough time, and the right tools, he could get almost any lock open, but he didn't have either.

With every thump of his hand against the wood, Spencer grew more and more agitated. Deciding to try around the rear of the mansion before resorting to plan B — break a window to get inside — he stepped off the porch.

As Spencer started down the sidewalk, Ivy rushed out of the house and shouted, "Uncle Spence!" He turned toward her and she ran to him, flinging her arms around his neck. "This man forced his way in here and he turned out to be a city cop, but he was really mean and Regina Bourne is dead and Dani and I are suspects."

Spencer patted his niece's shoulder as he sorted through her run-on sentence. Any way you looked at it, what she'd said was bad news.

Ivy finally stopped for a breath and Spencer asked, "Is the officer gone now?"

"Yes." Ivy's head went up and down as if it were on a spring. "He tried to make us confess, but Dani said if he had enough evidence to arrest us he should do it. Then he got really mad and I thought he was going to hit her, but when you showed up, he went out the back."

"Funny that I didn't see him come down the driveway." Spencer's stomach knotted. "And there wasn't a police vehicle parked anywhere in sight. I would have noticed even an unmarked cruiser."

"He must have left his car on another block and walked through the neighbors' yards." Ivy clutched Spencer's hand. "But why would he do that?"

"Good question." Spencer's neck muscles tensed. Something wasn't right.

As Ivy led him into the house, she related the rest of their encounter with Detective Mikeloff. Spencer grew angrier and more concerned with each word. A cold sweat glued his dress shirt to his back. Mikeloff sounded like the worst kind of cop. One with no respect for the rules and totally out of control.

Entering the kitchen, Spencer spotted Ivy's pals Tippi and Starr sitting at the table. Both were staring off into space. Tippi's normally fair skin was ghostly white and Starr's darker complexion had a definite gray tinge to it. They were as shaken as his niece. What in the hell had the detective done to scare them so badly?

He inhaled sharply and his senses were flooded with the yeasty scent of homemade bread. For some reason the cozy aroma made him even more upset. Fuming, Spencer looked around. Where was Danielle Sloan? She was supposed to be keeping these girls safe, but they'd been threatened while under her care.

Okay. That wasn't fair. From what Ivy had told him, he knew that none of what had happened was the Sloan woman's fault, but his gut hadn't gotten the message. Maybe it was for the best that he had a few minutes to calm down before talking to her. He didn't want to scare her.

Ivy tugged him to an empty chair and said, "Have a seat. Dani will be down in a minute." When he raised a questioning brow, Ivy explained, "Once I looked out the window and saw that it was you on the porch, I told Dani it was okay to go upstairs to change. That awful man broke a huge bottle of expensive vanilla and it splattered all over her shirt."

That explained the second wonderful smell in the air. Spencer allowed the memory of his mother's amazing baking to soothe him. She'd had warm-from-the-oven treats waiting for him every single day after school. One of the worst parts about his undercover assignment had been being unable to see his parents for months on end.

He hadn't realized how much he missed his family until he'd met Wally Boyd. The Scumble River police chief had been kidnapped by the motorcycle gang that Spencer had infiltrated. Hearing the man talk about his pregnant wife, Skye, and seeing the love between them had been the final nudge in Spencer's decision to quit his job and never go undercover again.

Spencer was still smiling from the memory when he heard footsteps behind him. He turned to greet his niece's landlady, but when his gaze locked onto the warm, caramel eyes looking back at him, all thoughts of Wally and Skye fled and a sizzle shot up his spine.

Ivy hadn't mentioned that her friend was so pretty. Maybe some idiots wouldn't consider her appealing, but Spencer thought she was stunning. The naturalness of her beauty was like a cold glass of water after being forced to drink nothing but artificially flavored soda his whole life.

The years of fake boobs, bleached-blond hair, and heavy makeup on the women who hung around the motorcycle gang made him appreciate Dani's genuineness. And as she stared at him, Spencer felt a spark jump between them. Tearing his gaze away, he called on every bit of his training to keep what he was feeling off his face. Instead, he shrouded himself in his cop persona and kept his reaction under wraps.

Danielle Sloan wasn't at all what he'd pictured. Her dark-blond curls bounced as she moved and her creamy skin had turned an adorable pink on her rounded cheeks. She wore faded jeans that clung to every delectable curve and her soft-yellow T-shirt lovingly cupped her breasts.

The last thing Spencer wanted was the flicker of attraction warming his chest, but he wasn't sure how to douse the ember. Still, he needed to put out that flame, because after his disastrous marriage and acrimonious divorce, he'd vowed to stay away from women. Especially ones that made his heart beat faster. He'd been fooled before and would never be as trusting again.

He winced as he recalled the whirlwind affair that had led to him marrying a woman he barely knew. Because he'd trusted her and foolishly thought that she wanted a home and to start a family as he did, he'd put her name on everything. Six years later, he was still trying to untangle their lives, not to mention recover financially from her duplicity. It would be a long, long time before he was ready to try a relationship again, so any attraction to Ivy's friend was a moot point.

Shoving away any lingering temptation, Spencer stood, held out his hand, and said, "Spencer Drake. You must be Danielle Sloan."

As if coming out of a daze, she sucked in

a shaky breath, then said, "Nice to meet you." Her expression held a strange mixture of strength and vulnerability as she added, "Call me Dani."

"Well, Dani." Spencer reluctantly let go of her soft fingers. "I understand you had an unwelcome visitor. Ivy's told me what happened, but I'd like to hear your version of the incident."

"Why is that?" Dani's demeanor changed and her sweet voice became guarded.

"Because I'm going to check into the detective that interviewed you, and I'd like to have all the facts before doing so."

"The thin blue line, right?" Dani's shoulders tensed. "Ivy mentioned that you're a retired police officer." She looked him up and down. "Although you seem a little young to be collecting a pension."

"True. I recently left my position in law enforcement," Spencer said carefully. "But as you pointed out, I wasn't old enough to retire. And while I support my fellow officers and the good work they do, I would never cover up for one who has gone rogue."

The only person who knew exactly who Spencer had worked for or the nature of his previous job was his boss, the university vice president. And even she only knew a part of the truth. He had helped put away too many outlaw bikers to be safe. If it ever became common knowledge that he had been the Tin Man, a member of the infamous Satan's Posse, the gang would descend on Normalton like an invading army. And they wouldn't leave until he was dead.

When he'd come out from undercover, the story had been circulated that the Tin Man had been shanked in prison and died. There was even a small marker on an empty grave in the penitentiary cemetery to prove he was six feet under. And it was best for everyone concerned that Tin Man was never resurrected.

"I see." Dani crossed her arms, clearly not really believing that he wouldn't take a cop's side against hers. "Would you care for something to drink? I could sure use some caffeine."

"You have to try Dani's special blend of tea, Uncle Spence." Ivy pulled him back into the chair next to her. "It's absolutely scrumptious."

Starr grinned, her teeth gleaming whitely against her light-brown skin. "Especially with her homemade honey-roasted peanut butter sandwich cookies."

"Or her special mocha cupcakes," Tippi added, bringing her small, pink-tipped fingers to her mouth and kissing them.

"They're to die for."

"Tea would be great." Spencer smiled at his niece and her friends, then glanced over at Dani, who was putting a kettle on the stove. "But I still want you to walk me through the detective's visit."

"If you feel it's really necessary." Dani's lips thinned, but she nodded her head.

Once they all were settled at the table munching on treats, Dani recounted her experience with the detective. Then after taking a sip of tea, she said, "That's when you arrived and he stormed out the back door."

Spencer looked around at the faces of his niece and her friends and prodded, "He didn't say anything else? Any reason he might be targeting Ivy or Dani?"

"I'm definitely an afterthought," Ivy said thoughtfully. "I think he sees me as more of a way to control Dani than a serious suspect."

"Why do you say that?" Spencer asked. Was his niece in denial?

Ivy finished her cupcake, licked her fingers, and said, "He shouted something at Dani like, 'This time, you'll pay for your sins.'"

"That's right." Tippi snapped her fingers. "I forgot that he also said to Dani, 'You may have had all the power before, but now, I'm in control.' "

"Do you know what the detective meant by that?" Spencer stared at his niece's landlord.

"I . . ." Dani didn't meet his eyes. "No. I don't really *know* anything."

"I remember something," Ivy yelped. "Detective Dickhead seemed real mad about something that happened when Dani was working for the insurance company."

"Yeah." Starr tapped her chin. "He said that Dani ruined someone's life, and he accused her of getting rewarded under the table to do it."

"Did he have his facts straight?" Spencer asked trapping Dani's gaze with his.

"Not entirely," Dani stammered. "I never received a penny beyond my normal salary." She looked away, sweeping cookie crumbs into a pile and crushing them under her thumb. "But I was involved in many hiring and firing decisions which could conceivably be construed as ruining someone's life."

"Tell me about that," Spencer ordered, touching her wrist to stop her fidgeting. "Does any one person or incident stand out?"

"Not really." When Dani shook her head,

making her curls bounce, Spencer was barely able to stop himself from brushing a butterscotch-colored ringlet off her cheek. "And I signed a nondisclosure agreement, so everything I did at my job is considered confidential."

"Why would the detective care what you did at your old job in the insurance company?" Spencer reluctantly released her wrist. "Was Mikeloff ever involved in anything having to do with the corporation?"

"Not that I know of." Something flickered in Dani's expression.

Spencer frowned. What was she hiding, and why she was hiding it? Was it simply a matter of not trusting him or something more ominous?

Spencer had all four women run through the incident with Mikeloff one more time, then tell him what they knew about Regina and the people who had been at her party. Finally, after finishing his tea and thanking Dani for the best cupcakes he'd had since his mother hung up her apron and retired to Florida, he rose from the table and said goodbye.

As he jogged back to his truck, a plan began to form. He could use the excuse that the vic was a student at the university and ask for a meeting with the police chief to feel her out about Mikeloff. But before he did that, he needed to gather some intel on the detective.

He texted his confidential informant requesting a meeting and she replied that she would see him at her favorite bar at seven thirty. It was only a little past six o'clock so he had ninety minutes to kill. He'd spend that time reaching out to a few of his ex-colleagues about Mikeloff.

Spencer also planned to do some research of his own on Little Miss Cupcake. Had something happened during her previous employment that she wasn't telling him? He hadn't pushed her about whatever she was hiding because he damn well knew that arguing with a woman was like trying to read the terms of agreement on the computer. Eventually, he always ended up ignoring everything else and just clicking I AGREE.

But he still wanted to make damn sure she was innocent of any wrongdoing before he decided to help her. All he needed was to be taken in by another con artist like his ex-wife. She'd left him bleeding money and involved in a long, drawn-out divorce, which is why Dani would have to earn his trust and assistance. He sure as hell was never giving it blindly again.

Nevertheless, his gut told him that Little

Miss Cupcake could worm her way into his heart if he wasn't careful. Good thing his undercover training had taught him to keep his emotions in check. He might lust for Dani, but he wouldn't act on it, and he certainly wasn't going to fall for her.

He was annoyed with himself at his fascination with Dani. He knew better than to let good-looking females past his defenses. Too many foolish women fell for the badge, not the man behind it. And once they were faced with the reality, they ended up hating the very job that they'd romanticized.

Still, later that night as he entered the bar where he hoped to find his informant, for one crazy nanosecond, Spencer considered stopping back at the Cook Mansion once he'd spoken to his CI.

But as he drank a bottle of beer, he reminded himself that he still had no idea what Dani was concealing. His research hadn't turned up much beyond the basic facts. She was twenty-nine, born and raised in nearby Towanda, and her father worked for a company that manufactured fast-food equipment. She'd graduated with honors from college and accepted a job at Homestead Insurance, where she remained until approximately eight months ago.

There hadn't been anything online about

why she quit her job. And her social media presence hadn't even hinted at a current boyfriend. Just as Spencer chugged the last of his Corona, he spotted Vivi O'Hara tottering toward him on impossibly high heels.

He blew out a frustrated breath at the mystery of Ms. Danielle Sloan, then shoved thoughts of her aside and concentrated on his CI.

Vivi's brightly painted red lips curved into a predatory smile as she wrapped her arms around Spencer's neck. She purred in his ear, "I haven't seen you in a long time, lover boy."

Grabbing Vivi's arms, he peeled her off him and plopped her onto a stool. The woman was buttoned into McClean County's underbelly, and she insisted that the only way she could talk to Spencer without putting herself in danger was to pretend they were hooking up.

"I've been out of town," he lied smoothly. "But I'm back for a while, so how about we move this to one of the booths in the back?"

"Aren't you even going to buy a girl a drink first?" Vivi put her hands on her tiny waist and tossed her long, black hair. The wrinkles near her hazel eyes deepened and she said, "Make it a double Jack."

"Sure." Spencer flashed a repentant grin.

"And get one for yourself." She winked. "I'm going to ply you with liquor until you think I'm too beautiful to resist."

"There isn't enough beer in Illinois for that to come true," Spencer muttered under his breath.

Vivi narrowed her eyes and demanded, "What?"

"I said you look good in blue." Spencer forced a smile. "I'll meet you at the table."

It was only a few minutes past eight and the crowd was still relatively quiet. But after another hour or two, with more alcohol under their belts, the noise would be deafening. Spencer planned on being long gone by that time.

After getting Vivi's drink and another bottle of beer for himself, Spencer joined her.

She threw him a flirty smile and said, "You know, we don't have to meet here. You could come to my place."

"Maybe next time." Spencer gave her the same answer as always.

Vivi touched a manicured hand to the back of her hair and said, "I'm beginning to think you don't find me sexy."

"It's not that." Spencer took a swig of beer to hide his annoyance. He noted the pique in Vivi's eyes and realized that unless he slept with her, he would lose her as a CI. And since there was no way he was banging her, he needed to make this Q & A a good one, since it might end up being the last bit of info he got from her. "I just don't mix business and pleasure."

"Well . . ." Vivi sipped her whiskey. "I think at this stage of our relationship, you need to make an exception."

Spencer made a noncommittal sound implying agreement, then asked, "So what do you hear about a city detective named Mikeloff?"

"Nothing." Vivi dropped her eyes. "I've never heard of him."

"Why don't I believe that?" Spencer forced himself to take Vivi's hand. "A beautiful woman like you knows all the important people."

"Well, he's not really important." Vivi's tongue traced her lips.

"So you do know him," Spencer said lightly.

"It depends." Vivi petted Spencer's arm with her free hand. "What's it worth to you?"

"A hundred?"

"Make it two."

"One fifty."

"Okay." Vivi licked her lips again. "But

you definitely didn't hear this from me." She glanced nervously over her shoulder, leaned forward, and whispered. "Mikeloff is a mean, crazy bastard."

"Is he on the take?" Spencer asked.

"Well . . ." Vivi fluttered her lashes. "Not that I've heard."

"But?"

"But, he has been known to do people favors." Vivi finished her drink. "Not for money, but he likes to have people in debt to him."

"Why's that?"

"Rumor has it he enjoys inflicting emotional torture . . ." She trailed off, then she blinked and added, "And he's a real stickler for a tooth for a tooth, if you know what I mean."

"Cross him and he wants revenge?" Spencer asked.

"Exactly." Vivi slid a stack of gold bracelets up and down her wrist. "You don't want to get on his bad side because he'll set you up and you'll end up in prison."

"Do you know anyone that happened to, or is it just gossip?"

"I only deal in certified facts." Vivi gave a high-pitched laugh and whapped Spencer on the bicep with the back of her hand.

"I see." Spencer noticed that Vivi had

avoided a direct answer, but he didn't press her. Instead, he asked, "Is there anyone you know who would be willing to talk to me about Mikeloff?"

"Hey." Vivi pursed her lips. "Do you doubt what I told you?"

"Of course not." Spencer shook his head. "Just wondering if there was someone he framed that might be willing to tell me the details."

"I'm sure that could be arranged." Vivi's tone was playful, but her expression was hard to read. "How about you come to my place tomorrow night, and I'll see what I can do?"

"That's not part of my flight plan."

"Then think of me as unexpected turbulence." Vivi stared at him. "Something you have to put up with to get where you want to be."

"That won't work for me." Spencer knew that if he showed up at Vivi's condo, there wouldn't be anyone there but her. "Thanks for the offer, but whatever you're looking for isn't something I can give." Standing, he dug out the money he'd promised her from his pocket, but before handing it over, he asked, "By any chance have of you heard of a Regina Bourne?"

"Why does that name sound familiar?"

Vivi looked at the ceiling for a long second, then snapped her fingers. "Now I remember. Her ex-boyfriend is one of my clients."

"Drugs or sex?"

"A little of both. The first to help the second." Vivi winked. "He used to complain that she was a spoiled brat and didn't understand the 'needs' of a man like him."

"Needs?"

"Vance likes to be in control and he needs to inflict a little pain to get off."

"Interesting." Spencer wondered if the cops knew about the guy's tastes. Touching his finger to his forehead, he said, "Be careful, Vivi. Regina was murdered, and nine out of ten times, the killer is the current or ex-boyfriend."

CHAPTER 8

The girls had gone upstairs to their rooms to put away their books when the doorbell rang. Dani seriously considered ignoring the bell, half-afraid it was Mikeloff, but she tiptoed down the hall and squinted through the window.

Seeing her ex-boyfriend standing on her porch, she started to back away. Kipp's sudden appearance after nearly a year was the perfect ending to a crappy day.

Before she could get out of the foyer, her ex yelled, "I know you're there."

"Go away!" Dani shouted. "We have nothing to say to one another."

"Don't be childish." Kipp's voice took on a cajoling tone. "I thought by now you'd have realized that you overreacted when you found out about my fiancée."

"Right." Dani snorted. "It wasn't as if you were married to her."

Dani rubbed the back of her neck. Why

was Kipp here? They'd had this conversation when she broke up with him, and he hadn't seemed all that upset.

"Look," Kipp said. "I know your father doesn't know about your new job, and unless you agree to talk to me face-to-face, I'm telling him that you've thrown away your education and are now basically a servant."

Shit! Even after she'd broken up with Kipp, he and her father had remained pals. Him getting to her father before she had a chance to talk to him would not be good. All she needed was to have Kipp put his spin on her new career into her dad's head.

"Fine." Dani unlocked the door and stepped onto the porch. No way was she letting her asshole ex inside. "You have five minutes."

Dani studied Kipp. There was something off about him. Although he'd never shown any signs of violence, he was emitting such a weird vibe, she wasn't sure what he'd do. He seemed a lot angrier than the situation warranted, and she was trying to figure out why when suddenly he smiled and tried to take her hand.

Dani jerked out of his reach and he *tsk*ed. "Now don't to be like that."

"Like what?" Dani gritted her teeth. "A

cheated-on woman who has no idea why her no-good ex-boyfriend has turned up on her doorstep after nearly a year? Or a woman who's concerned when said ex-boyfriend refuses to go away and blackmails her into talking to him?"

"Come on." Kipp's smile was flirtations. "The last thing I want to do is to fight with you." He moved closer. "I broke off my engagement." Then he gave her that stupid grin of his, the one that might have wiped out her defenses in the past, but now it just annoyed her. "Remember how much fun we used to have making up?"

"Yuck!" Dani made a face. "That line sounds just as cheesy as the other eight hundred times that I heard it."

"Just don't say I never gave us a second chance." Kipp shrugged.

"Well, now that we have that settled, you can leave." Dani crossed her arms.

"One more thing." Kipp paused. "Do you remember that book of poetry that I lent you when you helped me clear out Mother's house after she died? It was in a box of my great-great-great-grandmother's things that looked as if it hadn't been opened in the last century. We only found it because the carton's bottom broke and its contents fell out onto the floor."

129

"Lent?" Dani raised her eyebrows. "You gave it to me."

"Whatever." Kipp shrugged. "It turns out that Mother promised it to my cousin and she's been bugging me about it."

"What took you so long to ask you for it?" Dani asked. "Your mother died more than a year and a half ago."

"My cousin was out of the country doing missionary work and hadn't heard about Mother's death."

"I haven't unpacked all my boxes yet, but you can have it when I find it."

"I need it right now." Kipp grabbed her hand and tried to pull her toward the door. "I'll help you look."

"Hold it right there, mister." Dani jerked her hand from his grasp and poked him in the chest with her index finger. "There are a lot of boxes and I have other plans for the evening. I'll text you when I run across it."

"No!" Kipp yelped. "Get it now."

"If you don't leave this instant, I'm keeping the book."

"Fine." Kipp's expression smoothed. "Don't get yourself in a tizzy. I'll stop by tomorrow to pick it up."

"You need to wait for my text."

"Don't take too long," Kipp ordered and headed down the front steps.

"With that kind of attitude, I might never find it!" Dani yelled after him.

As soon as Kipp left, Dani called her best friend, Kelsey Zahler. After her stressful day full of crazy cops, irrational ex-boyfriends, and hot uncles, she needed a sympathetic ear.

Since Kelsey had gotten married and had a couple of babies, the two women didn't see as much of each other as they had in high school and college. But when Dani wanted a shoulder to cry on, Kelsey was still her number one choice.

Miracle of miracles, Kelsey answered on the first ring and suggested that they meet around nine for a drink at their old hangout. By then, Kelsey's kids would be in bed and her husband would be home to keep an eye on them.

Dani fed her boarders dinner and told them that she would be out for the evening, then went upstairs to get ready. She was dressed and pacing the floor by eight fifteen.

Although it was still a little early, she scooped up her purse and headed for the van. She was too twitchy to sit around the house and she could always buzz the gut — cruise around Towanda's downtown a few times if she got really desperate.

Climbing into the huge, white vehicle with

the Chef-to-Go logo painted on the side, Dani wished for the hundredth time that she had been able to keep her sporty little Audi. But she'd had to sell the Cabriolet to pay for the van. Besides, she certainly couldn't afford two vehicles.

As Dani drove toward her hometown, she realized that her route took her past the entrance to Regina Bourne's neighborhood and she impulsively turned into the development. Spotting Chelsea and Trent Karnes's house, she wondered once again if the couple would still want her to cook for them. After the dessert debacle at the luau when Regina had threatened to ruin Dani's business, her first thought had been that the Karneses would never hire her to be their personal chef again. And they certainly wouldn't permit her in their home if Mikeloff spread the word that she was a murderer.

Groaning, Dani pulled the van to the curb and studied the Bournes' house. She couldn't see anything out of the ordinary — not that she'd really expected a neon sign flashing MURDER. Still, something had compelled her to revisit the place. Good thing the detective hadn't caught her there. Wasn't it some kind of cop motto that criminals always return to the scene of the crime?

Suddenly, Dani felt as if someone was watching her and quickly eased the van back onto the street and headed to her hometown.

Clouds rolled overhead, playing peekaboo with the moon, and the darkness fit her mood. She turned on the van's radio, searching for some cheerful music. Instead, she found the Beatles singing "Yesterday," one of the most depressing songs ever recorded.

Hitting the radio's Off button, Dani drove the rest of the way to the bar and grill in silence. Dani secured a coveted corner booth to wait for her friend. Unfortunately, it was under a hyperactive ceiling fan and, shivering, she slid along the bench until she found a sheltered spot.

When a waitress wearing the establishment's obligatory short shorts and cropped football jersey approached, Dani asked for a pitcher of margaritas. As the girl trudged away, Dani wondered if the bar had ever had a male server, and if so, what kind of equivalently skimpy outfit he'd be required to wear. No shirt and bicycle shorts?

A few seconds after the waitress returned with Dani's order, a shapely redhead strutted into the room. When she saw Dani, she ran over, dragged her to her feet, and hugged her.

"Kel," Dani gasped. "Need to breathe."

"Wuss," Kelsey laughed as she released her hold and they sat down. She spotted the pitcher, grabbed the handle, and poured for them both. "Nectar of the gods!"

"I'm so glad you were able to meet me." Dani smiled at her friend. "It's been so long, and it's really good to see you."

"I'm sorry I keep having to cancel." Kelsey twisted her ponytail around her finger. "The kids seem to pick up every bug that goes around, and then they give it to me."

"Thank goodness for texts and emails." Dani sipped her drink, feeling her shoulders relax for the first time since Mikeloff burst into her kitchen. "How are the hubs and the little ones right now?"

Kelsey signaled the server. "For one brief shining moment everyone is okay." Turning to the waitress who arrived at their table, she said, "Bring us a pound of your naked wings with hot sauce." When the woman left, Kelsey continued, "The kids are healthy and Toby's next business trip isn't until the fall."

"Awesome." Dani knew how hard it was on Kelsey when her husband was traveling. "How's the writing going? Are the hero and heroine cooperating?"

"Good." Kelsey chugged half her drink, then added, "With the kids in daycare half a day, I'm actually making some progress on my opus. If the hero puts on his big-boy briefs, the couple might actually have sex in the next chapter."

"Shouldn't he be taking off his underwear?" Dani giggled at her friend's imagination.

Kelsey wrote romance novels, and the last time they'd chatted, her heroine had been reluctant to sleep with the hero. Unlike the characters in her friend's books trying to take over the story, Dani was thankful that the ingredients for her recipes never tried to take over the dish.

"Enough about me." Kelsey topped off each of their glasses. "Tell me about Ivy's uncle."

"That's what you got from everything I said when I called you?" Dani raised a brow. "You don't want to hear about the detective that went berserk in my kitchen or that I may be arrested for murder?"

"We'll get to that later." Kelsey waved her hand. "First, the good stuff about this Spencer."

"Okay." Dani nodded. "Well, to start with, I was shocked when instead of the fifty- or sixty-year-old tubby ex-cop I was expecting, I found a gorgeous thirtysomething man sitting at my table. Spencer Drake is nothing like I'd expected."

"Does he have a good bod?" Kelsey asked, then licked the salt from the rim of her glass.

"More like perfect." Dani frowned, her hand smoothing over her generous hips. "Muscles that have to take hours of hard work in the gym to maintain."

"So he's not sitting around collecting a pension," Kelsey teased.

"No." Dani inhaled sharply. "And when his dark-blue eyes locked onto mine, there was a flash of heat that nearly burned off my panties." Dani shivered. The memory of his striking good looks stole away her breath. "He's the devil's candy and I couldn't stop fantasizing about eating him up."

"Did he seem to realize how he was affecting you?" Kelsey asked.

"Maybe." Dani shrugged. "When he took my hand to introduce himself, he held it a beat too long."

"And?" Kelsey prompted.

"And the feeling of his fingers wrapped around mine was more erotic than all of Kipp's kisses and caresses combined," Dani admitted. "I was sorry I hadn't bothered to put on makeup, fix my hair, and worn something a little more flattering than old jeans and a T-shirt. Of course that was before he started asking a lot of probing questions about my old job. Then he didn't seem quite as attractive. You know that's the last thing I want to relive."

"Why was he asking about your job?" Kelsey's green eyes widened. "Did he know about the 'incident'? You didn't break the confidentiality agreement, did you?"

"I would never talk about it." Dani shook her head. "I never want to even think about it. You know that whole affair was horrific."

Before having her kids and starting to write romances, Kelsey had been a practicing attorney. She had represented Dani during the mess at Homestead Insurance, so she was one of the few people who knew the whole story.

"Then, I repeat, why did Ivy's uncle ask you about your previous job?"

Dani summarized Mikeloff's accusations, then said, "Unfortunately, the girls' memories were a little too good and they repeated verbatim the detective's allegations and threats to Spencer." Dani shook her head. "Mikeloff could have been referring to any one of a hundred hiring or firing decisions that I made, and the last thing I need is a guy like Spencer intent on exhuming one of the worst experiences of my life. Especially if it has no relevance to the detective's motive for harassing me."

"Well" — Kelsey wrinkled her nose — "that was the nastiest situation you dealt with; ergo, it should be the one you consider first regarding the issue with this Mikeloff."

"I can't let that particular cat out of the bag. It would claw my soul to shreds to relive that awful experience, and as you know, Homestead would sue me for everything I owned if I failed to uphold the NDA." Dani paused as the server slid a tray of hot wings onto their table and passed out plates and napkins. Once the woman left, Dani said, "Therefore, even if Spencer has chiseled cheekbones to die for, he's bad news because he doesn't seem like the type who's going to let this go."

"You can't be sure of that," Kelsey reasoned. "And it isn't every day you meet a hot guy."

"True." Dani picked up a wing. "But even with the long drought in my love life, let's not forget that I'm being accused of murder."

"Then you kicked Spencer to the curb?" Kelsey served herself from the platter in the middle of the table and began to gnaw on a wing.

"Not exactly," Dani confessed. "Actually I made him tea and served him cupcakes."

"Not your famous special mocha cupcakes?" Kelsey licked her fingers.

"Uh-huh." Dani's cheeks reddened. "And when he bit into one, he groaned in a way that isn't normally heard outside the bedroom. I could barely breathe."

Kelsey raised her brows until they almost disappeared into her hairline, then accused, "You do like him."

"Maybe," Dani sighed. "Every time I glanced at him and caught him looking at me, I could almost see the electricity zinging between us. It took all my willpower to keep a composed expression on my face and answer his questions in a tone that indicated I was the one in control and intended to remain that way."

"How did he take that?" Kelsey grabbed another chicken wing and sucked the meat from the bone.

"Let's just say that if he'd raked his fingers through his coal-black hair one more time, there would be a bald patch on the top of his head." Dani grumbled, "He was frustrated with my non-answers and it was clear that he wasn't used to having a woman say no to him, but I didn't have a choice. There's a legally binding document keeping me mute."

"Maybe he'll give you a pass on that." Kelsey emptied the rest of the pitcher into their glasses.

"It doesn't matter." Dani drew rings in the condensation on the table's faded laminate top. "No matter how intense the attraction is between us, Spencer isn't my type. I've always steered clear of men who are too handsome. I'm not in his league. Kipp wasn't even that good-looking and he had someone on the side. I'm not risking it with Spencer. I'd never be able to keep his attention for the long run."

"Not that I agree with you, but even if that were the case for some guys, I've never seen you this interested before." Kelsey took Dani's hand. "If he makes you go weak in the knees, it could be time to give in to the temptation and make sure that when you fall, it's into his arms rather than to the ground."

"It's a moot point for now." Dani squeezed her friend's fingers. "The murder has to come first."

"At least Spencer didn't automatically take the cop's side, and he's willing to look into Mikeloff's behavior."

"True. But that's because he's concerned about Ivy. It has nothing to do with me." Dani bit her lip. "I have to protect myself. The fact that Mikeloff is either just plain crazy or crazy with a sprinkling of revenge on top is a huge problem because, either way, he seems pretty darned intent on sending me to prison for Regina's murder."

"Spencer might be able to help you with that," Kelsey suggested. "He is head of campus security, so he has to have some pull with the local cops."

"But Mikeloff's second choice of suspect is Ivy." Dani frowned. "I'm not sure why the detective has it in for her, unless it's because she's close to me, but if it came to his niece or me, I'm certain that Spencer would throw me under the bus in a heartbeat. Which means I can't totally trust him."

"Mmm." Kelsey tapped her fingernails on the table. "So what's the plan?"

"Once Spencer left, I started making a list of who at the party had acted oddly toward Regina." Dani scowled. "But I only wrote one name — Vance King — before the doorbell interrupted me."

"Who was it?" Kelsey's tapping increased.

"My ex."

"Shit!"

"Exactly." Dani grimaced and related her

141

encounter with Kipp. "What an ass."

"Why in the world did you even go out and talk to him?"

"He heard that I quit my job and started cooking for people and somehow figured out that I hadn't told my father yet."

"I told you that would come back to bite you in the butt," Kelsey said.

"*Et tu,* Kelsey?" Dani scowled. "Must you always speak your mind?"

"Hey." The redhead shrugged. "It hurts too much to bite my tongue all the time."

"Anyway," Dani sighed. "I really didn't need Kipp popping back into my life."

"Definitely not!" Kelsey slapped the table. "I knew he was a creep. I should have never let you date him."

"I probably wouldn't have listened to you if you had tried to stop me," Dani said, trying to comfort her friend.

"You probably wouldn't have." Kelsey checked the time. "We better wrap this up. It's always an early morning at my house."

"Mine too. The girls seem to think they should have breakfast before they go to class." Dani rolled her eyes in mock exasperation.

After paying the check and hugging goodbye, Dani headed home. As she drove, she felt a shiver of fear. What if Regina's killer was targeting college girls? What if her murder was just the beginning?

If Mikeloff was convinced that Dani was guilty, he wouldn't be looking for other suspects. The only way Dani would ever clear her name and protect other possible victims was to find the killer herself.

Now all she needed to do was figure out how to investigate a crime.

CHAPTER 9

Tuesday morning arrived entirely too early
— especially since a conga drum was playing "Babalú" inside Dani's skull when she
woke up. She blamed her throbbing temples
on the weather front that had moved
through during the night, bringing uncom-
fortably high humidity and the threat of
rain. She refused to believe that a couple of
margaritas could cause such a bad headache, because if she admitted that she had a
hangover after two measly drinks, it would
mean that she was officially old. And she
wasn't even thirty yet.

After swallowing a couple of Advil, Dani
threw on a pair of cargo shorts and a T-shirt
before gingerly walking down the stairs to
the first floor. She was usually the first one
up, but judging by the raised voices that
greeted her in the hallway, the girls had
beaten her into the kitchen.

Ivy, Starr, and Tippi had varied tastes in

their cups of joe, and Dani had ruled that whoever made it to the coffeepot first got to choose. Evidently, espresso was not a popular choice among Tippi's friends.

Facing the squabbling coeds, Dani rubbed between her eyes and said, "Settle this now or stop by Starbucks on your way to school. Because I seriously need an *inoculatte* and the first cup is mine."

"Inoculatte?" Tippi's heart-shaped face scrunched in confusion.

"Coffee taken intravenously," Dani translated. "Because you can't wait for the caffeine to hit by drinking it the usual way."

Ivy studied Dani's face and said, "You look awful. Are you all right?"

"Thanks. You look cute too." Dani scowled. "My head is pounding, but the lunch-to-go sacks won't fill themselves. So whose turn is it to help me with them?"

"Mine." Starr raised her hand. "But none of us could sleep, so we checked the menu and got all the ingredients out on the counter for you."

"Thanks, sweetie." Dani hugged her. "Why couldn't you all sleep?"

"Maybe because the asshat of a detective accused you of murder and we're worried about you?" Tippi put her hands on her slim hips.

"Uncle Spence will straighten him out," Ivy said. Her tone sounded confident, but Dani could see the worry in her face. "He'll take care of it."

"I'm sure he will." Dani hoped by agreeing with Ivy, her prediction would come true.

Although she planned to look into Regina's death herself, there was no reason for the girls to know that right now. They'd find out soon enough, when Dani started talking to suspects.

Once the four of them were caffeinated, and Ivy and Tippi headed to class, Dani flipped on the overhead fluorescents and flinched when they flickered to life. The coffee and ibuprofen had tamped down her headache to a dull thud, but the bright lights still hurt her eyes.

Starr shot her a sympathetic glance, then they both got busy making the food for the lunch-to-go sacks. In her original plan, Dani wasn't going to name the daily specials, but when she was training the girls, Tippi had looked at an overflowing sirloin sandwich and called it the Beef of Burden. Soon the others were competing to come up with clever monikers like Lox of Love and Jean Claude Van Ham.

Today's choices were the Ides of March, a

Caesar chicken wrap, and the Chucky Cheddar, roast beef and cheese on sour-dough. As they worked, Dani asked her helper about Regina's friends. Hoping Starr wouldn't catch on that Dani was investigating the murder, she started with a few casual questions.

"Did you know many of the people at the luau?" Dani concentrated on cubing the sweet potatoes for the healthy options side dish.

"Not really." Starr's attention was focused on expertly folding the whole-wheat tortillas around the chicken filling. "That's not really my scene."

"Why did you agree to work if you weren't interested in attending the party?" Dani asked, then immediately answered herself. "Because it meant a lot to Ivy, right?"

"Uh-huh." The beads on Starr's braids clicked gently as she nodded. "But I have to admit that Ivy talked about them so much I was curious."

"You, Tippi, and Ivy have been friends a long time," Dani said carefully. "Did you feel rejected that Ivy was so set on becoming a part of Regina's crowd?"

"Nah." Starr's fond smile creased her round cheeks. "With her being a couple of years younger than us, she's always had a hard time with the whole boy/girl thing. Add her super-high IQ to the mix, and dating has been, let's say, awkward for her. But Regina was an expert at the social scene."

"Are you saying that Ivy was studying her?" Dani moved on to packaging the triple chocolate chip bars for the decadent lunch. "That she thought of Regina and her friends as lab rats in an experiment?"

"Maybe not quite that cold." Starr bit her plump bottom lip. "But yeah."

"Wow." Dani blinked several times. "I knew Ivy was hoping to meet guys by hanging out with Regina, but that's . . . that's . . ." Dani threw up her hands. "I don't know if I'm impressed with her thoroughness or appalled that she'd invade someone's privacy."

"She didn't manipulate them," Starr objected. "She only observed them."

"I guess." Dani frowned.

She couldn't put her finger on what bothered her about the situation, but it sure as heck didn't feel right to her. Maybe it was the age gap. Although Dani was only nine years older than Starr and Tippi, the explosion of the internet's popularity in the past decade had created a disconnect between them. Her boarders' generation was used to their whole lives being documented on social media, while Dani's still tried to retain a tiny bit of their privacy.

Starr must have sensed Dani's continued unease because she added, "And if you knew Regina's clique, you'd realize that they were so egotistical and self-absorbed, they'd think it was cool that Ivy considered them the ideal research subjects for how to be popular."

"Why do you say that?" Dani asked.

She'd gotten a little off target for her original goal, but sometimes it was best to let the conversation take its own direction. And her patience was now rewarded. Starr's comment was the perfect introduction to figure out if one of Regina's pals or her fiancé might want her dead. It was possible that a random stranger had bumped off Regina, or even that it had been a serial killer after college girls, but from all the mysteries she'd read and watched on television, it was much more likely Regina had been murdered by someone close to her.

"Well, there's Bliss Armstrong, Regina's best friend." Starr finished with the wraps and moved on to the roast beef sandwiches. "That girl does whatever Regina tells her to do." Starr spread horseradish sauce on slices of sourdough. "Ivy said they were both members of a sorority, but Regina did something and was asked to leave the chapter, and she made Bliss move out of the house too."

"That's pretty major." Dani wrinkled her brow. She knew how traumatic getting kicked out of a sorority could be for a girl. So much of college existence centers around their membership — friends, social life, and sometimes even who they date. "Why would Bliss do that for her?"

"According to Ivy, Regina has some sort of voodoo hold on her friends."

"From my experience with Regina, I'm sort of shocked that she didn't have her daddy sue the sorority." Dani began to bag the lunches. "Or did she?"

"I don't think so."

"What did Regina do to get kicked out?" Dani packed entrées, sides, and desserts into the red-and-white sacks, topping everything off with a napkin stamped with her company logo and social media links.

"Ivy never said." Starr shrugged. "But I'm thinking it had to be pretty bad for a sorority to risk getting rid of someone with Regina's money and connections."

"Hmm." Dani tucked that info into the mental folder labeled *Further investigation needed*. "How about the guys in Regina's inner circle?"

"Her fiancé, Lazarus Hunter, comes from old money but seems nice enough." Starr began transferring the completed lunches to the refrigerator. "He strikes me as a go-with-the-flow kind of guy."

"He sure was a drunken kind of guy at the party." Dani took an armful of dirty dishes to the sink.

"I've only met him a few times, but I never saw him drink before."

"What about Bliss's boyfriend?" Dani rinsed off dirty bowls and utensils. "Vance King? He sure seemed intent on talking to Regina during the party, and she kept brushing him off."

"Vance is sort of creepy. Super callous and self-indulgent, you know?" Starr loaded the dishwasher. "Regina dated him before dumping him for Laz."

"Why did she break up with him?" Dani shut off the faucet and winced as the water gurgled down the drain. She sure hoped there wasn't anything wrong with the plumbing. Pipes in an old house like the mansion could be a time bomb waiting to go off. "I would think a star football player with NFL hopes would be a prize she'd consider worth keeping."

"He seemed kind of bossy for a girl like Regina, but I have no idea." Starr wiped her hands on a paper towel. "You should ask Ivy."

"Now you've got me curious." Dani winked at Starr. "Guess I'll have to see what Ivy says."

Starr headed upstairs to study and Dani checked the microwave clock. She had fifteen or twenty minutes until customers started to show up. Time enough to wash and to put on clean clothes.

A quarter of an hour later, Dani smiled at herself in the mirror. The shower had felt heavenly and her headache was almost completely gone. She'd already combed her wet hair and wound it into a bun. Now she pulled on a pair of jeans and a peach button-down blouse, then brushed on some blush and mascara. Sliding her feet into a pair of loafers, she hurried downstairs.

As she stepped into the kitchen, the front doorbell rang. Her pulse raced and she froze.

Shit! That better not be Kipp wanting his darn book, or worse, Mikeloff back to arrest me. Her lunch customers would be arriving any second, and she couldn't afford to send them away empty-handed.

Dani shot a glance at the sliding window to assure herself that no one was waiting, then turned on her heel and headed down the hallway. Dread slowed her steps, and as she approached the vestibule, she stopped completely. Finally, she reluctantly crept toward the window, careful to keep out of sight.

Squinting, Dani saw a young woman who was a little taller than average and a lot curvier than was fashionable. One thing about living in a college town was the plethora of young, beautiful, thin females. The abundance of size-four young women often made anyone who wore a pair of jeans with a double-digit tag feel huge.

However, the woman tapping her toe impatiently on the front porch radiated a confidence that Dani envied. Between spending much of the last year with Kipp sniping at her figure, and all of her life having her father tell her she wasn't thin enough, her body image was at an all-time low.

Curious, since there was a sign directing Chef-to-Go customers to the rear entrance, Dani opened the door and said, "Can I help you?"

"Are you Danielle Sloan?" The young woman slid her foot over the threshold.

"Yes." Dani frowned. Was her visitor selling something? "And you are?"

Nearby a car door slammed and a motor

whined to life. Dani glanced past her visitor's shoulder but didn't see the vehicle.

"Frannie Ryan." The woman stuck out her hand. "I work for the *Normalton News.*"

"You're a reporter?" Dani had sent a press release when she'd started her business. It would be great if the newspaper did a feature article.

"Not exactly." The woman's long, brown hair swirled in the warm breeze, emphasizing her suddenly red cheeks. "But I am a journalist. I cover the obituaries and write the Miss Fortune column."

"Well, no one at this address has passed on or has submitted a request for advice." At least Dani didn't think so. She was distracted by the sound of chimes indicating someone was at the to-go window. Looking over her shoulder, she said, "Sorry, I need to get that."

"No problem." Frannie slipped inside. "I can wait until you're free."

The chimes sounded again and Dani gave up on the idea of pushing her back outside. Grudgingly, she allowed the woman to follow her down the hallway.

As soon as they entered the kitchen, Frannie's eyes widened. "Wow! Your kitchen is bigger than my whole apartment." She trailed her fingers on the counter and added, "Nicer too."

"Thanks." Dani waved her visitor out of her way. "Take a seat."

Turning her attention to the waiting customers, Dani sold lunches nonstop for nearly an hour. She was so relieved that Regina's death didn't seem to be hurting her business, she almost forgot the reporter sitting at the table.

However, as she handed over the last of the red-and-white sacks, Frannie said, "Holy cow! Those things are really popular. What a fabulous idea."

"Thanks." Dani smiled. "Would you like to taste some of the leftovers?"

"Sure." Frannie twisted a glossy, brown lock of hair around her finger.

"You never did tell me why you're here." Dani put a less than perfectly wrapped chicken sandwich and the last small scoop of sweet potato salad on a dish and slid it in front of her guest, along with a cold bottle of water.

"Regina Bourne." Frannie mumbled around a mouthful of the salad. "I heard one of the reporters say that she died after her annual SummerPalooza bash. So I asked around and found out you catered it."

"I see." Dani twisted her fingers in her apron. This wasn't good. "I did provide the

155

food, but Ms. Bourne was alive and well when I left the party."

"I know that." Frannie picked up the chicken wrap. "According to my source, the final guests left the luau at 2:37 a.m. and they were the last ones to see Regina alive and conscious."

"Who told you that?" Dani poured herself a cup of coffee, grabbed a plate of triple chocolate chip bars, and joined Frannie.

"I can't reveal my sources." Frannie opened the water bottle.

"How about the identity of the last guests?" Dani selected a cookie.

"That I can do." Frannie grinned. "It was her fiancé, Lazarus Hunter, and his pal Lance King. It seems Mr. Hunter was royally pissed with Ms. Bourne about something and, according to his buddy, the guy made quite a scene as he peeled out of the driveway."

"I wonder what they were fighting about." Dani chewed thoughtfully.

"My guess is" — Frannie tapped her pen on her lips — "Regina wouldn't let Lazarus spend the night."

"Perhaps," Dani agreed. "He probably would expect to, since they were engaged."

"Exactly." Frannie's brown eyes sparkled. "So why did she send him away?"

"Well . . ." Dani considered how much she should say, but there was no oath of confidentiality for a caterer and aiming the spotlight at another subject was a smart idea. "Laz *was* drinking heavily, as was his pal Vance. Maybe Regina didn't want to deal with a drunk."

"It's possible," Frannie said thoughtfully. "But I thought SummerPalooza was one big booze fest. Wasn't Regina drinking too?"

Dani wrinkled her forehead. "I don't know." Had she seen Regina drink anything? "I was pretty busy keeping up with the food."

"And saving everyone's bacon when that idiot King nearly burned down the place." Frannie nabbed a paper napkin from the holder in the center of the table and wiped her fingers. "Mr. Hunter said you were awesome."

"It wasn't that big a deal." Dani twitched her shoulders. "It was a small blaze and I just used my fire extinguisher to put it out."

"My friend Skye says we all have to learn to accept the credit for our accomplishments." Frannie shook her finger at Dani. "She says it's just as important as admitting when we screw up."

"She sounds like a smart cookie," Dani said. "But if you're assigned to the obituaries and Miss Fortune column, why are you asking me about Regina?"

"Because if I solve the murder and scoop everyone else with an awesome story, maybe I won't have to write obits or advice to the lovelorn anymore."

"I'd like to help you with that, but you seem to know a lot more about the case than me." Dani stirred sweetener into her coffee.

Frannie dug a notebook from her purse. "But you were there." Her voice was hypnotic. "Tell me everything that happened from the minute it started."

"It really just seemed like a normal party." Dani cradled her mug. "I mean it was very high end, with the best of everything, but otherwise, it had loud music, lots of people, and too much alcohol."

"Still . . ." Frannie drew out the word. "I doubt there's a fire or a hostess throwing a tantrum about desserts at every event you cater."

"You heard about that too, huh?" Dani was beginning to dislike Frannie's informant.

"Of course." Frannie beamed. "Another one of my sources is really convinced you killed Regina."

"What?" Dani squeaked. "Is that source a

certain obnoxious detective?"

Frannie ignored Dani's question. "The thing is, this guy or gal is a little too anxious for the perp to be you. Hence you have even more at stake in discovering who rubbed out Regina Bourne than I do."

"Why do I get the feeling this isn't your first murder investigation?" Dani narrowed her eyes.

"Because I have a friend back home with many unusual talents. Solving mysteries is just one of them."

CHAPTER 10

The automatic doors swished shut behind Dani as she pushed her cart inside the local Meijer superstore. She shivered and rubbed the goose bumps on her arms as the over-cooled air surrounded her.

Her mouth watered at the aroma of frying chicken coming from the nearby deli, but she ignored the temptation and headed into the produce section. She quickly skimmed her list and began selecting what she'd need for the rest of the week.

While she bought most of the dry and canned ingredients wholesale, she had yet to find a reliable supplier for fruit and vegetables. She had feelers out to various farms in the area, but with the Midwest weather, they'd only be able to provide what she needed for a few months out of the year.

As she tapped cantaloupes and sniffed honeydews, she thought about her morning visitor. Frannie Ryan was an interesting woman. She'd told Dani that she'd graduated from college in the spring and was thrilled to find work in Normalton because her boyfriend, Justin, had one more year to go. He was finishing his degree at the University of Illinois, which was less than half an hour away, so they could still live together.

Frannie and Justin had both grown up in Scumble River, a small town that apparently had more than its fair share of homicides. She had recounted several cases that she and her friend Skye had solved.

If Dani wasn't already convinced that she needed to look into Regina's murder herself, Frannie's stories would have persuaded her. She just couldn't trust her fate to a cop with a grudge.

As Dani continued to shop, she considered her next move. She and Frannie had agreed the best suspects were Regina's fiancé and closest friends. Which one would be the easiest to talk to first?

After contemplating the trio of potential culprits, she fished through her purse for her cell. Once she located the sneaky device, which had been hiding under her wallet, she sent a quick text to Ivy:

Has Laz Hunter returned your necklace
yet?

Ivy instantly answered: No.

ask him to bring it over tonight. he can stay
for dinner.

A short pause and Ivy responded: Okay.
You want to grill him about Regina, right? Do
you think he killed her? Cuz he's not like that.

In reply, Dani sent Ivy an emoji of a face
with wiggling eyebrows.

Turning into the meat aisle, Dani checked
the weight of a roast. She was scheduled to
cook for Trent and Chelsea Karnes the next
evening and planned to make them beef
tenderloin with port sauce.

They hadn't called to cancel her services
as their personal chef, so either they hadn't
heard that Mikeloff thought she murdered
Regina or they didn't care. Either possibility worked for Dani.

Maybe the Karneses would have some
insight on Regina's life. They were friends
of her parents and were supposed to be
keeping an eye on her while Mr. and Mrs.
Bourne were on their trip, which, considering Regina's age, was a little odd. But then
again, for some girls, twenty-one would be

too old to depend on parental assistance, but Regina hadn't struck Dani as a young woman who was really used to handling things on her own. Getting her own way, yes. Shouldering the responsibility of those choices, not so much.

Who would Regina lean on when her parents were on vacation? Chelsea Karnes didn't seem like the maternal type, but Regina would never confide in her housekeeper. The spoiled young woman was way too class conscious to give her servant that kind of power over her.

Even so, Dani needed to talk to Mrs. Carnet, who doubtlessly knew more about her employer's personal life than Regina had ever realized. The trick would be getting the housekeeper to share that information with a relative stranger — someone who was high on the police's suspect list and had little to offer in return.

Heading toward the checkout lane, Dani tried to figure out a way to approach Mrs. Carnet. Nearly two hundred bucks later, loading her van full of groceries, Dani still had no idea how to gain the housekeeper's trust.

Tucking that problem away for another time, Dani climbed behind the wheel and drove out of the grocery store's parking lot.

Turning onto the street, she tensed at the sound of a siren.

The fear of Mikeloff returning to arrest her was never far from her thoughts, and when an ambulance passed going in the opposite direction, she blew out a relieved breath. If this all didn't end soon, she would end up with a heart attack.

As tempting as it was to wallow in her troubles, Dani focused on the positive news. Ivy had texted that Laz accepted the invitation to dinner.

Of course now that he was coming, Dani had to come up with a way to make him spill his guts. If it weren't for her "no alcohol" decree for her boarders, she'd consider getting him drunk. On the other hand, at the luau, Laz had grown quieter and quieter as he tossed back Jell-O shots. So even if she were willing to break her rule, booze wasn't the answer. She'd have to loosen his tongue some other way.

Dinner was at six, which left Dani just under three hours to cook and come up with an interrogation plan. How would she ask a grieving fiancé why someone would want to kill his beloved wife-to-be? Or worse yet, if he had been the one to wield the syringe.

Which reminded her, when Dani had

agreed to share info with Frannie Ryan, the budding journalist had promised to get ahold of the autopsy results once they were final. Knowing the location of the injection might help zero in on possible suspects. After all, a causal acquaintance could probably get to one of Regina's limbs, but a more intimate site would point the finger of blame in a completely different direction.

After arriving home, checking her business voicemail for any inquiries regarding future bookings, and putting away her purchases, Dani spent the rest of the afternoon preparing a potato-and-leek gratin and chicken Kiev. She usually cooked much simpler fare for the girls, but she wanted to impress Laz. Besides, it was a good practice run of the menu she was making for a sorority alumnae dinner in a couple of weeks.

She was pleasantly surprised when Laz arrived on time. He was dressed in crisply pressed khakis and a blue button-down shirt.

As Dani ushered him inside, she said, "I just want you to know how sorry I am for your loss." She saw a flicker of sadness in the young man's eyes, but he blinked and it was gone. Leading him into the kitchen, Dani continued, "Although it isn't the same, I lost my mother at a young age, and

I can understand some of what you might be going through."

"Thank you for your kind words." Laz cleared his throat, then seemed to push away any lingering emotion. "I appreciate your thoughtfulness."

After handing Ivy her necklace, he presented Dani with a lovely bouquet of pink lilies and white daises. A woodsy fragrance drifted toward her and she sniffed appreciatively, identifying the scent as Dior Sauvage, a pricey fragrance that was her father's favorite aftershave.

While Dani put the flowers in a vase, Ivy showed Laz to the kitchen table and took the seat next to him. Starr and Tippi slid into the chairs on the opposite side and Dani served the food.

As they ate, she was shocked at how different Laz was when he wasn't drunk. Sober, he was charming. At the party, he'd been sullen and aloof, ignoring his friends and fiancée, as well as anyone else who tried to speak to him.

"This is delicious," Laz commented, holding out his plate for a second helping of the gratin. "What spice is it that I taste?"

"Cumin and garlic." Dani smiled at him as she slid a slice onto his dish. "I'm glad you like it. My guess is that most college guys prefer their potatoes baked or fried." She tilted her head pretending concern. "I was worried that you might not like my cooking since you didn't eat at the SummerPalooza bash."

"I have to apologize for my behavior that night." Laz fidgeted with his napkin, smoothing it in his lap. "I'd learned something upsetting and instead of handling it like an adult, I drank too much." His shoulders slumped and he shook his head. "I'd been doing so well since I got out of rehab. Although I've been clean and sober for three years, the compulsion to get numb was just too much." Straightening, he said, "But I've talked to my sponsor and gone to meetings every day and I'm back on the right path."

Dani watched Ivy give him a hug and whisper something in his ear. He shot her a smile, and Tippi and Starr glanced at each other but remained silent. Was Laz being sincere or playing for their sympathy?

"I'm a little surprised that Regina would have a party with so much alcohol if she knew what a temptation it would be for you." Dani passed Laz the bread basket and the crystal butter dish.

"She felt that others shouldn't suffer because of my weakness." Laz shrugged and selected a hot roll. "As you may have noticed, she wasn't the most compassionate person in the world."

"Knowing that, you were still in love with her?" Dani asked.

"It's hard to explain." Laz picked up his fork. "Reg and I grew up together. We went to the same schools, attended the same parties, and hung out at the same country club. We were always expected to get married."

"But Regina dated Vance King," Ivy blurted out. She turned toward him and, frowning her concern, asked, "Did she cheat on you?"

"No." Laz ate a few bites, then said, "We decided when we started college to both date other people. Although I didn't for a while because my rehab counselor suggested just concentrating on me for the first year. Our parents weren't happy with us going our separate ways, but they agreed we needed to sow our wild oats."

"What changed?" Dani asked, worried at the way Ivy was gazing adoringly at Laz. All Ivy needed was to fall for a guy with an addiction problem and parents who wanted him to marry a debutante.

"Nothing, really." Laz pushed his empty plate away. "It was just time."

"Time?" Dani raised a brow.

"The start of our senior year," Laz explained. "The plan was to have the wedding next June. That way wherever I went to law school, Reg would move there with me."

"No offense," Dani said, "but since you both could afford to go anywhere to college, I'm a bit surprised you and Regina chose to attend NU instead of a more prestigious university."

"Regina was happier as a big fish in a small pond, and since she wanted to be a writer, it didn't really matter if she had a diploma from an important school." Laz drained his water glass, then hung his head. "And I was drunk during most of high school so my GPA sucked. I probably wouldn't have gotten into NU if my grandfather hadn't endowed the new library."

"But you straightened up and have a 4.0," Ivy said, shooting Dani a warning look.

"That's wonderful, Laz." Dani stood and asked, "Ready for dessert?"

They all nodded and she took the bowls of banana pudding from the fridge. Ivy had told Dani that this was Laz's favorite sweet, so she had whipped up the old-fashioned summer treat in order to lull him into revealing all his secrets.

Once everyone had been served and was eating, Dani searched her mind for anything else she wanted to ask Laz. Maybe it was the food or the homey atmosphere, but he'd been more open than she had expected and she didn't want to waste the opportunity to grill him.

Cradling her coffee cup, Dani absorbed the warmth from the mug as she watched Laz flirting with Ivy. He'd been friendly toward Tippi and Starr, chatting with them throughout the meal, but his interest was clearly fixed on Ivy. Was he really interested in her or was seducing women just second nature to him?

As Dani observed him, thinking about what he'd revealed so far, she realized there was one last question she needed answered.

She waited for a lull in the conversation and said, "Laz, I hope you don't mind me asking, but after three years of sobriety, what in the world shoved you off the wagon?"

"I . . . I'm not sure how to put this." He glanced at Ivy, who nodded encouragingly. "As I mentioned, Reg wasn't exactly a sweet, cuddly person."

"So we all noticed." Starr tapped a sparkly fingernail on her cheek.

"Yeah." Tippi wrinkled her nose. "It was kind of evident when, instead of thanking

Dani for putting out the fire, she screamed at her."

"Right." Laz licked his lips. "Reg has always been sort of self-centered."

"Which I suspect her parents did nothing to discourage," Dani commented.

"True." Laz stared into his dessert dish. "Anson and Honoria wouldn't have seen anything wrong with Reg's attitude."

"I take it that's what's expected in their circle?" Dani asked.

"No!" Laz's blue eyes flashed. "My parents aren't like that."

"But they wanted you to marry into a family that was like that?" Tippi snapped.

Dani shot her a please-don't-blow-this look.

"Well." Laz dropped his chin. "They aren't like that to the same degree as the Bournes."

"It's difficult to achieve that compromise between acting selfish and watching out for your own interests," Dani said.

"Very." Laz smiled gratefully at her. "People do try to take advantage of you when they think you're more fortunate than them."

"It was probably especially hard for someone like Regina to find that happy medium." Dani's voice softened. "When you look like a Victoria's Secret model and have a trust fund that would allow you to buy your own private island, people treat you like you're special and you begin to believe you deserve to be treated that way."

"That's just it." Laz scraped the last bit of pudding from his bowl. "When we dated in high school, Reg was a little arrogant, although not in a mean way. But once we got back together, she seemed different."

"Did something happen?" Dani asked. "Can you pinpoint when she changed?"

"Not really." Laz shifted in his chair. "The thing is that although we still saw each other at parties, etcetera, since we weren't going out together and didn't have the same classes, I wasn't really around her on a day-to-day basis until we started dating again."

"So the difference could have happened gradually," Ivy said.

"Or . . ." Dani paused, wondering if she should complete her thought.

"Or?" Starr prodded.

"Or, maybe it wasn't Regina who changed." Dani got to her feet, grabbed another serving of pudding from the fridge, and slid it in front of Laz. "It could be that once you got sober, you saw her more clearly than you had through the alcoholic fog."

"Going through rehab and counseling could have made you more aware of others' feelings." Ivy patted his arm and he put his hand on hers.

"I'd like to think that." Laz grinned and dug into the new dessert.

"You were certainly kind to me when you offered to make sure my necklace was okay and bring it to me." Ivy beamed at him.

"If I had been sober, I would have been able to stand up to Reg and gotten the locket for you that night." Laz continued to eat.

"Does alcohol make it more difficult for you to do the right thing?" Dani asked. Hearing how dumb that sounded, she added, "I mean, even if you know what you should do, does being intoxicated make it hard to go against what others want you to do?"

"Not guys." Laz's cheeks reddened. "But it's hard to say no to girls."

Starr leaned over and hissed in Dani's ear, "Mommy issues, I bet."

Dani narrowed her eyes at Starr, then smiled at Laz. "When you're raised to be a gentleman, it makes it tough to act differently."

"I guess." Laz finished his second bowl of pudding and wiped his mouth. "That was awesome. I can see why Reg had you save some desserts for her."

"Thanks!" Dani got up. "Why don't you guys go into the family room while I clean up?"

Once she'd agreed to have Ivy, Starr, and Tippi live with her, Dani had removed the antique furniture from the back parlor, replaced it with a comfy sectional and a flat screen television, and renamed it the family room.

"Let me help." Laz leaped to his feet. "I'll clear the table."

"I'll help too," Ivy said.

"Nope, Laz and I have got this." Dani herded the three girls out of the kitchen. As she filled the sink with hot water, she considered how to reintroduce her original question to Laz. Finally, she said, "We got a little sidetracked and you never did tell me what happened to make you start drinking the night of the luau."

"Well . . ." Laz deposited a stack of dirty dishes on the counter next to Dani. "As I said, I'd noticed that Reg seemed to be getting meaner."

"Yes." Dani kept her back to him, hoping it would make it easier for him to talk about it.

"The afternoon before the party, she sent

me, and a hundred of her closest friends, a nude picture of Bliss Armstrong."

"I thought Bliss was Regina's best friend." Dani raised a brow and asked carefully, "Why would she do that to her?"

"A few weeks ago, I made the mistake of paying Bliss a compliment. Reg had been steaming about it ever since." Laz's voice faltered as he spoke. "In the picture, Bliss was obviously passed out and there was something written on her back."

"What?" Dani asked, not sure she really wanted to know.

Laz swiped the screen of his cell phone and handed it to Dani. She recoiled at the close-up of a nude girl lying on her stomach. When he enlarged the photo, Dani saw that *Not looking so pretty now* was written in lipstick down her spine.

CHAPTER 11

Dani and Ivy stood on the front porch with Laz. The threatened rain had never materialized, but the air was still muggy and Dani was thankful for the newly installed overhead fan.

While Laz and Ivy said their goodbyes, Dani stared at the front lawn. The streetlamps cast a harsh glow on the yard and she could see that the grass was getting long. It would need cutting again soon and she still hadn't done anything about the overgrown bushes. Since she couldn't afford to hire a landscaper, there was only one option: her live-in help. She just had to figure out which of the girls would complain the least if they were reassigned from food prep to lawn duty.

As Laz said his final farewell and walked down the sidewalk toward his car, Dani smiled and waved. After dinner, he had helped her with the dishes, then joined the girls in the family room for a rousing game of Cards Against Humanity.

It had been the first time any of Dani's boarders had had a guy over, and she hadn't been sure whether to stick around to keep an eye on them.

Although she had finally decided that the young women weren't her wards and she wasn't some sort of Victorian-era governess, Dani *had* agreed to take responsibility for them, so she'd compromised and remained in earshot of the group. As a bonus, since she was hanging out in the kitchen, she got a head start on the next day's lunches.

As she'd sliced and diced, she'd heard wave after wave of laughter. It had sounded as if they were all having a great time and Dani hadn't been able to resist slipping down the hallway and taking a peek.

Tippi and Starr had been seated on the sofa in front of the coffee table with Laz and Ivy sprawled next to each other on the floor. The four of them appeared to be having fun together, but Laz's gaze had constantly sought Ivy's and he'd repeatedly touched her arm.

Which was the real Laz? Was he the drunken jerk that he'd been at the luau? Or the nice guy he seemed to be now? Had he truly been upset with his fiancée's cruelty or had that just been a convenient excuse to drink?

"Right?" Ivy's excited voice interrupted Dani's internal debate.

"What?" Dani blinked in confusion.

"Isn't Laz's car awesome?" Ivy bumped Dani's shoulder with her own.

"I guess." Dani squinted at the vehicle backing into the street.

"You have no idea what it is, do you?" Ivy put her hands on her hips.

"A convertible?" Dani said, unsure of what her friend was getting at.

"Not just any convertible." Ivy rolled her eyes. "A Maserati."

"Really?" Dani sat on the porch swing. "How much does a car like that run?"

"About a hundred and fifty thousand," Ivy said breathlessly.

"I knew that crowd was wealthy, but wow." Dani chewed her thumbnail. "Just wow. Although I suppose I should have figured out how rich they were when he said his grandfather paid for the library."

"It's a really nice library." Ivy sighed dreamily, then her face fell and she sank into a wicker rocking chair. "Laz is rich and handsome. Way out of my league."

Dani cringed. She'd said the same thing to Kelsey about Spencer. Dani and Ivy really were a lot alike. Which for the most part was great, but Dani didn't want her insecurities to rub off on her friend.

With that in mind, Dani said slowly, "Money doesn't define someone's worth. And . . ." She trailed off, uncertain what to add.

In truth, Ivy and Laz didn't seem to have much in common. Middle-class family versus billionaire dynasty. Pretty versus gorgeous. Nerd versus in crowd. But Laz had given the impression that he really liked Ivy. Was it fair to discourage her from pursuing a relationship?

"You don't have to say it, Dani. I already know." Ivy drew up her legs and laid her cheek on her knees. "Like Tippi always says, it's hard to find a sensitive, caring, handsome man because they already have boyfriends."

"You think Laz is gay?" Dani asked. Maybe Regina had threatened to out him and he'd killed her to maintain his facade.

"Nah." Ivy giggled. "It's just that I have as much chance of Laz Hunter asking me out as I would if he were into guys."

"You can't know that," Dani objected.

"Realistically, there is no Laz Hunter for someone like me."

"Before you make any decisions or jump

to any conclusions, three things." Dani held up her fingers. "First, Laz is probably not ready to start dating since his fiancée has only been dead a few days. Second, until Regina's murderer is found, it's not a good idea to give Detective Mikeloff any ideas about you having a motive — like wanting to move in on Regina's boyfriend."

Ivy nodded after each of Dani's first two points, then asked, "And third?"

"Third. Once the case is solved and some time has gone by, if you still want to go out with him, you should ask him." Dani set the porch swing in motion. "If Ron Weasley can end up with Hermione Granger, anything's possible."

"Seriously?" Ivy screeched. "You're giving me advice based on Harry Potter books?"

"That wasn't what I meant." Dani frowned. She'd been going to say *Beauty and the Beast* but realized just in time how bad that sounded. "I just meant that novels are full of unlikely couples."

"Too funny," Ivy snickered. "But if you're basing your relationship expectations on romances, you probably need to stop reading them."

"Never." Dani shook her head vehemently. "I'm holding out for a hero and a happily ever after."

Ivy snorted, then looked toward the road. "Who's pulling into the driveway? You don't think it's that awful detective again, do you?"

"I sure hope not." Chills chased up Dani's arms as she watched the car door open. She was relieved, at least for a second, to see Kipp getting out of the sedan.

"Hey." Ivy jumped to her feet. "It's Dr. Doofus." She turned and glared at Dani. "You are not getting back together with him, are you?"

"Of course not." Dani got up from the swing. "Why would you even think that?"

This was the reason she hadn't told her friend about Kipp's previous visit. Ivy hated him almost more than Dani did, which was a little odd but sweet.

"Then what's he doing here?" Ivy moved to stop Kipp from reaching the porch.

"Not that it's any of your business" — Kipp tried to maneuver around Ivy, and she shifted to block him — "but I'm here for the book Dani borrowed."

"I told you that I'd text you when I found it, which I haven't." Dani joined Ivy. "And technically, I didn't borrow it; you gave it to me. I'm being gracious and letting you have it back."

"Gracious would be getting it for me

now." Kipp tried to move forward.

"I haven't had a chance to look for it yet." Although her eyes were watering from the stench of stale smoke and sweaty gym socks wafting off her ex, Dani refused to budge.

As Kipp put his hands on Dani's shoulders to shift her out of his way, a sexy baritone growled, "Take your filthy mitts off of her."

Dani peered around Kipp and saw a scowling Spencer Drake hurtling up the steps. How had she missed his truck pulling into the driveway?

Dani stared at Spencer and said, "I can take care of myself." Kipp continued to dig his fingers into her arm, and she turned her attention to him. "Release me this instant or I'm going to go all Wonder Woman on your ass."

Ignoring her threat, Kipp looked over his shoulder. Seeing the large, glowering man behind him, he immediately dropped Dani's arm and held up his hands in supplication. "All I want is my book and I'll leave."

"You'll leave now." Dani tilted her head. "Why are you so anxious to get it?"

"My cousin is driving me nuts about the damn thing. She calls all the time." Kipp's voice was as annoying as an unoiled hinge. "Listen, Dani. I'll hire you. Whatever your going rate is to cook a meal, I'll pay you that to take the time to unpack your boxes and find it." He looked at Spencer. "Can't get any fairer than that, right, bro?"

"It's not up to me, *bro.*" Spencer raised his eyebrows. "It's up to Dani."

"Fine." Dani wanted to get Kipp out of her hair. "I'm busy tomorrow, but I have an opening Thursday afternoon and I'll look for the book then."

"How much does he owe you?" Spencer remained behind Kipp, trapping Dani's ex between the porch and sidewalk.

"I'll give him three hours of searching for a hundred and seventy-five dollars." Dani narrowed her eyes at Kipp. "But I want the cash up front, and if I find the book sooner, I still get to keep the full amount." She stared at her ex. "Is it worth that much money to you?"

"I'll go to the ATM right now," Kipp snapped. "I'll be back in half an hour."

"Fine. I'll wait with Dani." Spencer stepped around Kipp to stand by Dani. His smile was predatory as he lifted the leg of his jeans to show an ankle holster. "I can use the time to clean my Glock."

"You do know that firearms kill people." Kipp's tone was condescending.

"If guns kill people" — Ivy moved next to her uncle and stared down Kipp — "then pens misspell words, cars cause accidents, and forks make people gain weight."

Kipp opened his mouth, then closed it and stomped away.

Once her ex was gone, Dani glanced at Spencer. Why had he stopped by? A part of her would like to ask his help looking into Regina's murder, but she wasn't sure if that was a good idea or not.

After hugging Ivy, Spencer looked at Dani and asked, "Who was that guy?"

"Dani's creeper ex." Ivy pretended to gag. "He's an ER doc and thinks he's irresistible." She made a face. "He hid that he was engaged to someone else the whole time he was dating Dani."

"Your uncle isn't interested in my history with an old boyfriend." Dani's cheeks burned. Could she look like any more of a loser? "When his mom died, Kipp gave me a book from one of her boxes, which, it turns out, was promised to a relative. I told him he could have it back, but since I haven't completely unpacked from my move, I don't know where it is and —"

"And, big surprise, Dr. Dipstick thinks his needs and wants are more important than anyone else's." Ivy finished Dani's sentence.

Spencer grinned at his niece, then turned to Dani and said, "All the more reason for me to stick around until that bozo gets back with your money."

"There's no need. As I said before, I'm perfectly capable of taking care of myself." Dani ignored the little voice in her head screaming at her to shut up. "I'm sure you have better things to do than making sure Kipp comes through with his part of the bargain."

"Nope." Spencer took a seat on the wicker rocker and set the chair in motion. "It's a nice night and I can't think of any way I'd rather spend it than with my favorite niece."

Dani shuffled from foot to foot before she decided to go with the flow and asked, "Would you like some coffee and dessert?"

"One of your mocha cupcakes?" Spencer arched a dark brow.

"Not this time." Dani grinned at his hopeful expression and said, "But I have homemade banana pudding."

"Wow. I haven't had homemade since I was in grade school and Mom discovered store-bought pudding cups."

Dani smiled and hurried into the house. Emerging a few minutes later, she heard Ivy telling her uncle about their evening.

As Dani put the tray of coffee and dessert on a table next to Spencer's chair, he said, "So you had Regina's fiancé to dinner?"

"It seemed like the least I could do since he was nice enough to return Ivy's necklace." Dani joined Ivy on the porch swing.

"And you could pump him for info about his dead wife-to-be."

"We chatted about her a bit." Dani couldn't tell if Spencer was amused or annoyed. "But mostly, Laz apologized about his own behavior during the party."

"Oh?" Spencer picked up the bowl and dipped his spoon into the pudding.

"He explained, but I'm not sure that I should share his personal information." Dani watched as Spencer ate the entire dessert in three or four huge bites.

"Laz said it in front of all of us." Ivy glanced at Dani. "So I really doubt he's trying to keep it a big secret or anything."

"He's an alcoholic who fell off the wagon and got blitzed." Spencer licked his spoon, then leaned back in his chair.

"How did you know?" Ivy demanded, stopping the swing's movement.

"Because your uncle found out that Laz was in rehab." Dani shot Spencer a knowing look. "I thought you were only looking into Detective Mikeloff. Did you investigate all the partygoers' backgrounds?"

"Just the ones that you all told me were close to Regina." Spencer poured sugar in

186

his coffee, stirred, and took a cautious sip. "The intimate method used to kill her leads me to believe the murderer was someone in her immediate circle of friends or a relative. And Regina doesn't have any family within a thousand miles of Illinois."

Dani was silent. She'd bet her brand-new Vitamix blender that Spencer had also run her name past his resources. She really didn't have anything to hide. Well, except for the Homestead Insurance incident. And none of that mess was her fault.

"Did you find out anything else interesting, Uncle Spence?" Ivy asked.

"Mikeloff has a reputation for being mean." Spencer paused, then added, "He likes having people in his debt and gets off on exacting revenge if he feels like he's been betrayed. Rumor has it he's framed a few people to get payback." Spencer looked at Dani. "Is there any reason he would feel the need to retaliate against you?"

"I never met him before yesterday," Dani said.

Her mind flashed to the detective's resemblance to someone she knew. She really needed to find out who he looked like. If it was someone from her previous job, she'd have to come up with a way to tell Spencer about the detective's conflict of interest without violating the contract she'd signed.

"I also heard that Regina's ex-boyfriend went to prostitutes for drugs and rough sex," Spencer said staring at his niece.

"What? Vance? Ew!" Ivy wrinkled her nose and held up her hand to Spencer. "I don't even want to know how you found that out."

"Wouldn't that make him a good suspect?" Dani asked, ignoring Ivy's antics.

"It would be if Regina had been killed in a different way." Spencer sipped his coffee. "But an insulin overdose doesn't really fit that kind of person. I'm not a profiler, but I took the course, and strangulation during erotic asphyxiation or a whipping that got out of control would seem more his speed."

"And I'm out of here." Ivy jumped to her feet and dashed into the house.

"Shit! I'd better go check on her." Spencer rose from his chair. "She's so damn smart that I forget how young she really is."

"She's fine. Just a little embarrassed." Dani recalled some of the conversations about sex she'd overheard among Ivy, Starr, and Tippi. "It's not the topic so much as it is having her uncle talk about it."

"Sorry." Spencer blew out a breath. "Too many years in law enforcement."

"I imagine it's difficult to change your habits," Dani murmured.

"It is." Spencer's voice deepened. "I hope I didn't embarrass you."

"Nope." Dani shook her head. "My job in HR wasn't quite as bad, but as you can imagine, it would be hard to remain too innocent."

"I suppose." His blue eyes sparkled. "But somehow, I think you've managed to cling to the best part of innocence — the willingness to trust people and the sweetness that makes you want to help them."

Dani's breath hitched as she stared at his handsome face. The porch light's yellow bulb cast a pale glow that left the corners in shadow but created a halo around Spencer, making him seem almost magical. His assertion was the nicest thing anyone had said to her in a long, long time. Her stomach fluttered. Did he really see her like that or was he playing her so she'd let down her guard?

She chose her words carefully. "Well, that's certainly very flattering."

Her track record with men stank. Her father, her boss, and her boyfriend had all ended up mistreating her. None of them had ever physically harmed her, but they sure as heck had wrecked her emotionally.

"Dani." Spencer scooted his chair until it faced the swing where she sat, then leaned forward and took both her hands in his. "I'm not trying to charm you or smooth talk you into anything." He waited for her to stop staring at their fingers and to look at him before he continued, "I promise you I won't lie to you."

"That would be a refreshing change," Dani blurted, then quickly added, "What I mean is, a lot of people either fudge the truth or omit the relative facts and tell themselves they aren't liars."

"I can't argue with your assessment of our society." Spencer chuckled. "But between us, let's have a no-bullshit policy."

"Whenever possible," Dani qualified, then eased her fingers from his grasp. There were matters she couldn't discuss and she certainly didn't owe Spencer any explanations.

"Okay." Spencer continued to stare at her. "But I think we both want the same thing." He raised a brow. "To make sure Mikeloff doesn't set up either you or Ivy for Regina's murder."

"Agreed." Dani nodded and told him about her morning visitor. She didn't see how telling him about the reporter could be an issue for her, and sharing that information with him might lull Spencer into trusting her more.

"There are two ways to approach the

problem." Spencer tapped her knee, refocusing her attention. "One, we get Mikeloff removed from the case."

"By proving he's a dirty cop?" Dani asked, then recalled her other idea. "Or suggesting some kind of conflict of interest?"

"Yes, but it probably wouldn't work. A lot of suspects claim the cops are targeting them unfairly and we don't have any concrete evidence to prove he's really doing that to you." Spencer's nostrils flared. "I can put a bug in the chief of police's ear, but even if she believes me and investigates, Mikeloff could really jam up you and Ivy in the meantime."

"So what then?" Dani asked, annoyed that what she thought were two pretty darn good plans apparently wouldn't work.

He didn't answer. His lips pressed together as if he had tasted something bad.

"You don't want to say it," Dani prodded. "But the best way to clear my name and prevent Ivy from becoming Mikeloff's next target is —"

"For us to figure out who killed Regina," Spencer said, finishing Dani's sentence.

"And you hate the idea of civilians interfering with a police investigation," Dani guessed, then added, "But you're a civilian too."

"Yes and no." Spencer crossed his arms. "I may no longer have a formal connection to a law enforcement agency, but I do continue to have some ties. And I also have the training to deal with bad guys. You do not."

"Still," Dani argued, "I'm the one with the most to lose if Mikeloff frames me for the murder."

"True." Spencer inhaled deeply, then added, "And even more than I hate involving a private citizen, I hate the idea of someone who's innocent being convicted and someone who's guilty getting off scot-free even more."

CHAPTER 12

Spencer had slept poorly. An unrelenting *drip-drop-drip* from the kitchen's leaky faucet, noisy neighbors — the curse of a town house in a college town — and unsettling thoughts about Dani had kept him awake all night. He'd tossed and turned, alternating between staring at the ceiling and the digital clock on his nightstand.

He'd finally given up on the hope of sleeping, and by 5:00 a.m., he was already showered, dressed, and leaving for work. It looked as if yesterday's weather had been a signal for a change from the pleasant temperatures they had been enjoying. Today was predicted to be hot and even more humid, which meant the security force would be miserable in their polyester uniforms. Another issue for Spencer to address on his unending list of changes that needed to be made.

Along with their discomfort about their

193

personal attire, the security staff would have to deal with another sticky problem. In the summer, the students spent a lot more time outdoors on the quad, and they often wore a lot less clothing than their parents would appreciate.

Girls in tiny shorts and barely-there tank tops mixing with boys high on testosterone and other less legal substances were a bad combination. The consequences of such a dangerous combo were one of the principal reasons Spencer had been hired. An important part of his job was to make it clear there was no excuse for sexual assault — no means no — and to enforce a zero-tolerance policy on or off campus.

The university administration wanted abusive students held accountable and potential victims protected. By employing someone like Spencer to beef up security's presence and outline appropriate prevention and responses, the college had proven its commitment to its students' welfare.

Pulling into his reserved parking spot, Spencer's thoughts were on the safety strategy he'd been creating for the upcoming rally against gender-based violence. As he marched down the sidewalk toward the heavy metal doors of the campus security building, he jerked to halt and frowned at the empty beer can and used condom sitting on the lawn. Clearly, he needed to have a chat with his staff about including their own perimeter in their routine patrols.

Spencer jotted a reminder to himself in his ever-present notebook, then proceeded to his office. The room was tiny, with barely enough space to walk from the desk to the file cabinet to the bookcase. When he'd come on board, he could have claimed one of the large conference rooms, but since he hadn't planned on spending much time sitting on his butt behind a desk, he was fine with the smaller area.

Once he was settled and working on the plan, his mind wandered back to the previous evening. Forcing Dani's asshat ex to leave her alone had felt fantastic. Urging Little Miss Cupcake to investigate Regina's murder, not so much.

Seeing that scumbag manhandling Dani had brought out every one of Spencer's protective instincts. He didn't like the obnoxious doctor breathing her air, let alone touching her.

And he liked that she was on the radar of a corrupt cop known for his vengeful behavior even less. What was he thinking encouraging a civilian to become involved in a police matter? Had he completely lost his fricking mind?

Although, as Dani had pointed out, he was now a civilian too. It was times like these that he missed his badge. He sure didn't miss being undercover, but the authority that came with his shield would have been mighty handy right about now.

If he were still in law enforcement, he would have never agreed to team up with Dani. But when she'd outlined what she had learned about the vic and her friends, he had to admit that, in a short amount of time, his Little Miss Cupcake had gathered an impressive amount of insider information. He doubted that the fiancé or the reporter would have been as open with either Spencer or the cops.

He frowned. Come to think of it, a journalist willingly sharing info was strange. He'd never met one he could trust. Most likely, the woman was using Dani. He needed to check out Frannie Ryan.

Dani had said the woman was from Scumble River. A community in which Spencer had spent some time undercover as a member of a motorcycle gang. And a place where he just happened to know the chief of police.

Spencer had kept in touch with Wally and his pretty wife, Skye. In fact, he still had the birth announcement containing a picture of their babies wearing T-shirts that read DADDY, I'VE GOT YOUR 6. The card was tacked to the bulletin board above his desk at home and he smiled every damn time he saw it.

Shaking his head, Spencer added a note to call Wally about the reporter to his to-do list, then tried to concentrate on the sexual assault awareness training seminar he was designing for his security team. But a few minutes later, he threw down his pen and stared out the window. What was it about Dani that attracted him so much?

Sure she was pretty and smart. But he was surrounded by good-looking, intelligent women, and none of them incited the intense lust or genuine warmth he felt toward Dani. Maybe it was exactly what he'd told her. Maybe it was her sweetness that drew him to her.

Last night, as they'd sat on her front porch, it had been rough ignoring the voice inside his head that insisted he ask her out. Insisted that he let her know he was interested in her as a woman not just as his niece's friend. Insisted that he move closer.

But in the long run, he knew it was better to keep Dani at a distance. That way, he wouldn't be lured into trying for something he'd already messed up once before. Something too fragile for the likes of him. Something out of his reach.

Relationships never worked for him, and his Little Miss Cupcake didn't seem the type who would be satisfied with just hooking up for a few nights of wild sex. Actually, if Spencer was totally honest with himself, neither was he. At least not anymore.

In the long years since his divorce, he'd played the field. Never seeing a woman more than once or twice. Never waking up in her bed or allowing her to visit his place. Never making it about anything but a fun, fast, and meaningless physical release.

But deep down in his soul, Spencer knew that he wanted what Wally and Skye Boyd had together. It was a damn shame that he was too much of a coward to risk opening up his heart again to find it. No. It was better to keep an emotional distance with Dani than go through the pain of another breakup.

Spencer rubbed the space between his eyes where a headache was forming. Working with Dani to discover who murdered Regina would give them a chance to get to know each other and develop a friendship. Which was the only relationship he really could handle right now.

All he had to do was keep Dani safe from

a shady cop and out of the path of a killer while they figured out who murdered Regina Bourne. Oh, and keep his own hands off the tempting chef and her luscious cupcakes.

Spencer ground his teeth, stomped out of his office, and went into the break room. Maybe a shot of java would cure what was ailing him. The look on his face must have deterred his employees from asking any questions, because the two men didn't attempt any conversation. Instead, they hastily finished their coffee, rose to their feet, grabbed their equipment, and headed out the door muttering about making their rounds.

As Spencer started to fill his cup, he stopped midpour. Breakfast. That was what he needed. A good old-fashioned breakfast with his friend Hiram. If anyone could advise him on the best way to handle the situation with Mikeloff, it was Hiram Heller.

Hiram had been Spencer's mentor since the academy. He wondered what his adviser would have to say about both the detective's behavior and Spencer's sudden urge to stick his nose into police business after years of steering clear of the local law enforcement officers. The old man usually had an opinion and wasn't shy about sharing it.

A quick text and twenty-five minutes later, Spencer arrived at the Downs Diner. The familiar double doors with their cloudy glass and fading red paint welcomed him. And the notices taped to the window informed him of an upcoming community garage sale as well as a lost bicycle.

As Spencer inhaled the wonderful scents of pancakes and bacon and coffee, he greeted Uriah, the café's owner. Then, marching to the back booth, Spencer slid into the bench across from his mentor. Before he was fully seated, Uriah approached the table and thumped a dish containing half a dozen slices of bacon, three eggs, and a generous portion of hash browns in front of Hiram. Wordlessly, the café owner cocked a brow at Spencer, who ignored the laminated menu and instead nodded that he would have the same. Uriah grunted and headed back to the kitchen.

The owner of the diner was a big, barrel-chested man in his sixties wearing his usual uniform of white cotton pants, T-shirt, and apron. Spencer wasn't sure of his ethnicity, but no matter the season, his complexion was always bronzed and his eyes were an unusual shade of light green. He never had much to say and he handled the cooking and serving without any hired help. His only employee was a cleaning lady he spoke to in something other than English.

Hiram glanced up from his newspaper, skewered Spencer with a sharp stare, and asked, "What's got your boxers in such a twist?"

His mentor had the rough voice of a heavy smoker, but Spencer knew Hiram had never lit up a cigarette. He was a compact man, barely able to claim five foot eight and 140 pounds. But his small stature hadn't kept him from being one of the best agents his unit had ever produced.

Grinning, Spencer said, "Hello to you too."

"Recruit," Hiram growled.

The old man didn't tolerate a lot of small talk. Not out of disinterest, but from years of getting to the point. Hiram had guided Spencer's career since he was twenty-two and had never given him a bad piece of advice — including the suggestion a year ago to get out from undercover and have a life.

Hiram was the one who had taught Spencer how to navigate the politics of the law enforcement profession and how to be a good officer. He was also the one with whom Spencer had shared his hopes, dreams, and troubles. And the one who, knowing Spencer would never be happy completely out of the protect-and-serve business, had recommended that he apply for the head of security job at Normalton University.

"Nothing's wrong," Spencer said to Hiram, then thanked Uriah who had returned with his plate of food.

"Uh-huh." Hiram set aside his newspaper, took off his glasses, and said, "Just a sudden urge to drive ten miles for breakfast?"

"Why not? I was up early and we haven't talked in a while." Spencer rose and walked to the coffee machine on the counter. "Want a refill?"

"Don't mind if I do." Hiram rubbed his hands together. "Uriah keeps this place too dang cold. It's icier than a whore's heart in here."

"You might be wishing for the AC this afternoon." Spencer grabbed the carafe, poured a cup for himself, and topped off Hiram's white crockery mug. "It's supposed to be a sizzler today."

"Thanks." Hiram leaned back and took a long sip. "So what's this really about?" He wiped his mouth with the back of his hand. "Something is on your mind and you might as well spill it."

"It's kind of complicated." Spencer stared

over Hiram's shoulder. "Did I tell you that my niece got into trouble and her parents made her move out of that apartment she was sharing with her friends?"

"You mentioned it." Hiram folded his glasses and put them in his shirt pocket. "She's living in some mansion with the woman who had been her neighbor. Something like a boardinghouse situation, right?"

"Yeah. Ivy's landlady has got herself a whopper of a serious problem." Spencer removed the napkin from around his silverware and put it in his lap. "And it could turn into something worse."

"That's a damn shame." Hiram's expression was mournful. "You said she'd been real good to Ivy and the other girls." He quirked his mouth. "Still. I don't see that as any of your concern."

"The thing is" — Spencer focused on spreading jelly on his toast — "it's entirely possible her troubles could also become Ivy's."

"Is that a fact?" Hiram tilted his head and examined his protégé. "So you're only worried about your niece's possible involvement?"

"Not entirely," Spencer admitted. "I don't want Dani hurt either."

"Dani, huh?" Hiram's lips quirked. "She

isn't the frumpy neighbor lady you thought she was after all. Just how good looking is she?"

"She's real pretty." Spencer squirmed on the uncomfortable wooden bench, uneasy with his thoughts. "But she's got this freshness. And although she's not a pushover, life hasn't made her hard."

"Interesting." Hiram took a sip of his coffee. "What's her problem?"

"In addition to renting out rooms to my niece and her friends, Dani has this business called Chef-to-Go." Spencer ate a strip of bacon, then continued, "One of her clients was murdered the night after an event that Dani and the girls catered. And the party didn't end on a good note for Dani or Ivy."

"I see." Hiram took a small red notebook from his shirt pocket. "So Dani's a suspect and Ivy could turn into one." He jotted down a note. "Do they have an alibi for the time of death?"

"Unfortunately, the TOD isn't as important as when the insulin was injected, and evidently, that isn't as easy to pin down." Spencer knew where Hiram was going and outlined the circumstances of Regina's murder.

"Ah." Hiram pinched his bottom lip

204

between his index finger and thumb and pulled it out. "You need to get a copy of the coroner's report to find out when and where this girl was injected."

"Any possibility you know someone who can get me a peek at it?" Spencer slid his cup in circles on the cracked plastic top of the table.

"I have someone who works in the coroner's office," Hiram said. "He'll want something for his trouble. A hundred bucks should do it."

"That's fine." Spencer dug out his wallet and handed over two fifties. At the rate he was paying for information, he'd better make an ATM stop on his way back to his office.

"Is the detective handling the case someone reasonable who you can work with?"

"Just the opposite." Spencer ate a bite of crispy hash browns. "In fact, the asshat's the bigger of the two problems." He explained to Hiram what he'd discovered about Mikeloff's penchant for using his position for revenge, then added, "And this jerkwad apparently has some sort of hard-on where Dani is concerned."

"Why is that?" Hiram leaned back in his seat and extended his arms across the back. "Does she know him? Have they had a run-in before?"

"She says that she hasn't and I believe her." Between bites, Spencer filled his mentor in on his conversation with Dani regarding the detective. "However, while I'm fairly sure she's telling me the truth about Mikeloff, she is holding something back. And I think it has to do with her previous job in HR at the insurance company."

"You want me to look into that?" Hiram asked. "I could call in a favor."

"No." Spencer dipped his toast into the yolk of a perfect sunny-side-up egg. Uriah was a genius with a spatula and frying pan. "At least not yet."

"You want to give her time to tell you herself." Hiram nodded approvingly. "That's smart. My policy has always been never to make a woman mad. She can remember shit that hasn't even happened yet. And that's no way to start a relationship."

"Relationship! What?" Spencer choked on the bite he'd just taken. "No! We aren't . . . I'm not ready yet."

"Keep telling yourself that, son." Hiram chuckled and drank some coffee.

Clearing his throat, Spencer said, "Getting back to problem number three."

"Which is?" Hiram clicked on his pen and

tapped it against his notebook.

"With Mikeloff's reputation for framing people he doesn't like and no way that I can see to get him off the case" — Spencer clenched his jaw — "I . . ." He blew out a breath and shook his head. "I suggested to Dani that we look into the murder ourselves."

"You advised a civilian to interfere with a police investigation," Hiram sputtered before understanding dawned in his bright-brown eyes. "You've got the hots for Dani and you want to spend time with her without actually committing to a date."

"No!" Spencer snapped. "That is yes, I'd like to get to know her as a friend, but mostly I'm concerned what Mikeloff might do."

"Okay." Hiram drew out the word and raised a brow indicating he thought Spencer was full of bull. "What's your plan of attack?"

"Since Regina was an NU student, I have an appointment with the police chief to discuss the case. She's been out of town and couldn't squeeze me in until tomorrow." Spencer finished his breakfast and pushed aside the empty plate. "I plan to feel her out about Mikeloff and see if she knows that Mikeloff is a bad cop."

"The chief's not going to remove him from the case without some ironclad reason." Hiram's thick, white eyebrows met over his nose. "Best scenario, she agrees to keep you in the loop regarding their progress. No way in hell is she showing you the file."

"That's my guess too." Spencer nodded. "Which means Dani and I will need to interview witnesses and interrogate suspects on our own."

"You didn't fool me back when you were a rookie, and you don't fool me now," Hiram snorted. "Hell, just come clean. You like this woman and you want to protect her and spend time with her."

"Maybe I do." Spencer's tone was stiff. "But all I can handle right now is friendship." He raised both brows. "And after meeting her ex last night, that's probably all she can handle too."

CHAPTER 13

Early Wednesday afternoon, Dani handed a red-and-white paper sack to Abby Goodman and watched as the girl tapped her credit card against the machine. Because she liked to make sure she had dibs if she wanted any substitutions, Abby was usually among the first to arrive, but today she was the last.

Even Smokey had beaten her to the counter. Dani noticed the girl's exhausted appearance and wondered if she had taken on too heavy a class load. Although they were technically sold out, Dani felt sorry for Abby and scraped together a healthy lunch-to-go bag for her.

After the girl hurried away, Dani turned and looked at the disaster that had once been her kitchen. Tippi, her assigned helper, had left an IOU saying she had to study for a test and would make up the hours she owed Dani.

Of the three girls, the tiny brunette was

the least reliable. She tended to show up late for work and leave early, always promising to make up the time but never following through. Her behavior wasn't something that Dani, or the other girls, would tolerate for long, but since they were all still settling into this new situation, Dani would wait a few more weeks before confronting her.

Previously, Tippi's actions hadn't been a real problem, but today, Dani had been late getting out of bed herself.

She'd been awake until well after 2:00 a.m., staring into the darkness and obsessing over her situation. An ex that was driving her crazy, Regina's murder possibly ruining her Chef-to-Go business, and a twisted detective trying to convict her of killing the young woman.

As Kelsey had pointed out, and Dani had tried to ignore, the cop's motives were almost certainly related to her participation in Homestead Insurance's biggest cover-up. As much as she wanted to pretend Mikeloff's vendetta against her could be connected to any number of personnel matters at her old job, logically, she knew it was probably the nastiest one.

Which meant Dani would have to pay a visit to her previous employer and try to figure out which of the people involved were connected to the vindictive cop. Although she heard that the entire HR department had gone through a huge shake-up when a chainsaw consultant had been brought in and reduced the employee head count by half, Dani could only hope that there was someone left who would be willing to give her access to the pertinent files.

As she cleaned up the kitchen, she mentally ran through the list of her colleagues. Although she hadn't burned any bridges when she quit, she also hadn't kept in touch.

Shuddering, Dani realized that Perry Sumac was the only person in her old company who might be willing to help her. He had invited her out several times, and it was clear that he had a crush on her. But even if she hadn't had a rule against socializing with colleagues, Perry creeped her out. Asking him for a favor would be tough, getting it without agreeing to a date with him even tougher.

Dani's mind veered away from the unappealing thought of her old coworker to the very appealing memory of Spencer Drake. Last night, it had been so nice sitting on the porch with him. Once Kipp had dropped off the money and left, she and Spencer had continued to enjoy the pleasant evening.

She had been shocked when Spencer

agreed to help her investigate Regina's murder. And as much as she could tell he wanted to take back his words, he hadn't whined or tried to blame her.

In fact, he had been funny and charming, telling her amusing stories about recent incidents campus security had to handle. He'd seemed genuinely interested in her Chef-to-Go business and hadn't shown any indication that he thought she was wasting her education or that should be working in HR. Maybe that was because they were both starting over and reinventing themselves.

Smiling at the thought of the two of them getting a fresh start, Dani inspected the kitchen. Everything was back in place, the dishwasher was humming quietly, and all the surfaces sparkled. Now she could turn her attention to figuring out Mikeloff's link to Homestead, which would require a shower and some makeup.

Ninety minutes later, with her hair curled and wearing a pretty summer dress, Dani walked into the Homestead Insurance building. The modern glass-and-brick high-rise had been her home away from home for seven years, and she was surprised to realize that she hadn't missed it or the work or, to be honest, any of the people.

The receptionist was on the phone and

waved Dani through. She took the elevator to the fifth floor and walked down the long hall until she came to the frosted-glass door with the inscription *Human Resources.*

The metal knob felt icy in her palm, but she pasted a pleasant expression on her face and entered the department. Taking a deep breath, she nearly choked at the artificial smell of room freshener. Lilies had never been her favorite scent and the imitation was worse than the original.

A few seconds later, Dani cringed when she heard, "Danielle, what a surprise to see you here. Are coming back to work for us?"

"Sorry, no." Dani faced Evie Hanger, the woman who had taken over after the boss's heart attack. "Since I was in the area, I just thought I'd drop by and say hello."

"How sweet." Evie's expression didn't match her words. "Well, there have been some personnel modifications and there may not be a lot of people you know anymore. Still, a quick hello to any of your friends who are remaining is fine, but this *is* a place of business."

"Of course." Dani held on to her smile. "Is Perry still working here?"

"Yes." Evie turned and marched away. "He's now in the last cube on the right."

Perry Sumac resembled a mushroom, a

brown blob on a stem of two skinny legs. When Dani entered his cubicle, he was frowning at his keyboard, hunched over a desktop overflowing with empty food wrappers and overturned paper cups. However, when he looked up and recognized Dani, his annoyed expression morphed into a huge smile.

He jumped to his feet and lumbered toward her. "Dani!" Perry's voice reminded her of oozing sap. "It's so good to see you."

"Thanks, Perry." Dani's skin crawled as she endured his hug. "Do you have a minute?"

"Sure." He held on to her a few beats too long, but when she squirmed, he let go and guided her to the chair next to his desk.

"I hear that there've been a lot of staff changes since I left." Dani searched her mind for small talk, putting off the inevitable when she'd have to ask for help.

"Yeah." Perry ran a hand through his greasy hair. "They had a blame-storming session and fired everyone they considered responsible for the disappointing profits."

"But you weathered the storm?"

"Yep." Perry's chest puffed out. "They can't do without me."

"That's great." Dani smoothed her dress over her knees. "Who else survived?"

Perry named half a dozen others, then went on a long tirade about corporate policies.

As he wound up his rant, he said, "When Webster kicked the bucket, I should have gotten the manager's job, but Evie was sleeping with one of the VPs and they gave it to her."

"Oh." Dani wasn't sure if that was true or not, but a disgruntled Perry was good for her plan. "That's so not fair to you."

"Evie's already screwing up, so I'll probably get the job once they fire her."

"Won't her lover protect her? Especially if she threatens a harassment lawsuit. It seems where the company's image is at stake, it has very little loyalty to their hardworking employees."

"They would definitely hush up her incompetence," Perry snarled. "After all, to err may be human, but to pin it on someone else shows administrative potential. The VP will make sure he has all his ducks in a row for that quack."

"That's so true. I saw it time and time again." Dani recognized her opening and said, "Which is one of the reasons I quit. I just couldn't go along with corporate's cavalier attitude toward people. Now that might be coming back to bite me in the butt."

"We all wondered why you left," Perry said. "If there's anything I can do to help you" — he leaned toward her — "just name it."

"I don't want to get you in trouble," Dani said, edging back from him.

She was starting to feel sleazy about her plan to use the poor guy but hardened her heart when he put his palm on her thigh, leered at her, and said, "I can take care of myself and you too, if you get my meaning."

"Well . . ." Guilt lifted from Dani's shoulders and she fluttered her lashes. "If I could have access to your computer for a few minutes, I might be able to figure out who's behind my problems."

"You know what?" Perry reluctantly withdrew his hand and stood. "I suddenly remember that I need to use the little boy's room." He gave her an exaggerated wink. "And since I'll be right back, it's really too much trouble to log off and back on. I wouldn't want to be accused of wasting precious work time."

"Hey." Dani waved him away. "When you gotta go, you gotta go."

As soon as Perry disappeared, Dani rose

and slipped into his chair. She held her breath as her fingers flew over the keyboard. Would the files still be there or had they been deleted?

Several clicks later, she blew out a relieved lungful of air. The personnel records for the three men who had been dismissed after the harassment incident came to light were still in the system. Dani drew a thumb drive from her cleavage, inserted it in the computer, and pressed save.

Peeking over the cubicle wall, Dani saw that the coast was still clear. Returning the flash drive to her bra, she quickly cleared the screen and deleted any trace of what she'd been searching.

A minute or two later, Perry returned. He was loudly clearing his throat as approached and made a big production of settling back in his chair.

As soon as he was seated, Dani jumped to her feet and said brightly, "It was so good seeing you, Perry, but I better get going."

"How about I take you for dinner tonight?" Perry waggled his eyebrows. "It's all you can eat for $9.99 at the Golden Round Up."

"Darn!" Dani shook her head. "I have a personal chef job tonight."

"Tomorrow is buy-one-get-one-free at the

Great Wall Buffet, so it will only cost us ten bucks each." Perry rolled his chair in front of her, caging her against the cubicle wall. "I'll pick you up at six."

"I have a huge catering contract on Friday and I'll be busy getting the food ready." Dani swallowed nervously. "Right now, my new business takes all of my time." She tried to edge sideways. "Maybe we can get together after Christmas."

"You owe me." Perry grabbed her wrist. "And you're going to pay up."

"How much?" Dani asked, wincing when his ragged, dirt-rimmed fingernails dug into her skin.

"You know what I want and it isn't dough." Perry scooted his chair closer until Dani could feel the rough material of the partition against the back of her knees.

"Money is all you're getting." Dani dug a fifty from her purse and thrust it at his chest. Thank goodness, she hadn't stopped at the bank yet to deposit the cash from the lunches-to-go.

A calculating looked crossed Perry's face and he said, "Make it a hundred, and we'll call it square." When Dani hesitated, he added, "A decent-looking pro will cost at least that much."

"Fine." Not wanting to hear more and

feeling like she needed a shower, Dani handed over two twenties and a ten, then fled.

Driving home, Dani was disgusted with herself. She should have figured out a different means of getting the files. But she hadn't been able to think of any other way, and the alternative to flirting with Perry had been the risk of doing nothing and having Mikeloff frame her.

When she got back to the mansion, Dani assembled the food and equipment that she would need for tonight's dinner for Trent and Chelsea Karnes. The salted beef tenderloin was already on a rack in the refrigerator along with the bacon, potato, and cheese tart. Both needed an hour in the oven. While they cooked, Dani would make the port sauce, as well as the Georgian green beans and the lemon fluff dessert.

Once Dani was sure she was prepared for the evening, she headed upstairs with a plate of sliced fruit, yogurt, and a piece of raisin toast. She wouldn't get to eat her own supper until after she finished at the Karneses', so this snack would have to hold her until then.

Putting her dish on a nearby table, she fetched her laptop and settled on the comfy chaise in her sitting room. Dani opened her computer, pushed the Power button, and impatiently waited for it to boot up. As she watched the various programs load, she thought about her course of action. Was she wasting her time trying to figure out what Mikeloff had against her when she should be trying to solve Regina's murder instead?

No. First things first. After she discovered the detective's motives, she'd concentrate on finding Regina's killer.

Inserting the thumb drive with the files from Homestead Insurance, Dani clicked rapidly through the documents. She wasn't sure where to start. Was Mikeloff connected to the woman who had been victimized or the men who had been dismissed? The detective had just said that she'd ruined someone's life. It could be any of the four people involved in the incident and its subsequent cover-up.

Popping a grape into her mouth, Dani decided to start with the men. While she had info on the three persecutors, the records regarding the woman and her case were password protected. Dani didn't recall the victim's name, so if she didn't find what she was looking for in the files she had, she'd have to do an online search using the few details about the woman that she remembered.

Having settled on a plan, Dani clicked open the personnel dossier of the first man. She ran her finger across the screen, careful to read each line. After studying the entire dossier, she opened the attached photograph and stared at the guy's picture.

She hadn't spent much time with the men involved in the scandal; most matters had been handled via email so that there would be documentation. And the few instances that she'd met with them in person, she'd been unwilling to meet their eyes and kept her gaze on the paperwork they were completing. As a result, she couldn't recall any of their faces.

This first guy she looked at was blond, in his late twenties. There was nothing to indicate that he had any connection to Mikeloff. Of course, there were a million things Dani didn't know about either man, so if she didn't discover something from the other records she'd have to enlarge her search.

The next possibility was a redhead in his thirties. Again there was nothing obvious to link him with the detective.

Feeling discouraged, Dani clicked open the last man's file and stared at Demetri Mitchell's picture. If this guy were twenty years older and fifty pounds lighter, he'd be a dead ringer for Mikeloff.

Oh. My. God! Dani closed her eyes, hoping she was wrong. But several seconds later, when she opened them, the photograph hadn't changed. Demetri, one of the men whom she had been instrumental in firing without severance or recommendation, was definitely somehow related to the detective who was trying to convict her of murdering Regina.

Demetri had maintained that while he was aware of what the other two men in his division were doing, he'd never participated. Dani had sensed he was telling the truth and suggested putting him on probation, but Homestead's CEO had wanted the entire department wiped clean. And when the woman had remained adamant that all three men had been a part of her harassment, Dani had had no choice but to fire Demetri along with his colleagues.

Feeling nauseated, Dani scrutinized the picture for a third time. She rubbed her temples. There was such a strong resemblance, she wondered if the detective might even be Demetri's father. The last name of Mitchell could certainly be an Americanization of Mikeloff. If so, Dani was in big trouble, and maybe Ivy by her association with her.

Sick to her stomach, Dani pushed away the fruit plate and fumbled with her cell. She had to call Spencer. Even keeping to the confidentiality agreement that she'd signed, she could tell him that there was a strong possibility that Mikeloff was closely related to an employee that she had been involved in firing.

She didn't have to give Spencer the particulars, but he needed to know that the detective had a good reason to persecute her. And that it was likely that Mikeloff would concentrate all his efforts on proving Dani had murdered Regina.

CHAPTER 14

After Dani had consulted with Kelsey regarding the confidentiality agreement she'd signed and determined exactly what she could and could not reveal about the detective's motivation for retribution, she'd phoned Spencer. As she had anticipated, he hadn't been pleased that the only thing she would tell him was that a man named Demetri Mitchell who bore a strong physical resemblance to Mikeloff had worked at Homestead Insurance while she was employed in the company's HR department.

Spencer had spent several minutes attempting to change her mind, but eventually he realized that Dani wasn't budging. Once he'd conceded defeat, he agreed to do some research on both Mitchell and Mikeloff to find out if the two men were related. Spencer had also promised to stop over Thursday afternoon to share what he learned from his appointment with the police chief.

By the time Dani got off the phone with Spencer, it was past five, and she swiftly changed into her chef coat and pants, gathered her supplies, and headed toward the ritzy side of town. It was a little early, since Trent and Chelsea Karnes wanted to eat at their customary dinnertime of seven thirty, but Dani didn't want to have to rush again.

As she pulled into the cul-de-sac, Dani crossed her fingers that in spite of everything that had happened with the luau and murder, the Karneses still wanted her to cook for them. They hadn't contacted her to cancel, but she was a little nervous about facing a couple who had been Regina's friends — or at least her parents' friends.

They were presently her only personal chef customers and she didn't want to lose them. She'd sent out flyers to all the addresses in Normalton's ritzier neighborhoods and intended to follow up with another round, but her best chance for finding clients for this branch of her business was referrals from people like the Karneses.

Not at all sure of her reception, Dani took a deep breath and grabbed the cooler of food by the handles. Balancing the box of equipment on top of the ice chest, she made her way down the sidewalk leading to the rear of the faux castle and used her elbow to ring the bell.

Several terrifyingly long moments later, in which Dani's imagination raced between rejection and another murdered client, Trent Karnes opened the back door. He held a cell phone to his ear with one hand and motioned Dani inside with the other.

After a distracted greeting, he continued his telephone conversation as he led Dani through the mudroom. When they entered the kitchen, Trent finally said goodbye to whoever was on the other end of his call and slipped the cell into his pants pocket.

With a guilty look on his handsome face, he turned to Dani and said, "I know this is impossibly last minute, and I truly hate to ask, but could you possibly serve dinner for four tonight?"

"Absolutely." Dani didn't bother to tell him that his wife routinely didn't give her any notice about either the change in number of guests or the time they wanted to eat and that she came prepared with extras of everything and a game plan for an unexpected time crunch. "Do you still want dinner served at seven thirty?"

"If that works for you." Trent flashed his dimples and when Dani nodded, he added,

"Friends of ours just phoned to say they were in town. We've been bragging about your skills and when the Ackermans asked if you were cooking for us tonight, I felt like I had no choice but to invite them to dinner."

"Are they vegan or vegetarians?" Dani asked. When he shook his head, she smiled and said, "Then it's no problem and we're in good shape."

"Outstanding. Maureen and Scott will be ecstatic." Trent started to leave the room, then paused and asked, "Do you need any help carrying in the rest of your gear?"

"Thanks, but I've got it," Dani assured him, hoping to get him moving out of the kitchen.

When he hesitated, she waved him away, then headed back to the van. Trent was a lot nicer than his wife, but she didn't like clients hanging around while she cooked.

Once Dani had everything inside, she laid out the food and equipment on the counter, then went to fetch what she needed from the walk-in pantry. Entering, she smiled. The pantry shelves looked as if nothing had been touched since her last visit. With the couple's aversion and/or inability to feed themselves, unless she was actually incarcerated for Regina's murder, her job as their twice-a-week personal chef seemed to be safe.

Relieved, Dani focused on preparing the tenderloin. It was a prime cut that would be delicious with the port sauce. The beef needed to be in the oven fifty minutes before it was served so that it would have a chance to rest prior to being carved; otherwise, the juices would run out, and the meat would be dry and stringy.

After rubbing the meat with oil and sprinkling it with cracked peppercorns, Dani programmed one of the double ovens to 425. While it was heating, she prepped the fresh green beans.

An hour later, the doorbell chimed the first few bars of "Dixie" and she heard Chelsea and Trent greet their guests. From the sounds coming from the living room, the couples were remaining inside instead of having drinks on the patio, as was the Karneses' habit. Evidently, Chelsea had decided that no matter how much she wanted to show off her fancy patio with the fireplace, lap pool, and flat-screen TV, the hot, sticky weather wasn't conducive to outdoor entertaining.

With her clients and their company nearby, Dani had to tune out their voices as she worked. The tenderloin and the potato tart were in the oven, due to come out in ten minutes, and she needed to concentrate on the tricky port sauce. She had already melted butter, sautéed shallots, and measured in Cognac, rosemary, and pepper. Then, after simmering, she had added port and beef stock. Now, she had to watch the mixture as it boiled, waiting for it to reduce to the perfect consistency.

When the timer sounded, Dani turned the burner under the sauce to low, slid the meat, potatoes, and rolls from the ovens, checked on the Georgian green beans, and grabbed the four seafood cocktails from the fridge. The Karneses and their guests could have their first course while Dani sliced the tenderloin and plated the entrée.

After putting the appetizers on the dining room table, Dani headed back to the kitchen. But a few steps down the hallway, she heard Regina's name mentioned. Hoping to catch an important tidbit, she paused, then tiptoed to the end of the passage and flattened herself against the wall.

The house was decorated in a starkly modernistic style and the brushed-steel arch lamps illuminated the two couples as if they were on a stage. The Karneses and the Ackermans were sitting across from one another with their profiles to Dani, and were so engrossed in the conversation that none of them noticed her peeking around the wall.

"I wasn't at all shocked when you texted me that Regina had been murdered." A slim strawberry-blond who had to be Maureen Ackerman crossed a white-linen-clad leg. "After what the beastly girl did to our wonderful sorority's reputation, I'm just surprised no one killed her back then."

Dani gasped, then clapped a hand over her mouth, hoping she hadn't just revealed her presence. What in the world had Regina done to bring out such vehemence from the sophisticated woman? Starr had mentioned that Regina had been asked to leave her sorority's house, but she hadn't known the reason for her banishment. This was Dani's chance to find out the details.

"Now, honey." A paunchy, fiftyish man who had to be Scott Ackerman shook his finger in his wife's face. "I know you love good old Alpha Beta Delta, but don't you think you're being a bit harsh?"

"No." Maureen swatted her husband's hand away and glared at him until he retreated. "She stole from a sister. There is no excuse for that."

"What did she steal?" Trent asked, shooting his wife a strange look.

"Well, certainly not money." Scott chuckled. "Her parents are filthy rich."

"Worse." Chelsea grimaced. "She stole intellectual property."

"Really?" Scott's eyebrows would have disappeared into his hairline if he weren't bald.

"Yes." Maureen's fair complexion reddened. "One of the pledges had written a novel, and although she kept it a secret, because Regina wanted to be a writer too, the girl confided in her. Regina expressed an interest in reading the girl's book and the pledge gave her the manuscript to critique. After a couple of months went by and Regina didn't give it back, the girl asked about it. Regina pretended she didn't know what the pledge was talking about. And when the girl went to her sorority big sister about the missing manuscript, Regina claimed that the girl was delusional."

"Couldn't she just print out another one?" Trent asked, finishing his martini and putting the empty glass on the coffee table.

"The manuscript was handwritten and there were no copies." Maureen explained. She held up a finger to prevent anyone from interrupting her and added, "Yes. The girl was incredibly stupid to hand over her only copy, but she thought she could trust Regina."

"Why in the world would Regina do something like that?" Trent asked.

Dani silently nodded her agreement with Trent's question. Was it another case of sheer meanness like Lazarus Hunter had described?

"Because Regina had submitted the manuscript to an agent friend of her mother's as her own work." Chelsea blew out a breath. "Apparently, the novel was amazing and the agent found an editor who made an offer to acquire it for her publishing house.

"But before any contracts were signed, the editor's assistant remembered reading a query letter with the same plot and character names," Maureen continued the story. "The assistant alerted her boss, who contacted the pledge, who took the matter to the standards committee, who turned it over to national."

"I don't remember Regina having a book published, and I'm sure her parents would have invited the whole country club to her launch party, so did the pledge get her novel back?" Trent asked.

"Unfortunately, no." Maureen shook her head, setting her shoulder-length hair in motion. "Regina refused to admit she'd stolen the manuscript and the publisher's attorney said that a query letter would never be enough to prove it was the pledge's work."

"So with a 'she said versus she said' case, the publisher backed away from the project." Chelsea's tone was grim. "And no other agent or editor would even look at the book, so it was never published."

"The poor girl." Trent seemed genuinely sympathetic. "Pouring her heart into writing a novel and having it stolen had to be devastating."

"Absolutely." Maureen recrossed her legs. "If Regina had been murdered back then, there wouldn't be much of a question as to who killed her." Maureen shrugged. "But it all happened over a year ago, maybe closer to a year and a half. I can't remember exactly when it took place."

Dani frowned. That was a long time to hold a grudge, but still she should at least find out the name of that pledge and talk to her. But how? Dani took a deep breath —

Shit! She'd been so engrossed in the conversation, she'd forgotten the food cooking in the kitchen. And now it smelled as if her sauce was burning.

Fighting the impulse to run, Dani eased away from the wall, cleared her throat, and announced, "Anytime you all are ready to eat, I've put the first course on the dining room table."

"Thanks, Dani." Trent rose to his feet and the others followed.

Dani forced herself to walk sedately down the hallway, making sure her rubber-soled shoes didn't squeak on the corridor's polished hardwood floor. Once she was out of sight and was sure no one would notice, she broke into a jog and sprinted toward the stove. Thankfully the port sauce was salvageable and she quickly strained it into another pan, then grabbed her knife and carved the beef.

Although Dani overheard snatches of conversation as she served dinner, nothing more about the stolen manuscript was discussed. And at eight thirty, when Dani entered the dining room with the lemon fluff, the couples were talking about a vacation they were planning on taking together during the holidays.

Dani hid her frustration and served the dessert, then stood there searching for a way to steer the discussion back to Regina.

Chelsea flicked Dani an irritated glance and stared pointedly at the doorway. "We have everything we need."

"Great," Dani mumbled and retreated to the kitchen. While she packed her equipment, she turned over in her head how she would get the identity of the pledge who Regina had betrayed, but nothing came to mind.

Too bad she couldn't just ask Chelsea. But there were two problems with that solution. One, she'd have to admit that she'd been eavesdropping. And two, Dani didn't want the Karneses to associate her with Regina. The more she could keep herself separated in their thoughts from the murdered young woman, the better.

Shelving that conundrum for another time, Dani continued to tidy up. An hour later, Dani heard the Ackermans leave, and she went to find her clients. As usual, Trent and Chelsea had retired to the professor's study for their after-dinner drink, but instead of their customary casual banter, tonight the couple was arguing.

Hesitating outside the partially opened door, Dani heard Trent shouting, "You knew that Regina was an unethical bitch. You knew what she was capable of doing. Why didn't you warn me about her?"

"It never occurred to me that my husband would fall for her tricks."

"I didn't." Trent's voice wavered. "I mean, I was flattered when she seemed attracted to me, and I may have flirted a bit, but I never had an affair with her. I wouldn't do that to our marriage."

"Of course you wouldn't." Chelsea's tone was mocking. "Why wouldn't I trust you? Just because Regina sent me a video of you kissing her?"

"Chelly, you know that I love you and only you," Trent said. "Regina set me up. She was incensed when I wouldn't change her C to an A."

"You didn't seem to be fighting her off too hard in the recording."

"I was in an awkward position." Trent's voice was pleading. "With her parents being friends of ours, I was trying to let her down lightly."

"How?" Chelsea sneered. "By shoving your tongue down her throat?"

"No!" Trent yelped. "As I explained before, I had just told her I wasn't interested and she was still getting a C when she threw herself into my arms. She must have set up her cell phone beforehand to record us. And she edited out the part where I shoved her away."

"What I still don't understand is why, despite your moral preening, you didn't take any legal measures when she stole your wallet and used your identity to open all those credit cards."

"I didn't want to get dragged into a messy

court case."

"Right." Chelsea's heels tapped across the hardwood floor and Dani heard liquid pouring into a glass. "We were lucky that her parents wrote us a check for what she charged."

"They seemed as confused as we were as to why she just didn't use her own cards." Trent sighed. "The Bournes said between what they gave her and her trust, she had nearly unlimited funds. To this day they claim the whole thing was a mix-up."

"When that all happened, I told Honoria to get that girl into therapy."

"Seriously?" Trent snorted. "Like either Ashton or his wife would admit there was something wrong with their perfect daughter."

Dani waited, but when it was obvious the discussion about Regina was over, she knocked on the door, entered, and said, "I hope you and your guests enjoyed dinner. There are leftovers for tomorrow night."

"It was delicious." Trent smiled from where he sat behind his massive, black-lacquered desk. "Maureen and Scott couldn't stop talking about the food. Thank you for extending dinner to four."

"Yes." Chelsea's smile was tight. "It's a good thing that they live a couple of states away or we'd have to worry about them stealing you."

"No worries. I can always fit in a couple of more clients," Dani said brightly, not adding that they currently were her only personal chef customers. "But original ones have priority." Dani pulled her phone from her pants pocket and held it out. "Are you ready to settle the bill?"

"Here you go." Trent reached into his pocket, pulled out his wallet, flipped it open, and handed over his American Express.

"I see you got your new card," Dani commented as she processed the transaction and returned his credit card.

Although she doubted Trent would talk about Regina in front of her, Dani hoped maybe he'd slip.

"Yes." Trent slipped his AmEx back into its proper slot. "Thank goodness."

"I was thinking about how scary identity theft can be," Dani said, walking toward the door.

"You don't know the half of it." Chelsea tapped a perfectly manicured red nail on her brandy snifter. "Right, dear?"

Trent nodded.

Dani wished the couple good night and headed out to her van. As she backed out of their driveway, she thought about all she'd heard at the Karneses'. At this rate, it would be harder to figure out who *didn't* want Regina dead than who did.

бізаl in the Karneses. At the rate, it would
to finish in hours, and she didn't want Re-
imo rest than from the tile.

CHAPTER 15

A cold front had come through while Dani
was inside cooking for the Karneses, and
the van's wipers were having a hard time
keeping up with the rain hammering against
the windshield. She turned on the radio
before scooting forward to the edge of the
driver's seat, trying to see out of the water-
logged glass.

Punching the button for the NOAA
weather station, she mentally crossed her
fingers. The past few years, Central and
Southern Illinois had been devastated by
several tornadoes. Because of that, everyone, including Dani, was a lot more concerned about the possibility of a twister
touching down than they had been in the
past. And this was exactly the conditions
that could produce a supercell. The cool,
dry air from the storm front meeting up
with the hot, humid environment that
they'd suffered through all day was a recipe

for creating a funnel cloud. And despite Dani's fondness for testing out new recipes, this wasn't one she wanted to sample.

There were no watches or warnings on the radio for the Normalton area, and Dani had relaxed a bit when a loud clap of thunder accompanied by a blindingly bright bolt of lightning sent a shiver down her spine.

Taking a deep breath, she willed her racing heart to slow down, then inched the bulky van through the open gateway that separated the secluded cul-de-sac from the rest of the development. Although there were a few cars parked along the curb here and there, the dark streets were empty of traffic. Not exactly a surprise at ten fifteen on a weeknight.

Tomorrow was a workday for most folks who lived in this upper-middle-class neighborhood and they were probably on their couches watching the news or getting ready for bed, rather than out driving around. Especially with the storm blowing through the region.

Dani gripped the steering wheel and drove slowly through the residential area. The pavement was slick, and as she stared out her windshield, she could see raindrops creating needlelike streaks in the light of the streetlamps.

Visibility was poor, and the last thing she needed was to be involved in an accident. She couldn't afford for her insurance to skyrocket or, worse yet, have her name pop up on any police reports. Dollars to doughnuts, Detective Mikeloff would seize any opportunity to drag her into the station and attempt to make her look like a habitual offender.

Between the dangerous weather and her thoughts of the even more dangerous detective, Dani's pulse was pounding as she tried to concentrate on her driving. She was only a few blocks from the main road when she caught a glimpse of a figure bent over next to an old Mercury station wagon ahead of her.

Squinting, Dani watched the person struggling to remove a flat tire. A sudden gust of wind made the figure stagger backward, and Dani saw that it was an older woman.

Dani tapped the brakes, then hesitated as the good and bad angels on her shoulders argued. Ms. Pitchfork whispered in her ear that she was tired and it was dangerous to stop for strangers, assuring her that the woman could call a garage for assistance. Ms. Halo pointed out that the poor lady was clearly in need of help and maybe she didn't have a cell phone or the money to pay for a tow truck.

Knowing she'd never be able to sleep if she didn't pull over, Dani parked the van behind the incapacitated car, then took a moment to consider the situation. She had an umbrella in an organizer on the back of her seat, but the wind would destroy it in seconds. And although it wasn't super cold, she didn't want to get soaked and have to drive home in wet clothes.

Deciding that the disposable poncho she kept in a pouch in her emergency kit would be her best hope for remaining dry, she dug the box out from under the passenger seat and rummaged until she found the sealed envelope. It looked a bit melted, but when she pulled apart the packet, the poncho appeared to be undamaged.

Once Dani was shrouded in plastic, she reluctantly emerged from the van. Tiny shards of hail stung her cheeks and she nearly jumped out of her skin when the van door slammed shut behind her.

After checking to makes sure she had her keys, Dani approached the stranded station wagon. Sickly moonbeams tinted the street an eerie silver, and when the woman looked up from her battle with the tire, she jumped to her feet, clutching her chest and stumbling backward.

With the headlights now illuminating the woman's face, Dani recognized her as the Bourne's housekeeper, Mrs. Carnet. Didn't she live in? What in the heck was she doing out this late in such bad weather?

Pushing her hood back a little so the woman could see her face, Dani said, "Mrs. Carnet, it's Dani Sloan. I don't know if you remember me, but I catered Regina's luau. I just finished cooking dinner for the Karneses and was heading home when I saw you."

"Of course I remember you. You and your girls were so sweet. Thank you for stopping." Regaining her footing, the housekeeper pushed her hair out of her eyes and trudged back toward the disabled vehicle. Abruptly, she stopped, her shoulders slumped, and she covered her face with her hands. "This is the worst day of my life and I don't know what to do."

The rain made it difficult to tell if Mrs. Carnet was crying, but Dani automatically reached for the packet of Kleenex she always kept in her pocket.

When she realized that in this weather offering her a tissue would be futile, Dani sighed and asked, "What happened?"

"The Bournes fired me this afternoon."

Mrs. Carnet started to sob. "I've been with them for twenty-one years and they told me I had eight hours to vacate the premises or they'd have me forcibly removed."

Dani glanced into the ancient station wagon and saw that it was loaded with boxes and suitcases that looked as if they had been hastily piled in the car.

"Why in the world —" Dani cut herself off. The older woman was shaking and Dani wasn't sure if it was from the cold or from the shock. Either way, she needed to get Mrs. Carnet out of the rain. "I'm not sure I could change your tire, so how about I drive you wherever you were going and you pick up your car tomorrow?"

"I . . . I can't leave it." Mrs. Carnet gazed at the station wagon. "Everything that I own is in there. What if it gets stolen?"

"If you want, we can call for a tow truck." Dani took the woman's elbow and tugged. "But let's wait for it where it's dry."

"My cell phone is dead." Mrs. Carnet allowed Dani to help her into the van. "With everything that happened, I forgot to charge it."

"No worries." Dani took her cell from her pocket, swiped the screen to unlock it, and handed it to the woman. "You can use mine."

Mrs. Carnet carefully placed the phone on the dashboard, took off her fogged-up glasses, then, realizing her clothes were soaked, she looked around helplessly. Dani handed her a stack of paper napkins and watched silently as the older woman carefully wiped the lens, then settled the frames back on her face. Finally, Mrs. Carnet picked up Dani's cell from the console and stared at the tiny, black rectangle as if she'd never seen a cell before.

Shaking her head, Mrs. Carnet said, "I don't even know who to call. The Bournes have always had me on their insurance plan, but I'm guessing that I'm not covered by that road assistance anymore."

"Most likely they haven't had a chance to cancel it yet," Dani said slowly. "You could probably use it this one last time."

Mrs. Carnet shook her head violently. "No! If I do that, they might have me arrested." She glanced at Dani. "They're merciless."

"Fine. How about if I call who I use?" Dani asked, tucking the info about the Bournes into the back of her mind to consider later.

"I guess that would be okay."

Mrs. Carnet returned the cell phone to Dani, who woke up the screen again, brought up her contacts, and tapped the icon. After she'd reached the emergency tire business and spoke to the serviceman, she held the cell against her chest.

Turning to Mrs. Carnet, she said, "The guy wants to know if you have a spare tire available, and if so, are you sure that it's good."

"I have no idea." Mrs. Carnet shredded the used napkin, forming a tiny, white paper mountain in her lap. "I'm not even sure where it is. I've had the car for thirty-seven years and never had a flat before."

"It'll be okay." Dani patted her hand, then spoke into her cell. She passed on the lack of info about the spare, along with the make, model, and age of the vehicle. Once she disconnected, she said, "They're super busy because of the storm, but the technician promised that he'll be here in thirty to forty-five minutes. An hour at the most. He'll bring a tire with him to replace the flat, but he said you'll need to get a whole new set before you drive any distance."

"You don't have to wait." Mrs. Carnet reached for the door handle. The older woman's head was held high and her voice was steady. It was clear that she wasn't the type who enjoyed sharing her troubles or accepting help. "I know you must be tired after cooking dinner for the Karneses."

"I don't mind." Dani smiled reassuringly, hoping her exhaustion didn't show. "Would you like something to eat while you wait? I have some sandwiches and fruit right here."

"Well . . ." Mrs. Carnet hesitated. "If it's no bother. I was so upset after Mrs. Bourne called and fired me that I forgot to have lunch or dinner."

"No bother at all." Dani reached behind her and grabbed an insulated bag and a couple bottles of water. "I like to have something available in case I'm starving after I finish cooking."

"I understand completely." Mrs. Carnet made a face. "The Bournes never allowed me to eat until they were finished. They didn't care that while I was serving them and cleaning up, I was hungry too."

"Isn't that the truth?" Dani chuckled. "Anymore, whenever I have a meal at a normal time, it almost seems as if I'm doing something wrong."

As the women shared the food, Mrs. Carnet talked about working for the Bournes. She reminisced about all the years she'd been with them, then had to stop to wipe away a tear and compose herself.

After taking a long drink of water, Mrs. Carnet sighed. "I came to them just after

Mrs. Bourne had Miss Regina. I took care of her more often than her mother. I was the one who did the potty training, helped her with her homework, and taught her to drive."

"Why in the world did they let you go?" Dani asked softly. It seemed coldhearted to question the woman when she was so obviously distraught, but she really needed to know more about Regina and her family. "And to make you leave so quickly seems needlessly cruel."

"They blame me for Miss Regina's death." Mrs. Carnet peeled the label off the water bottle and Dani noticed her unpolished fingernails had been chewed to the quick. "The Bournes said that I should have never left her alone. But it was supposed to be my day off. I only stayed as long as I did as a favor to Miss Regina, to make sure everything was in place for her party." Mrs. Carnet's lips thinned. "It was my sister's sixtieth birthday and I had to postpone seeing her, but I promised her that I'd drive up to Chicago, spend the night with her, and that we'd celebrate with a fancy Sunday brunch."

"It sounds to me as if you went above and beyond." Dani frowned. "And Regina was certainly old enough to be left by herself overnight." She wrinkled her brow, trying to recall if she'd seen Mrs. Carnet after the luau began. "What time did you leave the party?"

"I headed into the city as soon as I finished getting the bartenders situated," Mrs. Carnet answered. "It must have been a little before seven because I was at my sister's for the nine thirty news."

"You were the one who found Regina, right?" Dani asked gently, hoping she wasn't pushing the woman too far.

"Yes. I'll never forget the moment when I realized she was unconscious." Mrs. Carnet patted her chest, then fanned herself. "My sister and I had an early brunch and I got home about one. When I saw that Miss Regina was lying by the pool, I didn't think anything of it. She spent a lot of time sunbathing out there. But when I went out to tell her I was back, I could tell something was wrong."

"Oh?" Dani barely spoke, unwilling to interrupt Mrs. Carnet.

"There were empty plates and food wrappers all around her." Mrs. Carnet's breath hitched. "Miss Regina was —" Mrs. Carnet slapped a hand over her mouth and the crepey skin on her neck reddened. "I shouldn't be telling you this."

Dani, finally putting together everything she'd observed and heard about the girl, said slowly, "I noticed that she didn't eat much at the party, but a lot of hostesses are too wound up to eat. Then when she directed me to put food in the refrigerator that was not to be served under any circumstances, I thought it was odd but didn't put two and two together. Although now that you mention how you found her . . ." Dani trailed off, then said, "Regina was bulimic, right?"

"Yes, she was." Mrs. Carnet hung her head. "But Miss Regina hadn't binged in quite a while, so I was surprised to see the mess."

"Or maybe she'd just gotten better at hiding it from you," Dani suggested.

"Maybe." Mrs. Carnet bit her lip. "She'd had a couple of episodes where she was out of control and her parents threatened her with rehab."

"Out of control with her eating?" Dani asked. Had the Bournes been concerned with the manuscript issue and the identity theft? "Or was there something more? Other issues that involved Regina?"

"There were a few things that concerned them," Mrs. Carnet said under her breath.

"But it doesn't seem right to tell you about them."

Dani could only push the woman so far. She didn't want to burn any bridges. Maybe later, after Mrs. Carnet had a chance to realize just how badly she'd been treated by the Bournes, she'd be more willing to discuss this further.

"I understand." Dani offered the woman a plastic baggie containing several chocolate chip cookies and waited while Mrs. Carnet selected one. "So once you noticed the food wrappers and such, what did you do?"

"I started to speak to Miss Regina." Mrs. Carnet shook her head. "To ask if she wanted me to clean up or get her anything, but then I really looked at her. She was flopped on the lounge chair like a rag doll. I called 911 right away. But it was too late. They were never able to revive her."

"I understand you found a syringe in the driveway. Have the police figured out yet how she died?" Dani asked, wondering if the insulin overdose that the detective mentioned was common knowledge.

"No one has told me anything." Mrs. Carnet bit angrily into her cookie, chewed, and swallowed, then said, "Everyone just keeps asking me questions. The police, the reporters, the Bournes' friends. Was Miss Regina or anyone in the house diabetic? Was she depressed? Was there anyone who might want to harm her?"

"What did you tell them?" Dani wasn't sure how long the older woman would talk to her about Regina, but any little tidbit might lead to a clue that she could follow up on with Spencer or Frannie.

"I told the police no one in the house used insulin and Miss Regina was far from depressed." Mrs. Carnet ate another cookie, then added, "I didn't mention that the list of people who didn't like her was too long to write down. And I certainly didn't discuss the matter with anyone else." She crossed her arms. "The Bournes expect confidentiality, and until today, they had my loyalty."

"But maybe you gave a nice young reporter a little hint," Dani guessed.

"I might have passed along a few things that I overheard the police talking about, like who was the last to leave the party." Mrs. Carnet shot Dani a pointed glance. "And the fact that after you saved the place from burning down, Miss Regina was rude to you."

"Oh." Dani's cheeks warmed. "So you know about that."

"Certainly. Miss Bliss told me all about the incident."

"It really wasn't as big a deal as everyone is making it out to be. The fire was small and Regina's blowup wasn't that bad. She'd already paid me and I figured that in a few days, she'd get over it and move on to the next big drama in her life."

"Which she probably would have if someone hadn't killed her." Mrs. Carnet reached for the last cookie. "Too bad the murderer didn't have your patience."

CHAPTER 16

When Spencer woke up Thursday morning, his first impulse was to call Dani. His gut urged him to make sure her snooping hadn't stirred up any hornet nests of vengeful cops or panicky killers. He also wanted to confirm her dickwad of an ex wasn't harassing her. He grabbed his cell phone from the nightstand, unlocked it, and opened up his contact list.

He'd grabbed Dani's photo from her Chef-to-Go website and her pretty caramel eyes sparkled at him from the screen. The tiny dent in her cute, little chin tempted him, as did the memory of her lush hips and her heart-shaped ass. What would it feel like to hold her in his arms and taste her soft, soft lips?

As his finger hovered over the picture of her face, Hiram's words stopped him from tapping the icon. Despite his attraction to her and his mentor's encouragement, Spencer wasn't ready for a relationship.

Shoving away the image of Dani sprawled beneath him, Spencer jumped out of bed and headed into the shower. For once, he didn't mind how long it took the icy water to get hot.

After he was dressed and waiting for the coffee to brew, he texted Ivy to ask how things were going. His niece immediately answered that everything was same old, same old and that she and Dani were prepping the food for a football booster dinner that evening. Dani was excited since it was only her second catering gig and was driving them all crazy with her need for perfection.

Now that he knew Dani and Ivy were safe, Spencer's stomach settled and he could face the thought of eating breakfast. After quickly polishing off a bowl of cereal, he got into his truck and backed out of the garage. Noticing that the town house association's overzealous gardener had pruned his azalea bushes to within an inch of their lives, he made a mental note to inform the landscape company that, in the future, he'd trim the shrubs himself. Better a little work on his part than the decimation of the bright-red blossoms.

Puddles from last night's rain studded the

asphalt and Spencer deliberately steered through them. He'd always liked the sound of splashing water. Rolling his window down, Spencer enjoyed the cold front's cooler temperatures. With the blazing sun, the thermometer would soon rise and he'd be stuck breathing stale, air-conditioned air.

Driving toward his office, he recalled promising to stop by the mansion after his meeting with the police chief. Smiling, Spencer's mind drifted and he daydreamed about taking Dani in his arms when he saw her. Pressing her soft curves against his hard length and inhaling the spicy yet sweet fragrance that seemed to wrap around her. Was it perfume or her natural scent?

Shit! Spencer slammed on the brakes as an obviously suicidal pedestrian with a huge bullmastiff on a leash darted between two parked cars and directly into the path of his pickup. Wiping the sweat from his forehead, Spencer ground his teeth. He had to stop thinking about Little Miss Cupcake. Nothing could come of it and the distraction was annoying. Too bad Dani was so damn adorable.

His plan was to protect Ivy by figuring out who killed Regina Bourne and then step back into his role as the casual acquaintance who checked once a week on the girls. Ivy was his number one priority, but clearly anything bad that affected Dani had the possibility of spilling over onto his niece, so he had keep Dani safe as well.

Satisfied with his rationalization, Spencer turned his attention to Dani's ex. There was something off about the good doctor. Spencer didn't believe his reason for wanting the missing book for one single minute, and he definitely needed to be the one to deliver it once Dani found the AWOL tome.

After parking in his assigned spot, Spencer took the stairs to his office. His appointment with the police chief wasn't until eleven thirty and he needed to get schedules and timesheets approved for his employees or the security staff wouldn't get paid this week.

While Spencer loved being out from undercover and working security rather than living with motorcycle gangs, he hated the administrative bookkeeping. But he had to do it and as he dealt with paperwork that he could complete in his sleep, his thoughts wandered to what he'd learned about the man Dani had fired. It hadn't taken much in the way of detective skills to discover that Demetri Mitchell was Detective Mikeloff's nephew. The real mystery was the circumstances of Mitchell's dismissal.

None of Spencer's sources had been able to provide any light on what had gone on in Mitchell's department at the insurance company and Dani continued to refuse to divulge any details. Spencer was afraid that her pigheadedness would get her arrested for a crime she didn't commit.

It had taken every ounce of self-control that he possessed not to order her to tell him the whole story. His gut told him that if he forced the information out of her, those tactics would backfire and she wouldn't trust him with other important facts.

But that was only one of the reasons that Spencer hadn't persisted in trying to pry the details from Dani. Another was that if he angered her to the extent she shut him out of her investigations, he wouldn't be able to keep her safe. So even if it meant biting his tongue and allowing her to keep secrets, he had given in and stopped trying to find out why Demetri Mitchell had been fired and instead concentrated on making sure the man's uncle didn't take revenge on Dani for the dismissal.

Spencer thumped his head against the back of his desk chair and stared out the window at the white clouds dotting the morning sky. Why was his life always so damn complicated? What happened to minding his own business and keeping a low profile? Why did logic fly out the window and his carefully planned life go to hell the minute he got around Danielle Sloan?

Tuesday night, when Spencer had stopped by the mansion to talk to Dani, he'd had every intention of telling her what he'd found out about Detective Mikeloff, warning her to be careful, and leaving. But the minute he saw Dr. Dipshit with his hands on her, Spencer had allowed his emotions to take over. And instead of delivering his information and taking off, he'd pulled up a chair, eaten her addictive pudding, and offered to help her find Regina's killer.

A year ago, Spencer would have said no effing way would he ever get involved with another woman. Hell, six months ago, his fondest desire was to put as much distance between him and any female that showed a hint of wanting more than a few hours of mutual satisfaction. Then he met Dani, and now she refused to get out of his thoughts.

Spencer thumped his head against the back of his chair again. No woman had ever affected him this way. Not one of his girlfriends, and certainly not his ex-wife, had made him this crazy. Was it foolish to think that Dani might be what he'd always been looking for?

Spencer reminded himself that neither one of them was anywhere near ready to begin a relationship nor was there any reason to rush into anything. Ivy had mentioned — okay, he'd asked her — that Dani wasn't seeing anyone and that there weren't any guys she talked about wanting to date.

Which meant Spencer had time to think things through. He couldn't allow his feelings to outweigh his common sense. Undercover, emotions got you killed, and in this situation, it could be almost as disastrous.

Spencer took a deep breath, clicked the Send button for the file he'd completed, and got to his feet. This wasn't getting him anywhere and it was almost time for his meeting with the police chief.

Twenty minutes later, as Spencer steered his truck away from the university, he noticed the dense, green leaves of the trees that lined the road. During the summer semester, the campus quieted down. There were a lot fewer students in class, which meant activity around the college decreased.

Instead of crowds, smaller groups wandered the sidewalks and hung out in the quad. Spencer's goal had been to use this downtime for staff training and program development, and Regina's murder didn't change that plan. Although he might be looking into her death, his investigation couldn't interfere with the job he was being paid to perform.

Still, it was good that he had some flexibility and didn't have to punch a clock. He'd just make sure that the college didn't get shortchanged. The students' safety would always come first.

Driving downtown, Spencer tried to collect his thoughts and figure out a strategy for approaching the police chief. He'd never met Chief Cleary, having always dealt with the assistant chief of operations, and wasn't sure what his reception would be. Police officers weren't usually very happy with any outside interference in their investigations or questions about their staff.

After parking in the public lot, Spencer walked across the street and entered the building. The police station was like most other stations he had been in — a rectangular, brick structure with absolutely no personality.

The empty vestibule, bracketed by restrooms on either side, was painted a boring beige and smelled of heavy-duty cleaning products. But as he pushed through the heavy glass doors leading into the lobby the antiseptic odor faded and the stench of too many sweaty bodies crowded together took over.

To Spencer's right, the visitor seating section was overflowing. Several people sat on the floor, and one man wearing baggy jeans and a Hawaiian shirt was poking the man sprawled next to him.

When the guy got his friend's attention, he said, "Bro, I thought you weren't planning on running today."

The man shrugged and said, "I wasn't. But those damn cops came out of nowhere."

Spencer rolled his eyes and turned his attention to the people swarming the dispatch area.

The uniformed woman behind the counter was shaking her head and repeating, "Please take a seat. An officer will be with you shortly."

Spencer assumed the mob was due to the massive pileup that had shut down Trouper Avenue. He had heard about the mess on the radio. A semi had flipped over making a turn and cars had rear-ended each other like a line of falling dominoes.

Normalton was a small community, but due to the three colleges and the town's vintage car and motorcycle collection, there was always a lot of traffic. This week, adding to the congestion was the symposium that Normalton University's parapsychology department was hosting.

NU was one of only a handful of schools that had a department the focused on the study of paranormal and psychic phenomena, and it made the university unique among its Midwestern peers. So far, Spencer hadn't had any dealings with that part of NU, and he hoped that would continue to be true.

Edging his way through the throng, he caught the woman's attention and said, "Spencer Drake for Chief Cleary. I have an eleven thirty appointment."

The officer seemed relieved that he wasn't another accident victim and pointed up. "Second floor."

Spencer thanked her and fought his way past the horde. The elevator spit him out into another waiting area, but this one was unoccupied and blessedly quiet after the cacophony downstairs.

The doorway to the chief's administrative assistant's office was open and Spencer stepped inside. The front two-thirds of the room was lined with rows of gray metal file cabinets and shelves containing thick red, yellow, and blue three-ring binders grouped according to color. A teenager bobbing to whatever she was listening to through her earbuds was sitting behind the desk at the rear.

Spencer cleared his throat, and when that had no effect, he said, "Miss?"

Nothing. He repeated the word louder, but there was still no response, so he stepped closer and gingerly tapped the girl on the shoulder.

The adolescent jumped as if she'd been tasered, then shouted, "What the hell, dude! You almost gave me a heart attack."

"Sorry, miss." Spencer bit back a lecture about being more aware of one's surroundings. "I didn't know how else to get your attention."

Glaring, the girl said, "Maybe that's because I didn't want to be disturbed."

"The door was open," Spencer pointed out, then said, "I have an appointment to see Chief Clearly at eleven thirty. Is she ready for me?"

"Sure." The teenager smirked. "You can go in."

"Can you let the chief know that I'm here?" The girl was definitely up to something.

The teenager peered at him for a long moment, then demanded, "Who are you?"

"Spencer Drake." When the girl had screamed, Spencer had moved back from the desk, but now he leaned forward and held out his palm. "And you?"

The teenager tentatively shook Spencer's hand and muttered, "I'm Chloe."

"Good to meet you, Chloe." Spencer smiled. "I'm the head of campus security at NU. Are you thinking of going there when you graduate?"

"Seriously?" Chloe couldn't have been more than thirteen, but she had the teenage attitude down pat. "Why would I go to a second-rate school like that?" She examined her bright-blue nail polish and rubbed at a chipped spot. "I'm going to Barnard or Wellesley."

The girl wore a pair of denim shorts, a pink T-shirt with I'M A GENIUS printed in black, and metallic high-top sneakers. Her white-blond hair was in a braid, and she shoved her oversize, black-framed glasses on her head to hold back her long bangs.

She gazed at him, as if waiting for a response. But when Spencer remained silent, she shrugged, picked up the phone, and said, "Your eleven thirty is here." Hanging up, Chloe announced, "The chief will see you now."

Spencer still didn't trust her. "Are you sure?"

Chloe wrinkled her nose and said, "Of

course. Go ahead."

Spencer shrugged and walked over to the door the girl indicated. He grabbed the knob and swung it open. A fortysomething woman sat on the lap of a slightly older man. The couple was kissing, the remains of their brunch abandoned on the desktop in front of them.

At Spencer's entrance, they looked up and the woman checked her watch, then said, "Oops. I'm sorry to keep you waiting. Jet surprised me. He just got home from his latest tour of duty." She got to her feet and crossed to Spencer. "I'm Meredith Cleary."

"Spencer Drake." Spencer shook her hand and said, "I didn't mean to interrupt. Chloe told me you were ready to see me, but I guess she didn't really call you. I can wait outside."

"No." Chief Cleary chuckled. "My daughter isn't too thrilled about my second marriage. She wanted me to stay a widow forever."

"I see." Spencer waited until the chief's husband finished stuffing the remains of their meal into a paper bag, then introduced himself.

"Jet Porter." The men shook hands and Jet said, "Nice to meet you. My son is on your team at NU. He admires the direction you're taking with security."

"You're Robert Porter's father?" Spencer could see the resemblance. Both men were tall, lean, and had the same coal-black hair. "I enjoy working with him. He's been an asset in many situations."

Jet beamed. "I'm real proud of him." His dark-brown eyes sparkled as he turned to his wife, kissed her cheek, and said, "I'd better get going before I totally ruin your reputation as a hard-ass."

"Right." Meredith took her husband's hand and walked with him to the door. "Mustn't let the troops know that I have a personal life."

"Chloe and I will go do some father-daughter bonding at the mall."

"Really?" Meredith stared at her husband with a questioning expression. "Last time you took her shopping, you vowed to never set foot in a store with her again."

"Did I?" Jet looked at Spencer and winked. "I guess I should remember that every conversation with a woman is recorded for training and quality-assurance purposes."

Spencer snickered.

Meredith swatted her husband's arm and ordered, "Get out of here."

Jet twisted the knob. "If I'm not home by

dinnertime, send in the SWAT team."

"Watch your six." Meredith closed the door behind her husband, then gestured to the chairs in front of her desk. "Have a seat."

Once they were settled, Spencer said, "Thank you for meeting with me."

Meredith nodded. "I've been meaning to invite you in since you were hired." She leaned back in her chair and said, "Because Regina Bourne was an NU student, I'm guessing this is about her murder."

"Yes." Spencer adjusted the crease in his trousers, glad he'd decided to wear a suit today. "I was hoping you could bring me up-to-date on the progress your department has made on the case and let me know if any of the suspects are connected to the university."

Meredith picked up a gold pen. Hitting it against her palm, the chief gazed at him as if taking his measure, then said, "We don't usually discuss an active investigation with anyone outside the department."

"I understand." Spencer wasn't sure how to respond. It was hard to read Meredith's expression. "But I'd really appreciate it if you could make an exception." Recalling the chief's teenage daughter, he added, "My niece Ivy was at the Bourne girl's party."

"Yes, I know. Detective Mikeloff noted

that in his report." Meredith crossed her arms. "But she doesn't seem to be a serious suspect. At least no more so than Ms. Bourne's other friends and associates."

"Glad to hear it." Spencer met the chief's eyes. "So who is?"

"That's not something I can share with you." Meredith tapped some keys and peered at her computer monitor. "But I can assure you that person has nothing official to do with the university."

"And by official" — Spencer kept all expression from his face — "you mean that she runs a business that sells to-go lunches to the students."

"Perhaps." Meredith's voice was cool. "What's your interest in this person?"

"She's my niece's landlady," Spencer said, and when the chief raised her eyebrow, he added, "And I feel like I owe her whatever help I can provide. She's always kept an eye out for Ivy."

"Mmm." Meredith's mouth pursed, then her lips curved upward. She stared at him for a second, gave a small shrug, and said, "If you already know that Danielle Sloan is a suspect, why are you here?"

"Two reasons," Spencer answered quickly. It seemed as if the chief might be willing to throw him a bone or two and he wanted her to trust him. "One. Has the medical examiner completed his report yet?"

Meredith tapped a few more keys. "He finished it this morning."

"Anything you're willing to share?" Spencer asked. "I understand the preliminary finding was that an insulin overdose was the cause of death."

"That's true," Meredith confirmed.

"Was there anything else found?" Spencer leaned forward. "Anything that would help nail down an alibi?"

Meredith hesitated, then said, "When you asked for this appointment, I reviewed your employment record and spoke to several people in law enforcement about you." She brought her fingertips together. "Everyone assures me that you are a good guy."

"That's nice to hear." Spencer smiled. Who had vouched for him?

"But all I can tell you is that there's nothing in the ME's report that will help anyone establish an alibi."

"Shit," Spencer muttered, took a deep breath to calm himself, then said, "Okay. On to my second reason for this meeting."

"Detective Mikeloff." Meredith chuckled and Spencer realized that his mouth had dropped open. She sighed. "Yes. I'm aware there's an issue with my officer."

Meredith rose, unlocked a file cabinet, and took out a thick folder. Returning to her seat, she placed the file precisely in the center of her desktop.

"You know that, but Mikeloff is still working for you?" Spencer asked, frowning.

"There's no proof he's done anything wrong . . . yet." Meredith's straight, white teeth gleamed in a predatory smile. "Tell me why he concerns you."

"First, there's his reputation as a vengeful prick who is willing to set up innocent people if he has a grudge against them." Spencer held up one finger, then added another. "Second, he was out of control when he interviewed my niece and her friends."

"And third?" Meredith asked.

"Third, his prime suspect is the person who fired his nephew."

"Ah." Meredith flipped open the folder and jotted something down. "Ms. Sloan was previously employed in the HR department of Homestead Insurance. I take it Mikeloff's nephew worked there."

"Yes. His last name is different, but he's a dead ringer for his uncle."

"I wish that was enough to remove Mikeloff from the case, but it isn't." Meredith scowled. "His union rep would make too big a stink."

"Because solving this murder is a sure step up the ladder to sergeant?"

"Yep." Meredith gazed into space, then said, "Although there's nothing I can do right now about removing Mikeloff, I will make sure he understands that I expect him to focus on more than one suspect and that I'm aware of his nephew's relationship with Ms. Sloan."

"That would be terrific."

"I would be very interested in any evidence you can give me that can be used to get rid of him. I'd consider it a favor to the department." She paused. "And in return, I will keep you informed regarding the Bourne investigation."

Spencer stood and shook the chief's hand. "You've got a deal."

As he left the chief's office, Spencer grinned. The meeting with Chief Cleary had gone much better than he'd expected, but he still needed to see the complete ME's report, so the hundred he'd given Hiram wasn't wasted.

Spencer's pulse raced. And even better, he had something positive to tell Dani. But first he wanted to talk to the reporter. After that, he'd call Dani and find out the title of the book Dr. Demented was so interested in getting back.

CHAPTER 17

Dani had been sitting in the frigid room for over an hour. Shivering, she stared at the mirrored wall, which she was sure was two-way glass. Her stomach knotted. Was someone observing her? Was this some kind of test?

The overhead lights flickered as chills chased up her spine. In a futile attempt to get warm, Dani wrapped her arms around herself. She was an idiot. She should never have opened her door, let alone agree to come to the station with the scary detective. She should have called Spencer.

Dani had just finished with the lunch rush and had been about to look for Kipp's book when the doorbell had started ringing. Rushing into the foyer, she saw Mikeloff's face peering through the side window. When she'd hesitated, he'd pounded on the old glass so hard she was afraid the pane would break.

As soon as she'd unlocked the door and opened it a few inches, Mikeloff had snarled, "If you don't want Ivy Drake to spend the night in jail for the murder of Regina Bourne, you'll accompany me downtown right now and tell me everything I want to know." He'd poked her in the shoulder and repeated, "Everything. Are we clear?"

Mikeloff had ignored Dani's questions, barely giving her time to grab her purse and lock up before hurrying her into his unmarked Chevy Impala. Although she'd been relieved that it wasn't a squad car with sirens, flashing lights, and a steel mesh cage between the front and back seats, her heart had thudded so loud, she could barely hear the detective's rantings.

Then when he'd nearly rear-ended a truck, passing it half on the sidewalk, she'd yelped and clutched the dashboard, positive they were about to crash.

Mikeloff had glanced at her and sneered, "No. I do not have road rage. I just assertively maneuver around morons that don't know how to drive."

"Why don't you simply give them a ticket?" Dani had asked.

"I'm a detective, not a patrol officer," Mikeloff had snapped.

The detective had then proceeded to ignore Dani during the remainder of the short drive. He'd refused to explain his statement about Ivy or reveal if the girl was already in custody. Once they arrived at the police station, Mikeloff had parked in the staff lot behind the building, hustled her in through the back entrance, up the stairs, and into the room where she now sat, her emotions vacillating between boredom and fear.

Dani took a deep breath. The overwhelming smell of vomit mixed with disinfectant made her gag. Breathing through her mouth, she eyed the door. Could she just walk out?

Had Mikeloff locked it? The detective had secured her purse in a file drawer and she had nothing in her pockets, but surely someone would give her a ride home. Or at least let her make a phone call.

She'd just pushed back her chair, determined to leave, when she heard shuffling footsteps and the rattle of the doorknob. Mikeloff marched into the room. He had a folder under his arm and a steaming mug in his hand. The concerned expression on his face confused Dani, and she wrinkled her brow. What had changed the detective's attitude from belligerent to sympathetic?

Mikeloff leaned close to her — his breath reminded her of rotten vegetables and sewer water. Barely keeping the repulsed look off her face, Dani scooted her chair back from him and made a show of crossing her legs.

The detective placed the coffee near her hand, dropped into the seat across from her, and said conversationally, "I don't know why they keep it so cold in here."

"That's for sure." Dani warmed her fingers on the cup. "Thank you." Straightening her spine, she said, "Now that I've had a chance to think about this, I'm not sure what I can tell you. If Ivy is in trouble, it would probably be best for me to call her uncle."

"Mr. Drake is a busy man and I bet his girlfriend isn't too thrilled with all the time he's spending helping you and Miss Drake." Mikeloff rubbed the back of his neck. "Why don't we see if you and I can straighten this out before we bother him?"

Spencer had a girlfriend? Disappointment hit Dani like a fifty-pound sack of flour, but she shook it off and, ignoring the tiny voice inside her head that was urging her to shut up and leave, asked, "How?"

"I just need to know what happened." The detective's voice was as sticky as melted tar. "Once we get that cleared up, you can go, and we probably won't even have to bring Miss Drake into the station."

"Well . . ." Dani took a sip of the coffee and grimaced. It was not only unsweetened; it was also more like motor oil than a tasty beverage.

"Let's start with you spelling your first and last name for me."

Dani complied.

"Although your name is Danielle, most people call you Dani, right?" When she nodded, the detective recited her address. "Is that correct?" When she nodded again, he asked, "How long have you lived there?"

"About two months."

"And you rent out rooms to Ivy Drake, Starr Fleming, and Tippi Epstein."

"Uh-huh." Dani wondered why he was asking her stuff he already knew.

Mikeloff then went over her age, marital status, and her work history.

The questions were easy and just as she was beginning to relax, the detective said, "Dani, do you know the purpose of this interview?"

"To talk about Regina Bourne's murder." Dani tensed. "Right?"

"Correct." Mikeloff flipped open the folder that he'd placed in front of him. "We're here to figure out what happened that night after everyone left the party."

"I don't see how I can help you with that." Dani crossed her arms.

"You should realize that if you had something to do with the murder, we will eventually find evidence against you, so in the long run, it would be better for you if you told me whatever you know right now."

"But I didn't do anything." A weight descended on Dani's chest, stealing her breath. "I didn't even know she was dead until Monday when you told me."

"But you're the only one who had an argument with the victim just before she died." Mikeloff pointed his pen at Dani. "If she'd spread the word around through her parents' friends that you were an unreliable caterer, she'd have ruined your business."

"I told you before —" Panic clogged Dani's throat. Swallowing, she took a few seconds to come up with a response that wouldn't make her look guilty. "It wasn't that big a deal. Would I have lost a few referrals? Probably. Would it have slowed down the growth of my company? Possibly. But it wouldn't have bankrupted me."

The detective curled his lip and waved his hand dismissively. "You can't be sure of that. Especially in the heat of the moment."

Tendrils of fear shot through Dani's body,

and she blurted, "There are lots more people with better motives to kill Regina than me."

"Oh? Who do you think killed her?" Mikeloff pounced. When Dani didn't immediately respond, he added, "Let me assure you that even though your suspicions might be completely wrong, it's important that you let me know about them. No one you tell me about will ever know it was you who brought them to my attention."

Dani squirmed in her chair, her pulse pounding in her ears. Evidently, innocent until proven guilty wasn't working for her. She hated to do it, but surely she wasn't telling the detective anything he didn't already know.

"Who do you think might have killed Regina Bourne?" Mikeloff prodded, his voice whining through Dani's skull like a dentist's drill.

"I really have no idea." Dani twitched her shoulders. "But a lot of people didn't like her. Her own fiancé had some pretty harsh things to say about her. Plus, she pulled some really mean crap on her friend Bliss and her professor Trent Karnes. And her ex, Vance King, was obsessed with trying to talk to her at the party."

Dani watched the detective jotting down

what she'd said and immediately felt guilty for throwing the others under the bus. Still, she wasn't saying anything but the truth. It wasn't even gossip. And Mikeloff needed to focus on someone other than her or Ivy.

"Which one would you put your money on?" Mikeloff asked watching her closely.

"I don't know any of them very well, but I have to think that Bliss might have the most compelling motive." Dani chewed her bottom lip. "Regina sent a nude picture of her to Laz and all their friends."

"I see." Mikeloff stared into space. "But who do you think would have the best opportunity to get the insulin into the victim?"

"It's really hard to say because I don't know where it was injected." Dani nervously tapped out a jazz rhythm on the tabletop. "If it was an arm or leg, almost anyone might be able to do it, but a more concealed place, then it would have to be someone with whom she was more intimate."

Mikeloff leaned forward until his nose nearly touched hers, then he said so softly she almost couldn't hear him, "Can you think of any other way that Regina might have overdosed on insulin?"

"No." Dani frowned, considering what little she knew about the medication. "Is there a form of insulin that isn't injected?"

"No. I don't believe so." Mikeloff narrowed his eyes. "What was your first reaction when you found out that Regina was dead?"

"I couldn't believe it." Dani stared at her hands. "I mean, she was so young."

"But like you said, she wasn't a very nice person." Mikeloff's nicotine-stained fingers played with the edge of the file folder. "Maybe the killer did everyone a favor."

"No!"

"Come on," Mikeloff coaxed. "Can you really tell me that it never crossed your mind? Even if it's not something you would actually condone?"

"Never." Dani sucked in a breath. "Regina was young. She could change."

"Well, here's the thing," Mikeloff said. "I've talked to all the people you mentioned. I've gone over all of the evidence. And" — the detective's voice oozed satisfaction — "it all comes back to you."

"What?" Dani pushed her chair back from the table. "No! It wasn't me."

"The medical examiner finished the report and sent it to us today." Mikeloff's smile reminded Dani of a great white shark — hungry and relentless. "And guess what? Regina wasn't injected with insulin, which means the only way for her to get an overdose was to consume it."

"You mean eat or drink it?" Dani tugged at the neck of her T-shirt. "Is it even possible to die by ingesting insulin?"

"A single therapeutic dose wouldn't kill her, but with the amount Regina ingested and the fact she was taking ulcer medication that neutralized the stomach acids and enzymes that would normally destroy the insulin . . ." Mikeloff's grin widened. "And who was it that prepared the food that night? And left trays of goodies just for Regina?"

"But . . . but . . ." Dani stopped and shook her head to clear it. "There were wrappers from foods other than mine found around her body. And anyone could have added insulin to the stuff in her kitchen after I went home." Getting to her feet, Dani said, "Now, I'd either I'd like a lawyer or I'm leaving." Although she was shaking inside, she looked the detective coolly in the eye. "Your choice."

Twenty minutes later, clutching her purse to her chest, Dani wobbled into the hallway outside of the detectives' suite of offices. She felt lightheaded and sick to her stomach. She needed to sit down, but before she could do that she had to get as far away from Mikeloff as possible.

As she stood in the corridor, unsure of where to go, warm hands encased her upper arms and a familiar voice asked, "Are you okay?"

Confused, she looked up and demanded, "What are you doing here?"

"A little bird told me that Mikeloff had you in an interrogation room." Spencer's expression darkened. "How did that happen?"

"What little bird?" Dani wondered if she was making any sense. After all that had just happened to her, her brain might have jumped its tracks.

"I had a meeting with the chief. Her daughter, who was playing receptionist, is apparently keyed in to all the PD gossip and is in a state of teenage rebellion. She left a note thumbtacked to the admin's door informing me that Mikeloff had brought you into the station and was taking bets that he'd get you to confess."

"Oh." Dani drew in a deep breath to stop herself from falling apart. "Well, he didn't succeed, so I hope she bet against him."

"I'm sure she did." Spencer smiled. "Do you need a ride home?"

"Yeah." Dani swayed. "That would be great. I feel a little dizzy."

"Stress." Spencer wrapped an arm around her and guided her to the elevator. "Let's get you out of here and you can tell me all about it."

Silently, he led her through the station and out to his truck. Helping her in, he buckled her seat belt and headed toward her house.

They didn't speak until they were seated at her kitchen table drinking tea and nibbling on the leftover lunch-to-go peanut butter s'mores bars.

"Tell me everything you can remember from the moment Mikeloff showed up to the minute you walked out of the interrogation room." Spencer ate his cookie in two bites and stared expectantly at her.

"Mikeloff said that if I didn't go with him to the station, Ivy would spend the night in jail." Dani hesitated. Did she trust Spencer enough to believe that he'd still want to help her if she revealed that his niece continued to be the detective's second choice of suspect? Taking a fortifying sip of tea, she quickly added, "But it was a trick. I don't think Mikeloff has any real interest in Ivy."

"Go on." Spencer took a pen and notepad from the inside pocket of his suit coat. "Once he got you to the station, what happened?"

Dani described her wait in the chilly interrogation room, then repeated as much of the detective's questions and her answers as she could recall. Finally, she said, "So after I demanded to leave or to have a lawyer, he stormed out of the room. It took forever, but he eventually came back with my purse and let me go."

"So what Chief Cleary wasn't willing to share with me was the lack of injection site. She must have known that Mikeloff would use that as an excuse to fixate on you." Spencer relayed the rest of his conversation with the chief.

"So." Dani clutched her cup. "Even though she suspects that Mikeloff is a bad cop, the chief can't, or won't, take him off the case?"

"That about sums it up." Spencer gently peeled Dani's fingers from the mug. "Chief Cleary is sympathetic and would love it if we turned up any evidence against Mikeloff, but the union would fry her if she tried to remove him without cause."

"So we're still going to keep going with our own investigations?" Dani's shoulders slumped.

"Yes." Spencer kept his hands covering hers. "But we now know that the insulin wasn't injected. We just need to discover which of our suspects knew that Regina would eat all that food after the luau."

"I may have some insight on that." Dani pulled away from Spencer's grasp. "Last night, after I finished cooking for the Karneses' dinner party, I found Regina's housekeeper by the side of the road. The Bournes had fired her, and when she tried to leave, she got a flat tire. While we waited for help, she admitted to me that Regina was bulimic."

"Which means we need to figure out who knew about her disorder." Spencer's eyes gleamed. "Certainly her fiancé would know."

"And probably her ex and her best friend." Dani sighed and pursed her lips.

"So we still have three possible suspects." Spencer reached for another dessert bar.

"More than that." Dani pushed the plate closer to him. Seeing anyone enjoy her food always warmed her heart. "While I was preparing dinner last night, I overheard the Karneses and their guests discussing the reason Regina was kicked out of her sorority."

"Oh?" Spencer chewed and swallowed. "I didn't know she had been."

"She stole one of the pledge's manuscripts." Dani repeated the conversation she'd heard.

"We need to get that girl's name," Spencer said as he jotted down a note.

"Any idea how?" Dani asked. When Spencer didn't answer, she said, "I have one more person for our suspect list: Professor Karnes."

"Did he have an affair with her?" Spencer's eyebrows went up.

"Not exactly." Dani described the recorded kiss and the identity theft.

"It seems as if Miss Regina has been a very naughty girl," Spencer drawled. "It's going to be hard to find out who hated her the most."

Dani crossed her arms. "Well, like I said to the detective: I think Bliss has the best motive. At least, the most recent best one."

"True." Spencer tapped his chin. "And who would know more about Regina's bulimic habits than her best friend?"

CHAPTER 18

A few hours later, as Dani loaded the van with the food and equipment for the football booster dinner, she scowled at the memory of her telephone conversation with Kipp. Her ex had thrown a hissy fit when she'd told him that she hadn't yet found his book.

Dani had explained that she would look for it on Friday and that her Thursday schedule had been disrupted — although she didn't tell him it was due to a police interrogation — but he didn't care. At first he'd tried to charm her, but when that didn't work, he'd just stated in that annoying you-have-always-disappointed-me tone that he would be at her house first thing Saturday morning to pick up his book. He'd then hung up without giving her a chance to respond.

Tomorrow was back-to-back gigs. The usual lunch-to-go would occupy her morning. In the afternoon she had a hundredth-birthday celebration at an assisted-living facility; in the evening, she had a personal chef engagement for a new client. Dani had no idea when she'd be able to go through all her boxes, but she wanted to get Kipp out of her life for good, so she'd have to carve out some time.

When she'd packed for the move, Dani thought she'd been smart to put a few books in each box so no one carton would be too heavy. Now she wished that she had been a bit more organized and labeled the boxes with something more descriptive than the word *stuff.*

Pushing her irritation with Kipp aside, Dani checked the last item off her list and climbed into the van. Ivy, Starr, Tippi, and Spencer were meeting her at the venue. While the girls were helping to plate and serve, Spencer's presence was due to his desire to talk to Vance King and Bliss Armstrong.

When he and Dani had decided that Bliss was their prime suspect, they'd discussed the best way to approach her. Spencer had said that something casual, like running into her, would be best, and Dani had pointed out that Bliss was bound to accompany Vance to the football dinner.

The event was a gathering of the coaches,

top current players, their girlfriends, and the boosters who had donated the most money to the team. It was being held at the Normalton University Union. Dani's contract called for no more than a hundred guests and included a table of cold hors d'oeuvres for a social hour that started at six.

The boosters could help themselves to prosciutto crostini with lemony fennel slaw, mango shrimp in endive leaves, and red pepper and goat cheese crisps with radicchio while mingling with the players and reliving their own glory days. Dani had been a little surprised that the organizer hadn't wanted pigs in a blanket and hot wings, but she'd been given carte blanche for the menu. Now all she could hope for was that her more sophisticated food choices weren't a mistake.

When Dani pulled behind the building, Spencer and Ivy were already there, waiting at the back entrance. They helped her haul the food and equipment into the service elevator and rode with her to the union's top floor. This level was rented out for meetings and private events, and the football dinner was being held in a suite of rooms connected to a small kitchen.

Once the three of them had everything

from the van spread out on the counters, Dani pushed through the swinging doors to inspect the party space. As she had specified, there was a long table covered in a white linen cloth on either side of the room. And the two bars were set up on the opposite walls, which should solve the issue of any one food or beverage station being mobbed.

Next, Dani scrutinized the dining area. The team colors had been used to decorate. Spaced evenly around the floor were twelve round tables covered in red cloths and set with white napkins, black-handled utensils, and goblets bearing the image of the school's mascot, the red-tailed hawk.

Returning to the kitchen, she found Spencer and Ivy speaking in low voices, but as the swinging door swished open, Spencer turned and said to Dani, "I'll go move your van and park it in the lot."

"Thanks." Dani dug into the pocket of her chef pants and handed him the keys. His fingers brushed hers and her cheeks heated with the flicker of electricity that shot up her arm.

The minute Spencer disappeared from the kitchen Ivy spun around and, with her lips twitching, said, "So, you and my uncle, huh?"

"Me and your uncle what?" Dani busied herself unpacking her gear.

"Seriously?" Ivy yelped. "You're going to pretend that you're not interested in him and that he's not interested in you?"

"Why would you think that?" Dani asked, unwilling to admit her attraction since nothing was going to come from it.

"Let's see." Ivy snickered. "He can't take his eyes off you. You blush every time he touches you." She paused. "And he's here."

"The first two are purely your imagination." Dani loaded the trays of appetizers on a rolling cart. "And he's here to help figure out who killed Regina and keep your butt out of jail."

"More like to keep yours out." Ivy began filling a second cart with small china plates, utensils, and napkins. "That awful detective is obsessed with you, not me." She leveled a stare at Dani. "And as soon as you left the kitchen, Uncle Spencer started grilling me about you."

"What did he ask?" Dani frowned. Her trust issues flared. She didn't like being the subject of their conversation.

"Did your ex show up again?" Ivy recited. "Did you seem okay after being hauled into the police station?" Tossing a smirk at Dani, Ivy added casually, "Was I sure that you weren't currently seeing anyone?"

"I'm sure that was professional interest," Dani said quickly. "You know, to find out if there's someone else who might be involved, with what's been happening with the murder and all."

Not waiting for Ivy to respond, Dani wheeled her cart into the dining room and nodded at the two bartenders setting up their stations. She pushed thoughts of Spencer aside and concentrated on arranging the platters on both of the serving tables.

When Dani glanced up from what she was doing, Ivy had followed her. The girl had a knowing smirk on her face and was tapping her foot.

Dani wanted to mention Spencer's girlfriend but bit her tongue. Ivy would jump to the wrong conclusion if Dani brought up his love life. "Your uncle is just helping me because of you. There's no reason to read anything more into it."

Ivy opened her mouth to reply, but was interrupted by the first wave of people flowing into the room. They rushed toward the bars, but Dani knew that as soon as they had their drinks, they'd head for the appetizers. Staring at the huge men, she hoped she had enough food.

As she and Ivy quickly finished putting

out the hors d'oeuvres, Dani studied the guests. It was easy to spot the current players, muscled young men in their late teens or early twenties with petite, blond, animatronic-like women clinging to their massive arms.

Conversely, the boosters seemed to fall into two groups: nice-looking men in business suits who obviously still frequented the gym, and more casually dressed guys whose bodies had begun to show the effect of too much beer and not enough exercise. However, all their wives looked like older versions of the players' girlfriends.

As Dani and Ivy hurried into the kitchen to work on the meal, Dani pondered the difference. Were men less concerned with their appearance? Or maybe it was more a matter of societal expectations.

Before she could decide, Spencer returned from parking the van, returned her keys, and asked, "Do you need any help in here?"

"I'm good," Dani assured him. "I saw Bliss out there with Vance, so this might be the perfect opportunity to get her alone for a conversation."

"Great." Spencer smiled. "I'll text you to join me if I'm able to corner her."

Ivy shot Dani an I-told-you-so look but kept her mouth shut. Dani was in full chef mode and she appreciated the girl's restraint. She was too focused on the food to take the time to deflect Ivy's teasing.

She and Ivy had just finished plating the wilted radicchio, endive, and asparagus starter when Tippi and Starr appeared. Seeing that it was ten to seven, Dani sent the girls out to place the salads on the tables and turned her attention to the pork tenderloin with Italian tapenade.

While Dani frantically finished up the main course and sides, she realized that in the future, she would need more help for a seated dinner of this size — someone to assist her with the cooking, as well as an additional server. She'd thought that by prepping most things at home it was doable, but she was in the weeds for most of the meal.

As Ivy, Tippi, and Starr rushed in and out of the kitchen, they kept her informed as to what was happening in the dining room. Ivy reported that Bliss never left Vance's side and that Spencer was still watching for a chance to talk to their suspect.

Finally, as Dani added the last touches to the coconut shortcake with strawberry-lime compote, her cell vibrated. She snatched it from her pocket and read the message.

Bliss and Vance just had a big blowup. She is headed to the bathroom and he just walked out. I'm going after him. Ladies' room is a good place for you to accidentally run into her.

Dani threw down her cloth, and as Ivy entered the kitchen, Dani said, "Make sure the desserts get out to the guests."

Pushing through the swinging doors, Dani ran toward the women's restroom but skidded to a stop at the entrance. What on earth would she say to Bliss? *Hey, knowing Regina was bulimic, did you put an overdose of insulin in your BFF's junk food stash?*

Her mind blank, realizing that she'd just have to make it up as she went along and hope for the best, Dani took a deep breath and walked into the restroom. It smelled of hairspray and expensive perfume. Pausing, her gaze swept her surroundings.

As ladies' rooms went, this one was pretty nice. To her left was a trio of oval vessel sinks and to her right were three partially open white, wooden doors leading into the toilet cubicles. No metal stalls with barely functioning locks for the folks who rented this space from the university.

Straight ahead, somewhat obscured by a half wall, were two armchairs and a small sofa. Curled up crying on one end of the couch was Bliss Armstrong.

Stepping around the wall, Dani sat in one of the chairs that faced the weeping girl and waited until Bliss's sobs had subsided. Once there was only an occasional sniffle, she reached into her pocket and handed the distraught young woman a packet of tissues.

After Bliss had wiped her eyes and blown her nose, Dani said, "I don't know if you remember me. I'm Dani Sloan, a friend of Ivy's."

"You own that cool mansion that Ivy and her friends live in," Bliss said, her voice still raspy from her tears. "You're the caterer."

"That's right." Dani smiled. "In fact, I cooked tonight's dinner."

"It was really yummy," Bliss said. Then her breath hitched and she added, "At least until Vance . . . until Vance." She buried her face in her hands. "I can't say it. It's too awful to repeat."

"I understand." Dani patted the girl's shoulder. "But sometimes it feels better to talk about it and get it out in the open."

"I'm probably just being silly." Bliss dabbed at her eyes with a wad of disintegrating Kleenex. "My mom always tells me that I'm a drama queen. She says that no one wants to hear my first-world problems."

"Well . . ." Dani searched her mind for the right response. "I'm sure your mother means well, but I have to disagree with her on this. Just because your troubles aren't life-threatening, doesn't make them trivial."

"Don't you have to get back to the kitchen?" Bliss stared down at her pretty dress. She attempted to smooth the wrinkles from the pale-green gauzy fabric. "I mean you're probably too busy to just sit and talk to me."

"It's fine, sweetie." Dani would have comforted Bliss even if she weren't trying to investigate Regina's murder, but guilt still coated the back of her throat like a swallow of milk that had gone sour. "Dessert was being served as I left, so I'm all yours."

"Really?" Bliss asked, and when Dani nodded, the tiny redhead licked her lips and said, "Did you know that Vance dated Regina before he and I got together?"

"I think Starr may have mentioned that after Regina's party," Dani said, hedging, unwilling to reveal just how much she'd discovered about their group. "Did Vance still have feelings for her?"

"Feelings?" Bliss snickered, then blew out a scornful breath. "No. Vance was definitely not still in love with her. Regina and Vance were never" — she paused, clearly searching for the right way to explain the couple — "in an emotional relationship. And Vance knew from the beginning that Regina and Laz would eventually get back together, because neither of them was willing to go against their parents' wishes and risk their trust funds."

"Oh." Dani was again astounded at the whole idea. It was practically an arranged marriage. She'd had no clue that sort of thing still happened.

"Believe me. Vance didn't want Regina back in his life."

When Bliss didn't continue, Dani asked softly, "So what did he want? He seemed extremely anxious to talk to her at the luau."

"That's one of the things that we were arguing about at dinner." Bliss wrapped her arms around her waist and rocked back and forth on the couch. "He won't tell me exactly what was going on that night. He just says that Regina had some things of his she wouldn't return."

"Other than his persistence in attempting to have a conversation with Regina, was Vance's behavior different than usual at the party?"

"He drank more." Bliss stopped rocking and started nibbling on her thumbnail. "I mean, although he always has liked his beer, he usually stops before he gets totally wasted."

"But not that night?" Dani recalled Vance's staggering walk and glassy eyes.

"And ever since." Bliss twisted the gold signet ring on her pinkie.

Dani saw that it bore the letters of her sorority. Evidently, when Regina was kicked out and she made Bliss leave the house too, Bliss hadn't entirely disavowed her affiliation.

Before Dani could think about that significance of that fact, Bliss said, "Our fight started when I tried to get him to slow down on the booze." She shook her head. "His coach was glaring at him and some of the boosters were starting to notice."

"So you quarreled about his drinking and about his refusal to give you details about why he wanted to talk to Regina." Dani leaned forward. "Was that it?"

"Yes." Bliss closed her eyes. "I should have just done what he wanted."

"I doubt that would have been a good idea." Dani recalled what Spencer had said about the football player's sexual preferences. "It's almost always best to go with your gut in those situations."

"Maybe." Bliss sighed. "But I'm not sure how much longer I can hold out."

"If he pressures you to do something you don't want to, he's not the guy for you." Dani wondered how she'd gone from interrogator to pseudo-parent. "You're a smart, beautiful girl. You don't need him."

"I really do." Bliss stared at the ceiling. "I'm graduating this year in the most useless major ever created. The only job I'll be able to get with a B.A. in fashion design is retail sales." She sucked in a lungful of air. "The plan has always been to find the right husband, and Vance is perfect. He's good-looking, his family owns a successful religious supply company he's being groomed to take over, and he needs a wife for the position."

"Still . . ." Dani paused, gathering her thoughts. "You want to be with someone because you love them, not because you feel trapped."

Bliss ignored Dani's words and said, "All I have to do to get that diamond on my left hand is to let him into my dead best friend's house, allow him to paw through her stuff, and then look the other way when he removes whatever he's afraid someone will find there." Bliss's pretty face twisted, showing her struggle with the intimate facts she'd just revealed. Then, in a bitter voice, she added, "Oh, and not ask any questions."

CHAPTER 19

"Wow!" Dani wasn't precisely sure what Vance wanted from Regina's house, but she had a pretty good idea about what he wanted to keep secret. However, before she said anything, she needed to get some more information from Bliss. "I can see why you'd be reluctant to give in to your boyfriend's demands."

"Exactly."

They sat in silence until the sound of a toilet flushing made them both jump.

Bliss clutched her chest. "I thought we were the only ones in here."

"Me too." Dani got up and checked the stalls. "They're all empty. The automatic flush mechanism must be out of whack."

At least, Dani hoped that was the explanation because the last thing she needed was a ghost popping into her life. Thinking that they both needed a breather, Dani walked to the bathroom's entrance and opened the door.

Miraculously, the hallway was empty and all she could hear was the rattle of cutlery and, over the PA system, the guest speaker. He was an alumnus who had gone on to play professional football and was droning on and on about his illustrious career as a defensive linebacker for the Louisville Lions.

She'd have bet money that by now someone would have come to use the facilities, but so far, so good. While providence was smiling on her, Dani hastily returned to where she'd left her suspect and sat down.

"I'm confused. How are you supposed to let Vance into Regina's house?" Dani figured she might as well start with the easier questions.

"I have a key to her place," Bliss answered. "Regina wasn't the most organized person. A lot of times she'd forget something she needed for class and send me over to pick it up."

"That was nice of you." Dani tucked away the fact that Bliss had just admitted that she had access to Regina's food and could be the killer.

"Not so much nice as a requirement." Bliss tugged at her necklace.

"What a pretty pendant." Dani noted that

the Greek letters were from Vance's fraternity. If she understood the process correctly, wearing a guy's lavalier was something akin to being pre-engaged.

"Thanks!" Bliss touched the tiny ruby at the end of the epsilon. "Vance gave it to me when he picked me up tonight. I can't wait to show my sorority sisters and have my candle ceremony."

"Congratulations." Dani's smile was skeptical. Vance's timing was sure convenient. Bliss yearned for a fiancé and her boyfriend had just presented her with a carrot to get her to do what he wanted.

"Thank you." Bliss's own smile dimmed. "I can't believe our evening started out so wonderfully and ended up this way. I'm such an idiot. I should have just agreed to take him to Regina's."

"Aren't her parents home from their trip?" Dani asked, refusing to give in to the impulse to point out that if Vance treated Bliss this way now, chances were he would only get worse once they were married.

"Actually, no." Bliss continued to finger her necklace. "The day after she was killed, Mrs. Carnet told me that they had informed her that since the police weren't releasing Regina's body, they didn't see any point in rushing back."

"That's . . ." Dani was at loss. What kind of parents would continue their vacation when their only daughter was lying dead in the morgue?

"Yeah, hard to believe isn't it?" Bliss puffed out her cheeks. "In a way, her parents' behavior makes me feel a little better about myself. I've always been sort of jealous of Regina. She was beautiful, smart, knew that Laz would marry her, and her folks are filthy rich."

"But you can't compare yourself to someone else." Dani tried to reassure the girl whose self-confidence was so low she was ready to marry an obnoxious jerk like Vance because she didn't think she could do any better for herself. "You have no idea what that person's life is really like."

"Look." Bliss waved off Dani's words. "I know that I'm pretty, but I'm not drop-dead gorgeous like Regina." Bliss heaved a heavy sigh. "And I'm intelligent enough to make it through college, but Regina was majoring in creative writing and acing all her classes." Bliss shook her head. "Not to mention that my parents are comfortable, but I certainly don't have a trust fund."

"I can see how Regina's life would cause some envy," Dani said. "And I imagine it wasn't always easy being her best friend."

As she learned more about Regina, Dani still disliked her, but she certainly felt a lot sorrier for her than she had previously. No one chose to be bulimic. And working in HR, Dani had come to realize that everyone had a story, and most didn't have a happily ever after. Which is exactly why she liked to read romances. At least with those books she was guaranteed a heartwarming ending.

"Regina was well aware of the advantages associated with being her friend." Bliss's expression was thoughtful. "And she certainly demanded equal compensation in return. But it was worth it."

"What did she make you do?" Dani asked. "Besides run her errands."

"Whatever she said." Bliss crossed her arms. "She expected absolute loyalty."

"Like not living in the sorority house when she was kicked out?"

"Definitely." Bliss glanced at her ring. "She wanted me to quit the sorority completely."

"But you didn't," Dani guessed. "How did you manage to go to meetings and stuff? I understand there are certain required activities."

"Instead of quitting, I deactivated, which is like a leave of absence."

"Now you can go back," Dani murmured.

She knew there was something she should ask Bliss while they were on the subject of the sorority, but she couldn't come up with it.

"Uh-huh." Bliss bit her lip. "Vance wants me to do it right away."

"Of course he does." Dani couldn't keep the sarcastic tone from slipping out. But having just thought of what she needed to find out from Bliss about the sorority, she quickly asked, "Is the girl who Regina stole the manuscript from still living in the house?"

"As you can imagine, although the sorority handled the incident perfectly, Gail left before she finished pledging." Bliss made a face. "I bet she doesn't have too many fond memories of her time in Alpha Beta Delta."

Bingo! Dani kept the elation off her face. Now all she needed was a last name. Could she ask Bliss for it?

No. Dani didn't want her to feel like she was being interrogated and there was no casual way to get that information. She'd have to hope *Gail* was enough.

Now on to the next issue. Which would be the most innocuous? Vance's reason for needing to get into the Bournes' house or Regina's bulimia?

Dani widened her eyes as if she had just

thought of something and said, "You know, I almost forgot that I heard something about Vance that might give you a clue as to what he needs to get from Regina's." She reached out and squeezed the girl's hand. "But I should warn you, it may not be something you want to know."

"Who told you?" Bliss pursed her lips. "A lot of people are jealous of Vance."

"This person claimed it was from her own personal experience."

"Her!" Bliss screeched. "This was from a woman? A woman he dated?"

"I don't think they were exactly dating." Guilt stung Dani, but truly Bliss would be better off without a guy like Vance. "Do you want to know?" When the girl nodded, she continued, "He and this person had a sort of" — Dani searched for a nice way to put it — "a professional arrangement. While Vance was involved with Regina, this woman supplied him with sex."

"Why?" Bliss tipped her head. "I know for a fact Regina put out for him."

"Maybe not in the way he wanted her to do it." Dani hesitated, but Bliss absolutely needed to be aware of her boyfriend's true tastes regarding sex before she married him. "From what I understand, he was into BDSM — bondage, discipline, sadism, masochism — and Regina must have something that shows his participation in that lifestyle. You said his family owns a religious supply company so I'm pretty sure that's not something he'd want made public."

"I . . . That can't be true . . . He never . . . We never . . ." Bliss's freckles stood out in stark relief as her face lost all color and she collapsed against the couch. "He's been strictly . . . uh . . . you know . . . normal with me."

"Maybe Regina reacted so badly when he told her, he decided to keep that part of himself away from his girlfriends," Dani offered.

"That makes sense." Bliss rested her head against the sofa back and said, "I can't imagine her allowing anyone to tie her up or beat her." Bliss's tone was thoughtful. "Although she might enjoy it the other way around. I mean, if she were the one in control and the guy was handcuffed to the bed."

"You know," Dani said carefully, "Regina refusing to give him whatever proof she had of his unusual inclinations could make Vance really desperate. Did he know that Regina was bulimic?"

"No!" Regina glared at Dani, clearly understanding what she was suggesting.

"Regina would never have told him. She was too ashamed."

"But if they dated, he could have figured it out for himself."

"Regina stopped binging and purging after she was kicked out of the sorority. She always thought that was part of the reason they made her leave." Bliss stood up. "She was only fasting and exercising when she and Vance were together."

"When did she start binging again?" Dani asked, holding her breath.

"Within the last month." Bliss paced in front of Dani. "You know, bulimia isn't only about the fear of gaining weight. It's feeling in control and soothing you in stressful situations. Something was worrying her. I think it was the notes she was receiving, but she wouldn't show them to me. She always threw them away and refused to discuss them." Bliss shrugged. "She almost seemed to feel guilty about something, which was bizarre. Regina never felt ashamed about anything."

"But you knew she was binging again?" Dani looked up into Bliss's eyes.

"Yeah." Bliss rubbed her temples. "She always made me go buy the junk food."

Well, heck! Dani was really hoping that Vance was Regina's killer, but Bliss was shoving herself higher and higher onto the suspect list.

It was time to ask the hard question about the nude photo of Bliss that Regina had sent out, but Dani wasn't sure how to bring it up. She'd decided the only way was just to say it when her luck ran out and the door banged open. Evidently, the speeches were over and the women who had been holding it for the length of the dinner were all now rushing toward relief.

When Bliss spotted the other team girlfriends and boosters' wives pouring into the bathroom, she turned to Dani and said, "Thanks for staying with me, but I better get back. Vance is going to be furious at me for being in here so long. He hates it when I'm gone." Then as she began to push her way through the crowd to leave, she asked, "Is it okay if I come by sometime and we can talk some more?"

"Definitely!" Dani shouted as Bliss quickly disappeared into the mob. And although she doubted the girl could hear her, she yelled, "Vance left the dining room right after you did."

As Dani made her way to the bathroom exit, she silently repeated everything she'd learn from Bliss. She needed to get all the information down on paper before she forgot something important.

Digging her cell out of her pants pocket, she checked to see if there was any word from Spencer. It had vibrated a couple of times while she'd been occupied with Bliss, but she hadn't wanted to interrupt the flow of their conversation to look at her phone.

There were two texts from Ivy. One that said desserts have been served and the second stated Tippi, Starr, and I are cleaning up. Spencer's message was even shorter: following suspect.

Curious as to where Vance had headed, Dani replied: Where are you?

There was no immediate response, so she continued on to the kitchen.

The party was breaking up, and as she walked through the dining room, several alumni complimented the meal and asked for her contact information. Glad she kept a stack of business cards in the sleeve pocket of her chef coat, Dani happily chatted about the food as she handed them out. Word of mouth was always the best advertising for a small company.

Once she'd finished promoting her services as a personal chef and caterer, Dani was pleased to discover that her workers had done the dishes and were packing up. Dani gave the kitchen a final wipe down, then helped the girls stow the equipment.

The four of them pushed the loaded carts into the service elevator and when they reached the hallway at the ground floor, Dani dug her keys from her pocket. As she held the plastic fob, it dawned on her that Spencer had never told her where he parked her van.

Shit! He still hadn't responded to her last text, so hoping he'd answer his phone, she tried calling. When it went directly to voice-mail, she cursed herself for not asking where he'd parked. Another reason not to allow Spencer into her life — help from men never turned out to be the good thing she thought it would be at the time.

Explaining the problem to the girls, Dani left Ivy guarding their gear while she, Tippi, and Starr each took one of the Union's three parking lots. As Dani walked down row after row, she berated herself for her stupidity.

The lots were well lighted and Dani could clearly see each bird dropping, blob of chewing gum, and piece of litter on the black asphalt. But the infrequent hum of a car passing on the street behind her empha-sized the area's isolation, and uneasiness quickened her steps.

Worried about the girls, Dani grabbed her

phone out of her pocket and blew out a sigh of relief when a text from Tippi popped up on the screen. She had found the van and gave directions to its current location.

Chuckling, Dani knew she was getting old because she now considered finding her van in the parking lot as getting lucky for the night.

Because the girls had done such a great job at the football dinner and to compensate them for having to search for the van, Dani offered to treat them to ice cream at Izzy's Ice Cream Factory, a Normalton institution.

Walking into the shop, Dani inhaled the sweet, creamy aroma and her mouth watered. She hadn't had anything to eat since the dessert bars she'd shared with Spencer and she was starving. Once they were all served and sitting at a table, Ivy licked her cone and said, "What did you find out from Bliss?"

Dani realized that there was no way to keep her investigations secret from the girls. Especially after Ivy's guess about her motive for inviting Laz to dinner and then admitting to the girls that she and Spencer planned to talk to Vince and Bliss.

"Let me get a pen and paper and write it down before I forget." Dani dug through her purse and found a dry cleaning receipt and a ballpoint advertising a local farmers market. "Let's see, earlier this evening Vance lavaliered Bliss."

"Ah, that's sweet," Ivy cooed. "I know she'd been hoping he would."

"I'm not sure about sweet," Dani said, then explained about Vance's demand that Bliss get him into Regina's house and his unusual sexual tastes.

Making a face at the latter piece of information, Tippi waved Dani's words away like a bad smell and asked, "Anything else?"

"The pledge that Regina ripped off is named Gail." Dani looked around the table and asked, "Do any of you know a Gail from Alpha Beta Delta?"

They all said no, and Starr commented, "That could be a sorority nickname. A lot of times, they pick a name that only the sisters use. Did you ask if it was her real one?"

Dani shook her head. "At the time, I was trying to keep the conversation casual and not let Bliss know I was interrogating her."

"We can ask around," Tippi offered. "My cousin's in a sorority and the Greek system is pretty small at NU, so even though they aren't in the same house, she might know a girl called Gail."

"Be careful," Dani warned. "Don't tell her the real reason you want to know."

"Don't worry." Tippi ate a spoonful of hot fudge sauce. "I'll come up with something."

"You found out quite a bit about Vance and the pledge," Starr said. "Anything about Bliss?"

"Sadly, yes." Dani popped a maraschino cherry in her mouth. "She knew Regina was bulimic and had keys to her house."

"Shoot!" Ivy scowled. "I like Bliss. I don't want it to be her."

"Me either." As Dani talked, she jotted notes down on her list. Now she folded the paper and asked, "Ready to go?"

It was almost ten thirty when Dani and the girls rolled the loaded carts up the ramp at the mansion's rear entrance. Dani unlocked the door, flipped on the lights, and froze. Her kitchen had been trashed. Food was splattered everywhere and broken glass littered the floor.

Realizing that whoever vandalized the place could still be there, she shouted, "Everyone get in the van."

Once they were inside the locked vehicle she shivered, cold sweat trickling down her sides. Wishing she hadn't traded her chef coat for a T-shirt, she dug out her cell but hesitated. Did she really want to involve the police? Not only was she reluctant to come under their scrutiny again, but she was also afraid that her intruder might be one of them — namely, Mikeloff.

Deciding to try Spencer one more time, she dialed his number. It rang twice and when he answered on the third ring, she had to fight back tears in order to speak.

Finally, she cleared the lump from her throat and said, "This is Dani. The girls and I just got home and we're sitting in my locked van. Someone broke into the house and wrecked it. Can you come over?"

"Drive away now." Spencer's tone was clipped. "I'll meet you a couple blocks south of your place. I'll be there in ten."

CHAPTER 20

When Spencer disconnected from Dani, it felt as if he'd just been punched in the gut. He knew she and the girls were safe, but his knee-jerk reaction to the idea of someone having the gall to break into Dani's home and ransack it was to track down the asshat and put him in the hospital. Evidently, refusing to acknowledge his feelings for Dani and keeping a certain emotional distance between them was turning out to be a lot tougher than he'd imagined.

Spencer was as furious with himself as he was with the punk who vandalized the mansion. How did he manage to forget every damn bit of his determination where Dani was concerned? It was a freaking miracle that he'd been able to regain his cool so quickly and tell her to meet him, rather than flooring the gas pedal of his truck and charging toward the scene of the crime. Wouldn't that have helped Spencer maintain the facade of just friends?

The whole situation with Mikeloff and the murder was eating away at his self-control. He was frustrated as hell that he couldn't protect Dani from the dickwad detective. It was bad enough he'd had to put her in danger by including her in a murder investigation, but the thought of some prick breaking into Dani's home and terrorizing her was almost too much to take.

He just had to make sure that he wasn't by himself with Dani. As long as they were in public or the girls were around, he'd be okay. He would keep things in the friendship zone with her if it killed him.

With his headlights slicing through the darkness, Spencer drove along the shadowy roads toward Dani's street. He forced aside all thoughts of her and concentrated on the matter at hand. Someone had violated her home and he needed to find out that person's identity. Nothing was more important than keeping her and the girls safe.

Was it possible that he'd been wrong about Regina's murderer and there was some serial predator out there obsessed with bumping off college girls?

No. Spencer didn't buy the crazed-killer theory. It was much more likely that one of three people broke into the mansion. And his first guess was Mikeloff. He wouldn't put it past the renegade detective to conduct an illegal search in hopes of finding something incriminating.

Second on Spencer's hit parade was Dani's jerkoff ex-boyfriend. Dr. Dumbass was a little too interested in the book he wanted back for it to be just a matter of fulfilling his mother's promise to a cousin. Which reminded Spencer that he still needed to get the title and do some research.

And the final possibility, the worst one, was that whoever murdered Regina had heard that Dani was investigating and smashed up her place as a warning for her to back down. If that was the case, they needed to make a list of who she'd contacted and what had been said.

Depending on when the home invasion had taken place, Vance and Bliss could have alibis. They both had been in Spencer's presence or Dani's from six to nine o'clock.

Spencer had followed the football player when he'd left the dinner and gone to a local bar. As King had pounded down bottle after bottle of beer, Spencer had studied the hulking young man. Something was eating at the kid. Whether it was a guilty conscience from murdering Regina Bourne or a different matter completely, King wasn't a happy camper.

The guy had still been drinking when Dani called a few minutes ago. Fortunately, Spencer knew that the bar's manager had a taxi company on speed dial and the football player wouldn't be allowed to drive.

While Spencer had no jurisdiction away from campus, he'd made it a point to meet all the employees of the local watering holes. As head of university security, he felt responsible for the students no matter where they sought after-school entertainment.

Pulling behind Dani's parked vehicle, Spencer jumped out of his truck. Just as he made it to the van, Dani swung open her door and hopped out. Her eyes were red and her breathing was ragged, and Spencer's chest clenched as if a giant fist were squeezing his rib cage. It was all he could do not to take her in his arms.

With a hitch in her voice, Dani said, "Thank you for coming. I was so scared and I was afraid to call the police. I didn't know what to do."

Spencer's stomach knotted, but he kept his face expressionless and said, "That's understandable."

Although he hated it, he had to agree with Dani that calling the cops was probably not their best option. It would be too easy for Mikeloff to hijack the case and make any evidence against him disappear.

"But if I don't report it, my insurance company probably won't cover the damage." Dani's chin trembled. "Either way, I'm screwed."

"We'll figure something out." Spencer realized he'd taken her hand and was running his thumb across the soft skin of her palm. Dropping her hand as if it burned him, he said, "I'll go see what's been damaged and take pictures, then once we have it documented, if you want to make an insurance claim, we'll call the police. It's possible the repairs won't be much more than your deductible."

"I don't want you to go inside alone. It could be dangerous." She frowned. "What if the criminal is still there and shoots you?"

Spencer watched as Dani's plump lips pursed into an adorable pink rosebud of concern and forgot she'd asked him a question.

"Well?"

He forced himself to focus. "I'm sure the perp is long gone," Spencer assured her. "If he wasn't before you got home, he sure is now."

"I still don't like it." Dani's jaw firmed.

"I'm going with you." When he started to object, she added, "Or I'll just call 911 and take my chances that Detective Mikeloff isn't assigned to my case." She nodded to herself. "That's probably best."

"No!" Spencer barked, then said more softly, "Let's go take a look first."

"Okay." Dani glanced over her shoulder into the van's interior, where Ivy, Tippi, and Starr were avidly listening to Spencer and Dani's conversation. She pointed a finger at them and said, "You girls stay here with the doors locked. We'll be right back."

"Be careful," Ivy called as Dani followed Spencer to his truck.

The short ride to the mansion was silent, but as Spencer backed the pickup into Dani's driveway, he said, "This is how we're doing this. You will stay behind me at all times. You will immediately comply with my commands. And you will not touch anything."

"Yes, sir." Dani saluted, slid out of the truck, and narrowed her eyes. "But only because you're the one with the gun and the training. Otherwise, as I told you, I've been taking care of myself for years and have done a damn good job of it." Gesturing to the front entrance, she said, "I see how the guy got in. The front door's ajar. I didn't notice it before."

"Who has a key?"

"Just the girls and me." Dani's cheeks reddened. "But I keep one hidden in a specially designed stone next to the steps."

"As soon as we finish here," Spencer said, "you need to call a locksmith and have a double dead bolt installed on all the doors. And no more hiding keys outside. Everyone and their grandmother know about those fake rocks."

"Back off. I will entertain suggestions, but ordering me around isn't going to fly." Dani put her hands on her hips. "You're right about the lock, but I'll call tomorrow. I'm not paying after-hours prices."

"I'll contact my friend. He'll come first thing in the morning, before his regular shift." Spencer put his hands on his hips too. "And I'm sleeping here tonight."

"Fine." Dani's smile was mocking. "But the sofa isn't very comfortable."

"You don't have a guest room ready?" Spencer lifted an eyebrow.

"Not yet." Dani's pretty amber eyes twinkled. "But maybe you can talk Ivy into bunking with Tippi, who has twin beds in her room and you can have your niece's suite."

"I suppose that's one solution. I mean if

you aren't willing to share," Spencer drawled, then shook his head. He really had to stop flirting with Dani. "Now that we've figured out the sleeping arrangements, let's get this show on the road."

Before they could take a step, a loud howl ripped through the quiet. Spencer's scalp prickled and he froze.

Giggling, Dani patted his shoulder and said, "That's Petunia, my neighbor's dog. She thinks she's a wolf."

Spencer chuckled, then gestured for Dani to get behind him. When she moved into position, he cautiously stepped into the foyer, paused, and listened for any sign of an intruder. The only sound was the ticking of the old grandfather clock in the parlor.

As they went from room to room taking pictures, it became clear that the place had been searched more than it had been vandalized. Downstairs, shelves were emptied onto the floor and cushions were sliced, with their stuffing bleeding out of the gaping wounds.

On the second floor, in the girls' rooms, drawers were open and the contents thrown aside. The closet rods had been stripped of hangers with the clothes flung helter-skelter on the ground. As a final hurrah, the mattresses and box springs had been shoved off the bedframes.

With the two remaining suites empty and not yet remodeled, the only evidence the intruder had been inside the room were the footprints on the dusty hardwood.

Dani's quarters were a mess, just as the girls' had been, and Spencer sensed more than heard her small sigh. He gazed at the disorder and knew she had to be having a rough time dealing with the invasion of her personal space, but she didn't break down. Glancing at her, he saw her straighten her spine and paste a stoic look on her pretty face.

However, reentering the kitchen, Dani's impassive expression slipped, and Spencer witnessed the full impact of the experience as it slammed into her soul. The rest of the mansion had been searched, but the kitchen shambles displayed a malicious intent to cause destruction. Broken dishes and shattered glass were everywhere. And the fragments were mixed with piles of flour and sugar. Pools of milk and broken eggs decorated the stainless steel counter, while molasses and honey oozed down the dark wood cabinets.

Despite his assurances that the home invader was long gone, Spencer had been on the alert for an ambush. Now that they'd been through all three floors, he allowed himself to stow his gun in his ankle holster and stand down.

Putting an arm around Dani's bowed shoulders, he said, "It's not as bad as it looks. There's very little damage anywhere but here."

"Just a few cushions ripped open," Dani murmured, staring at the kitchen.

"Even here, it's mostly a mess." Spencer squeezed her arm, then forced himself to take his hand away before he started stroking the soft flesh. "It looks as if the perp only smashed a few dishes and glasses."

"Right." Dani perked up a little. "All of the expensive equipment seems fine." She walked over to the china hutch by the table. "Mrs. Cook's vintage milk glass and Waterford are still intact too."

"It looks as if your loss is minimal and you don't have to worry about filing an insurance claim." Spencer smiled encouragingly.

"True. With my deductible, it wouldn't be worth the hassle." Dani rubbed her hand across the back of her head. "Is it safe to let the girls come home?"

"Sure." Spencer sent Ivy a coast-is-clear text. "After cooking all night, you're probably exhausted. Why don't you wait for the girls down here and I'll go put the beds back together?"

"Adrenaline must still be rushing through me because I'm not at all tired." Dani followed him up the stairs. "I'll help with the beds."

As Spencer and Dani worked together, he couldn't help notice her lush curves, especially when she bent over. It wasn't too bad while they were dealing with the girls' beds, but entering Dani's room, he suddenly felt like a perv staring at her heart-shaped bottom as she reached for a pillow on the floor.

Turning away, he shoved the mattress onto the box springs and asked, "Where are the moving boxes that your ex wanted you to go through?"

Dani jerked upright and put her hand over her mouth, pointing to the ceiling. "They're in the attic. I couldn't stand living with cartons all around. Do you think Kipp is the one who did this?"

"The good doctor is certainly high on my list of suspects." Spencer raked his fingers through his hair. "How do you get into the attic?"

"Through the walk-in closet." Dani trudged over to it. "The steps are hidden behind shelving that swings out on concealed hinges."

"Interesting." Spencer followed her into the closet, then watched as she swung open a rack filled with shoes and revealed a narrow set of steps.

"I'm not sure if this house was a stop on the Underground Railroad or maybe it had something to do with prohibition." Dani grinned. "But I love this hidden staircase."

As they entered the attic, Dani pulled a string attached to the overhead bulb. With the light on, the mountain of cartons stacked against the back wall was visible and it was evident that the boxes hadn't been disturbed.

"Guess your intruder didn't find his way up here," Spencer commented as he and Dani retraced their steps into her bedroom. "Which means if it was your ex, he didn't get what he wanted and he might come back."

"I can't really see Kipp breaking and entering over a book." Dani stepped briefly into her bathroom to grab a fresh set of sheets from the linen closet, then started to make the bed. "I told him I'd give it to him."

"Yeah." Spencer helped her get the fitted sheet in place. "About that. I'm wondering if there's something about that book we don't know. And I for sure want to be here when you hand it over to him."

"Like the book's worth a lot of money?" Dani asked, then shrugged. "It crossed my mind, but I can't remember the dang title. And it really doesn't matter. Even if it is valuable, I'd let him have it."

"Mmm." Spencer couldn't help but lose a tiny piece of his heart. Very few women would willingly give an ex something expensive.

"Well, if it was Kipp, I have to find that darn book tomorrow morning and put an end to his nonsense." Dani finished with the sheets and said, "Now we need to go downstairs and make sure the girls are okay."

"I'm sure they're doing better than you are." Spencer smiled.

Spencer led the way, and when they reached the first floor, he heard female voices coming from the kitchen. Entering it, they found Ivy, Tippi, and Starr cleaning up the mess on the floor.

"You don't have to do this," Dani said, tears welling up in her eyes.

"Yes we do." Starr was closest and slung an arm around Dani. "This way you can still make and serve the lunch-to-go sacks tomorrow."

Tippi paused and asked, "You weren't calling the cops, right?" Dani shook her head. "Phew! I just realized that if you were, we might be destroying evidence."

"No." Dani grabbed a dustpan from the pantry. "Spencer and I decided that it was better not to involve the police or the insurance."

"Glad that you and Uncle Spence are on the same page." Ivy smirked and then mouthed *I told you so* to Dani when Spencer wasn't looking.

After they got the kitchen back to normal, the girls went to bed.

Once her boarders were gone, Dani turned to Spencer and asked, "Can I get you a beer or something?"

"Ivy told me you don't keep any booze in the house." Spencer cocked his head to one side. "Do you have a secret stash?"

"Promise not to tell?" Dani asked, and when he nodded, she opened the refrigerator, took out a rack full of water bottles, and reached into the compartment they had been concealing. Reaching in, she grabbed two Coronas and handed them to Spencer along with the opener she retrieved from a nearby drawer.

When Dani joined Spencer at the table, he uncapped both bottles and placed one in front of her, then said, "I kind of pictured you as a wine connoisseur."

"I'm not much of a drinker at all." Dani took a swallow of beer. "Maybe a margarita with my girlfriends once in a while, but that's about it."

"So you have the Corona why?" Spencer's throat tightened. Maybe Ivy didn't know about the man in Dani's life.

"It's silly." Dani's cheeks turned a sweet shade of pink.

"No judgment here." Spencer traced a finger over the hand she had resting on the table.

"My dad drinks Corona." Dani stared at the bottle she held in front of her eyes. "Not that he has ever visited me, but I always keep a six-pack just in case he ever does come see me." She shook her head. "Enough about that, let's talk about the case."

Spencer scowled. Dani's father lived less than half an hour away. Why the eff didn't he visit her?

Deciding to allow her to avoid what was obviously a painful subject, Spencer told her about what he'd seen when he followed Vance, then asked, "Did you get anything from Bliss?"

"I did." Dani put down her beer, grabbed the list from her purse, and handed it to him.

Scanning the document, Spencer was once again impressed with Dani's ability to get people talking. After copying her notes, he was silent as he considered everything Bliss had revealed.

As if reading his mind, Dani said, "I realize that Bliss seems like a good bet, having the key and knowing about Regina's bulimia, but I still don't think it was her. She just doesn't seem like the type."

"They never do," Spencer said wearily. "But having your best friend post the kind of photo you described could send anyone down the rabbit hole."

"Yeah." Dani bit her lip, clearly struggling to find the words. "But Bliss has had reason to snap before, and she never did."

"Okay." Spencer tapped the rim of his bottle. "Let me see if I can find out to what extent that picture was distributed."

"Fine, but my money is on Vance King." Dani narrowed his eyes. "With his family's business catering to a Christian market, if Regina had something that proved that he was into BDSM, it could really hurt him."

"Good point," Spencer conceded. "But if it's him, that makes me more concerned about your break-in."

"Why?"

"Because one of three people vandalized

your house." Spencer held up his index finger. "Your ex." He held up a second finger. "Detective Mikeloff looking for evidence to frame you." A third finger joined the other two. "Or Regina's murderer trying to intimidate you into stopping your investigation."

"Well, hell!" Dani yelped. "I never thought I'd see the day Kipp was the lesser of three evils. Especially when there are so many to choose from nowadays."

CHAPTER 21

Friday morning, Dani yawned and stumbled bleary eyed into the kitchen, wrinkling her nose at the artificial lemon scent of the cleaning product they'd used last night to mop up the floor. Six a.m. had come much too early, but she couldn't ignore her obligations. The girls had classes to attend and she had food to prepare.

But she didn't regret the lost sleep. She and Spencer had sat up talking until well past two. He'd been so sweet. So protective. So understanding. So why did he seem reluctant to touch her?

Dani frowned. Every time he'd absent-mindedly put his hands on her, he'd jerked them back as if she were kryptonite and he were Superman. Was Mikeloff telling the truth about Spencer having a girlfriend, or was Dani that repulsive to him?

It was a shame he didn't find her as attractive as she found him, but if she'd learned anything with her father, there was no way to make someone love you. You can't change the size of your breasts, the width of your hips, or the person inside of you. All you can do is be someone who can be loved. The rest is up to them.

Anyway, it was probably for the best. Her luck with men was already bad enough, and if Spencer *was* seeing someone else, Dani would never steal another woman's boyfriend. She'd never be some guy's side chick again.

Besides, even if Spencer was the first guy to pique her interest since she broke up with Kipp, she didn't have time in her life for a relationship. *Heck!* She didn't have time for a date, let alone any kind of romantic involvement.

Heavy footsteps in the hallway interrupted her internal dialogue and Dani spun around to face the door. Her heart was thudding in her ears, and although she knew there were four other people in the mansion, after the break-in, she was too jittery to stop the tiny scream that escaped from between her lips.

An instant later, Spencer rushed into the kitchen, an alarmed expression tightening his handsome features. "What's wrong? Is someone trying to get in? Lock yourself in the pantry."

"No. Uh . . ." Dani thought fast. She didn't want to seem like a wuss. "I stubbed my toe on the corner of the island. Sorry for screaming."

"Which one is it?" Spencer knelt down and tugged her foot into his palm. "Are you all right? It's really easy to break a toe."

"The little one," Dani lied, enjoying the sensation of his warm palm on the sole of her foot. "But it's fine. I'm sure it's not broken."

After running his finger over her toe, Spencer nodded, put the foot back on the floor, and got up. Leaning against the counter, he asked, "Did you sleep all right? I thought I heard you moving around."

"Oh. I forgot that you were below me." Dani's cheeks heated at the unintentional innuendo. "I couldn't stand the mess so I cleaned up a bit. I hope I didn't keep you from falling asleep or wake you up this morning."

"Nah. My friend has already been here and changed the locks for you." Spencer handed her four sets of keys and a bill. "Didn't you hear the drill?"

"I guess not." Dani stared at the coffeepot, willing it to drip faster. "I was dead to the world until my alarm started shrieking."

"Good. You needed your rest. Last night

was tough on you." Spencer reached toward her, then jerked back his hand. "So . . . uh . . . is the coffee ready?"

"Coming right up." Dani scanned the locksmith's invoice, relieved to see the total was much less than she'd feared, then she tucked it in her pocket along with the keys. "How do you take it?"

"Black with three sugars." His ears reddened. "I have a bit of a sweet tooth."

"Me too." Opening a cupboard, she reached into it for a mug. "Thank goodness my intruder only busted the dishes and glasses that were sitting out in the sink rack drying or we might be drinking our coffee from a gravy boat or a ramekin."

"I'd take it intravenously if necessary," Spencer joked and tapped a vein in his forearm.

"You're singing my song." Realizing that her sugar bowl had been broken and the bin of sugar dumped on the floor, Dani grabbed the freshly washed containers from the sink. Holding them up, she said, "One second. I need to get some supplies from the carriage house. I have storage shelves and an extra refrigerator out there."

"I'll give you a hand." Spencer followed her toward the back door.

A few minutes later, Dani and Spencer

returned carrying a couple egg cartons, a half-gallon of milk, tubs of flour and sugar, and bottles of honey and molasses. As they walked into the kitchen, they found Tippi in the kitchen staring into the open fridge as if it held the answers to her next test. She had on sleep shorts with a thin tank top, and when she saw Spencer, she squealed, crossed her arms over her chest, and ran out of the room.

"Guess she forgot you were here," Dani said, glad she'd remembered to put on jeans and a T-shirt before coming downstairs.

"I bet she's warning the others right now." Spencer chuckled and poured both of them a cup of coffee, stirring three heaping spoonfuls of sugar into his own mug.

"Waffles, pancakes, or French toast?" Dani asked, taking a cautious sip of the steaming hot beverage.

"Whichever is easiest." Spencer rubbed his stomach. "I usually have cereal, so no matter what, it will be a real treat."

"Pancakes it is." Dani took a package of bacon from the fridge.

Grabbing a cookie sheet, she lined it with parchment, then arranged the bacon slices flat across the bottom and sprinkled them with brown sugar. After placing the pan in the oven, she programmed the temperature to four hundred, set the timer for seventeen minutes, and started on the pancakes.

"The girls will be down as soon as they smell the bacon." Dani paused for another sip of coffee and saw Spencer watching her with a strange look on his face. Frowning, she asked, "What?"

"You really love this." Spencer's voice grew husky as he gestured to the stove and counter. "Cooking. Feeding people. Even after what happened last night, you just keep on taking care of everyone."

"Well, I can't send the girls off with empty stomachs." Dani's chest tightened defensively. Did he disapprove of her wasted education? Was he like her father? "What's wrong with that?"

"Nothing." Spencer shoved his hands through his hair. "But most women I know, after your experience, would be demanding someone serve them breakfast in bed, not up making it for everyone else."

"Then you know the wrong women." Dani hid her pink cheeks and relieved smile as she turned the heat on under the built-in griddle and continued to mix the batter while she waited for it to get hot.

"I'm beginning to think you're right about that." Spencer grinned.

Before he could go on, Ivy and Starr

rushed into the kitchen. They both squinted at the bright sunshine pouring through the sliding window and put up their hands as if warding off a death ray. Dani shook her head. What was it with college kids? Were they part vampire?

A fully dressed Tippi followed close at her friends' heels. She kept her eyes down, avoiding Spencer's gaze and headed straight to the coffeepot. Dani shook her head again. She'd seen Tippi wearing a bathing suit that was no bigger than two potato chips and a Post-it Note. Why was she so embarrassed to be caught in her pj's?

After good mornings were exchanged and Dani gave the girls the new keys, she started pouring out pancake batter. Fifteen minutes later, they were all enjoying breakfast.

As they ate, Dani asked, "Whose turn is it to help me with the lunch-to-go prep?"

"Mine." Tippi stuffed a huge bite of pancake in her mouth. "But my study group is meeting this morning to review for a test."

"Tippi." Dani infused a note of warning into her tone. Tippi's excuses for getting out of the hours she owed Dani were getting annoying. "You know that I count on you working when you're scheduled."

"I'm sorry." Tippi attempted puppy-dog

eyes, but Dani stared back without flinching.

"When are you finished with your classes today?" Dani asked.

"Noon." Tippi crunched a slice of brown-sugar-glazed bacon between her perfect, white teeth.

"Then how about this?" Dani said. "I have a hundredth-birthday celebration at an assisted-living facility this afternoon. Tippi, you can put in the time you owe me helping serve. Then you can do the clean-up afterward, which will free me to search my boxes for Kipp's book."

"Fine." Tippi wrinkled her nose and muttered, "Sounds like a blast."

"Since I'm working on Saturday and have today off, I can stick around and give you a hand with your lunch-to-go preparations," Spencer offered. When Dani started to shake her head, he admonished, "Don't. I want to do this and you need the help."

"Well" — Dani bit back her inclination to turn down any assistance — "thanks."

When they had finished breakfast and the girls had gone upstairs to clean up the debris in their rooms before leaving for school, Spencer asked, "When do we need to start the lunch prep? Do we have time to tackle any of the downstairs mess?"

Dani glanced at the clock. "Unfortunately not. I like to have the sacks filled and ready by ten thirty, and it's past seven thirty."

"Okay." Spencer found a dish towel in a drawer and tied it around his waist. "What do you want me to do?"

After a few seconds' thought, Dani rattled off a list of instructions. Twenty minutes later, she was shocked at how well he took direction. She'd been afraid that an alpha guy like Spencer would have difficulty following her lead, but he listened carefully and did exactly what she told him to do.

At ten fifteen, with the lunch-to-go bags ready and in the fridge, Dani and Spencer relaxed over a cup of tea and a slice of date-nut bread. She'd just taken her first bite when the doorbell rang.

They both stiffened and Spencer asked softly, "Are you expecting anyone?"

"Only my lunch customers." Dani pushed back her chair and stood.

"Wait." Spencer touched her hand. "Let me go. If it's Mikeloff or your ex, it'll be easier for me to get rid of them than you."

"I can take care of myself." Dani had been on her own for a long time. Once her mother died, her father had expected her to function without much support from him. Still, it felt nice to have some backup. "But

I'll accept your offer. I really don't want to deal with either the detective or Kipp."

Dani followed Spencer down the hall but waited out of sight. She could hear his footsteps crossing the vestibule's marble floor, then the rattle of the security chain as he eased the door open. She and the girls frequently forgot to put the chain in place, but with recent events, Dani vowed to be more conscientious about using it.

"Who are you?" a young woman's voice echoed through the foyer.

"Better question," Spencer countered. "Who are you and what do you want?"

"My name is Frannie Ryan and I'm here to see Dani." A pause and the woman added, "Is she okay? I noticed all the wrecked stuff in the trash."

"You went through Dani's garbage?" Spencer's tone was outraged.

"Back off, dude," Frannie snapped. "I saw it by the side of the house. I didn't put on waders and sift through for private information."

"But clearly you've considered doing that." Spencer's voice roughened. "You're that reporter, aren't you? Why don't you leave Dani alone?"

Realizing she needed to intervene, Dani rushed into the foyer and said, "Spencer, it's fine. Frannie and I have an agreement. Please let her in."

Grunting, Spencer closed the door to unhook the chain, then swung it open. He stared at Frannie as she passed him and approached Dani.

"You promised to keep me updated on Regina's murder." Frannie waved her finger in Dani's face. "But you never called me."

"It's only been three days." Dani heard the *ding* indicating someone was at the sliding window and dashed back into the kitchen.

Spencer and Frannie followed her, and she gestured for them to take a seat at the table. The customers were lining up and as Dani served them, she kept an eye on her guests and an ear on their conversation.

"A lot has happened in the past three days." Frannie helped herself to a slice of the date-nut bread, grabbed the teapot, and looked around for a cup. "For instance, I managed to get a peek at the autopsy report."

"We already know what it said." Spencer got up, found a clean mug, and handed it to the young woman. "So we really don't need your information."

"Why don't you like me?" Frannie poured the tea. "We're on the same side."

347

"Not quite." Spencer leaned forward. "The majority of the time reporters think that the First Amendment is more important than catching and putting away the bad guys. More important than keeping people safe. Those of us in law enforcement feel the exact opposite is true."

"I . . ." Frannie's face reddened. "I want the bad guys behind bars too." She swallowed. "But I also believe in the public's right to know. Surely, there's some compromise we can reach and work together."

Spencer was silent.

Dani was about to intervene when Spencer turned to Frannie and said, "So you're from Scumble River. Do you know Chief Boyd and his wife? I've been meaning to call to see if he'd vouch for you."

"That's a great idea." Frannie beamed. "Wally and Skye will definitely tell you that you can rely on me."

While Spencer stepped out of the kitchen to make his call and in between serving customers, Dani brought Frannie up to speed on what she'd learned. Spencer may have had concerns about trusting the young woman, but Dani had made a deal with her and wasn't reneging.

Frannie took copious notes and often stopped Dani to add her own information.

The reporter had discovered much of what Dani had found out. She knew about the bulimia, the nude picture of Bliss, and Laz's alcoholism, but she hadn't heard about the identity theft.

"Are you aware that the Bournes haven't returned from their trip, but they did call and fire their housekeeper?" Dani asked Frannie just as Spencer returned.

He frowned when he heard Dani's words. "I see you didn't wait for me to clear Ms. Ryan." He rolled his eyes. "Good thing her friends say she's trustworthy."

"Told you so." Frannie smirked, then turned to Dani and frowned. "I hope Mrs. Carnet wasn't canned because she talked to me."

"That wasn't it," Dani reassured her. "They blamed her for Regina's death."

"The Bournes think Mrs. Carnet killed her?" Frannie squealed.

"Not exactly." Dani paused to sell a lunch, then explained, "They just think that if the housekeeper had been there, Regina wouldn't have died."

"Which is entirely unreasonable." Spencer shook his head. "Once the insulin was in the food, unless the housekeeper was able to persuade Regina not to eat it, there was nothing the woman could have done."

"And if Regina was in a bulimic episode, nothing would stop her from binging." Dani sold the last lunch and flipped the sign on the window around to indicate she was closed. Taking a seat at the table, she asked, "Frannie, have you found out anything else about the victim or her clique?"

"Besides the fact that Regina might be the meanest person that I've ever run across?" Frannie made a face. "I mean what she did to that pledge at her sorority was beyond heinous."

"Do you know that girl's name?" Dani asked excitedly.

Frannie shook her head. "The sorority refuses to talk about it, and since it happened a while ago, other people's memories are fuzzy. I've heard Greta and Gloria and Grace."

"It's Gail," Dani said. "But we don't have a last name. Anyway you could get that?"

"I'll work on it, but . . . ." Frannie's lips twitched, then she said, "We may not have to worry about it."

"Why?"

"In the wee hours of the morning, the cops arrested Regina's killer." Frannie wiggled excitedly in her seat. "And I got the scoop."

"Who?" Spencer asked.

350

Dani talked over him. "Then why in the heck did you come here asking me about what I found out?"

"My editor wants a follow-up to the story of the arrest, which is in today's afternoon edition." Frannie hugged herself. "She said that if it was good, I could do a whole series on Regina's sordid life." Frannie beamed. "We're calling it 'Posh Mortem — Deathstyles of the Rich and Famous.' "

"Who did the police arrest?" Spencer repeated his question.

"Vance King." Frannie giggled. "They caught him breaking into the Bourne residence and stealing a video camera memory card. It turned out to be a recording of him dressed in leather pants and a vest, jerking off while he flogged some woman wearing a ball gag, spike collar, and not much of anything else."

Dani glanced at Spencer. "Evidently, Vance got tired of trying to convince Bliss to let him in the house and decided to take matters into his own hands."

"So to speak." Spencer snickered. "So to speak."

CHAPTER 22

"I know I should be happy that someone's been arrested and Mikeloff will have to leave me alone, but it doesn't feel right," Dani said as she and Spencer cleaned up the kitchen. "Do you think Vance King really killed Regina?"

Frannie had left a few minutes ago to turn in her first piece on the life and death of NU's three-time homecoming queen. A lot of the university boosters and Normalton's upper crust would be extremely unhappy with the reporter's exposé on one of the town's wealthiest families and their socialite friends.

"It's a reach." Spencer stretched to slide a huge Pyrex bowl onto a top shelf and his shirt pulled away from his waistband.

With his washboard stomach exposed, Dani checked to make sure she wasn't drooling before she asked, "Why do you say that?"

"First, if King is the killer, why didn't he return to the house and grab the memory card right after she died?" Spencer continued to put away dishes and pans according to Dani's chart. "He should have been keeping an eye on the place and gone in when the housekeeper left to follow the ambulance to the hospital."

Dani had drawn up the diagram Spencer was using for the girls. She liked everything to be in its correct spot. Searching for what she needed while she was in the middle of a recipe annoyed her to no end.

"Second" — Spencer looked around for any stray items — "King doesn't seem smart enough to come up with as elaborate a plan as insulin in food."

"True." Dani finished drying the last couple of spoons, pulled open the nearby drawer, and placed them in their proper compartment. "How would he even know that an overdose of insulin would kill someone? Let alone think to inject the desserts or her snacks?"

"And you said that Bliss was adamant that King was unaware of Regina's bulimia," Spencer reminded her. "If that's the case, he couldn't be sure it would be Regina who ate the food from the party?"

"Excellent point," Dani said thoughtfully.

"The other thing that bothers me is when would Vance have had time to sneak into the Bourne kitchen and put the insulin in the food? He was falling down drunk by the time I left, and if he'd done it earlier, there was no way to tell which of the pastries I would put away for Regina. They were all together before I served the desserts."

Dani checked her watch. It was going on one o'clock. She had to start getting organized for the birthday party. She shot Spencer a quick glance. How long was he planning on sticking around?

"And third" — Spencer rested a hip on the counter — "King doesn't fit the profile for this kind of murder. If he kills someone, it will be in the heat of the moment. He'll lose his temper or his sex games will go too far. He'd do it with his bare hands or whatever is nearby. And then he'd run home to his mommy and daddy."

"I know you mentioned that you weren't a profiler, but were you with the FBI?" Dani began taking the tea sandwiches from the massive restaurant-size refrigerator. "I don't recall you or Ivy ever specifically saying what you did in law enforcement."

"The program at Quantico is available to other agencies." Spencer lifted the plastic-wrapped tray of smoked salmon and dill from her hands and put it on the counter.

Dani remained silent, aware that Spencer had avoided naming his previous employer. Wondering what he was hiding, she slid the platter of stilton and pear next to the first tray, quickly following with the cucumber and cream cheese and the egg salad. The party's head count was set at twenty-five and she had prepared 150 tiny sandwiches. Any that were left could be shared with the residents and staff of the assisted-living facility.

"What would be the profile of Regina's killer?" Dani asked, fetching the containers of linzer and shortbread cookies, then going back for the lemon-curd tartlets and the ginger scones with cardamom.

Dani had only been able to squeeze in this gig because the birthday cake was being provided from a specialty bakeshop and the assisted-living facility was taking care of the tea and punch. At first, the grandniece who had booked the event had said that if Dani couldn't make the cake, they'd just skip it. But Dani had pointed out that a party without a cake was really just a meeting.

Dani had been brusque with the grandniece, hoping the woman would either book someone else or reschedule. But she hadn't, and Dani had had to get up at five in the morning on Thursday to prepare the food. She could only hope that the sandwiches held up okay overnight.

Spencer broke into Dani's thoughts. "Regina's killer was probably an intelligent, precise woman with a great deal of self-control and determination." He scratched his head. "Although a meticulous man is a slight possibility."

"I hope you didn't share that with the police chief." Dani went into the pantry and came back with a rolling cart. "Your description sounds a lot like me. Or any other successful businesswoman."

"Or college student." Spencer helped Dani load the trays and containers onto the cart. "I think Bliss is still our best suspect."

"I hate to admit it, but that's true." Dani rolled the filled cart outside and toward her van. "Bliss is by no means as empty-headed as she pretends to be. And she had to have a lot of self-discipline to put up with Regina's demands." Dani and Spencer lifted the loaded cart into the cargo area and Dani added, "Not to mention that Bliss is certainly unwavering in her determination to marry Vance."

"But you don't want it to be her." Spencer patted Dani's shoulder.

"No." Dani headed back inside to change

clothes. "I would much rather have it be Vance. But I can't hope that an innocent man goes to prison."

"Good thing it isn't up to us." Spencer followed Dani to the bottom of the stairs. "As long as you and Ivy are off the hook, I consider our part of the investigation over." He shot her a firm look. "You need to keep off of Mikeloff's radar. Understand?"

"I know you're right." Dani's answer was grudging. "Which is why I'll do it." She narrowed her eyes. "Not because you issued an order."

Spencer looked a little sheepish and nodded, then stood staring at her. Dani shuffled from foot to foot. Was he staying? Did he plan on going with her to the party?

As if coming out of a fog, Spencer said, "Okay. I'd better let you get ready." He walked down the hallway toward the front door. "Don't forget to lock up behind me. You really should get an alarm system."

"As soon as money gets a little less scarce, it's on the top of my list," Dani said, then remembered her manners and yelled, "Thank you for everything."

"No problem." He turned and smiled at her.

When she'd discovered the mansion had been vandalized and Spencer had not only made sure she was safe, but also agreed that she shouldn't call the cops, Dani had known he was a good guy. However, it was him sticking around this morning and helping her out with the lunches and everything else that sealed the deal.

Ignoring the voice inside of her that said even though she now knew she could trust Spencer, she shouldn't get involved with him, she added, "I owe you a fabulous dinner."

Spencer paused. "You really don't." Then, his expression unreadable, he said, "But anytime you want to cook for me, just tell me when and I'll bring the beer."

"How about tomorrow night?" Dani said before realizing it was a Saturday. Feeling her cheeks heat up, she blurted, "Unless you have a date with your girlfriend. I mean you're welcome to bring her."

"Where did you get the idea that I have a girlfriend?" Spencer frowned.

"Detective Mikeloff." Dani looked anywhere except at Spencer.

"He lied," Spencer said firmly. "There isn't any other woman in my life."

"Other?" Dani whispered, her heart fluttering. When Spencer didn't respond, she said, "So, dinner tomorrow?"

"Sure." Spencer studied his shoes. "I have to work the rally, but after that I'm free. Is six o'clock okay for you, or do you prefer later?"

"Six is good." Dani waited for Spencer to leave, and when he didn't, she couldn't figure out how to end the conversation so she waved. "See you then."

The birthday party went very well. The guest of honor had loved the food and even shared her recipe for making green tomato–raspberry jam. Tippi was punctual and was a huge hit with the older guests. When the festivities began winding down, Tippi assured Dani she had everything under control and sent her back to the mansion to search for Kipp's book.

Once Dani was home and changed into shorts and a T-shirt, she headed to the attic. She had a decent chunk of time before she needed to pack up and go to her personal chef gig and she was determined to get through every single carton until she found the damn book.

Although she couldn't recall the exact title, Dani did remember the book's appearance. It was slightly larger than a paperback, but less than a quarter of the usual thickness, not more than seventy or so pages. That thinness was one of the reasons it would be so hard to find in the boxes.

A couple of hours later, tired, dirty, and

dying of thirst, Dani grabbed one of the three remaining cartons. With only ten minutes left before she had to get ready to leave, she was running out of time.

Slitting the packing tape, she reached inside and started piling the contents on the floor. A stack of padded hangers was followed by a pair of terry cloth slippers and a package of plastic spoons. Why on earth had she kept disposable cutlery?

Ooh! This was where her favorite summer Coach purse had been hiding. Although she hadn't lost her taste for high-end handbags, she could no longer afford to indulge in buying them so she was especially happy to find this one. As she lifted out the pistachio-green bag, she caressed the soft leather. Gently setting it aside, she peered into the box to see if there was anything else at the bottom and gave a victorious whoop.

Sitting on top of a pile of old *Gourmet* magazines was Kipp's book. She picked up the tattered volume, flipped it open, and saw:

Al Aaraaf,
Tamerlane,
and
Minor

Poems By Edgar A. Poe

Clearly it was old, but was it really as valuable as Kipp obviously thought? Dani checked her watch.

Shoot! She was going to be late if she didn't stop right this second. And tardiness was no way to impress a new client. Particularly one who had made it clear that she didn't usually hire people from brochures left at her front door and that this was a trial run.

Dani hurried down from the attic, tossed her find on the dresser, then hesitated. Feeling a little silly, she went back and tucked the slim volume into a package of tampons and hid the box in her underwear drawer. Rushing into the shower, she decided that although she planned to give the book to Kipp no matter what it was worth, she'd definitely Google the title before she handed it over.

The dinner party had gone smoothly and Dani got home at a reasonable hour. But as she walked up the stairs to her suite, the last couple of days' frantic pace finally caught up with her. Pulling off her clothes, she stumbled over to the bed and collapsed facedown on top of the covers. It was a good thing that she didn't sell lunches on the weekends because she fell asleep without setting her alarm.

Dani woke to the sound of Elvis Presley's "Little Sister" and fumbled for her cell phone. It wasn't on the nightstand, or the dresser, or the floor. Still fuzzy from the deep sleep she'd been enjoying, she finally found the device in the pocket of her discarded pants.

Dani fumbled to answer the phone and swiped across Ivy's picture. "What?"

"Are you all right?" The volume of Ivy's voice was just a shade below a shout.

"I'm fine." Dani squinted at the sun pouring through her windows. What time was it? "Why? What's wrong? Did something happen?"

"That's what we want to know," Ivy said. "It's nearly noon. You never sleep that late. And Dr. Dingleberry has already been here twice pounding on the door and demanding to speak to you."

"Dingleberry?" Dani repeated. Where did Ivy come up with that stuff?

"You know, the poop hanging off an animal's butt," Ivy explained.

"Got it." Dani trudged into the bathroom and turned on the water. "After I shower, I'll text Kipp to come over. Keep the door locked."

As Dani shampooed her hair, she hummed

Katrina and the Waves' "Walking on Sunshine." Everything was finally going in the right direction. Mikeloff had his killer and no longer had an excuse to harass her. Today she'd hand over the Poe book to Kipp and get him out of her life for good. And she had a date tonight.

Okay. Not exactly a date. A thank-you. But she was having dinner with a ridiculously handsome man, and yes, she was cooking it, but it was just the two of them and he didn't have a girlfriend. And despite both their efforts to ignore it, there was unquestionably chemistry between them.

After she was dressed, Dani reached for her phone to text Kipp but paused. She had a vague memory of Spencer telling her that he wanted to be with her when she gave the book to Kipp. But she didn't want Spencer to get the idea she was a helpless little lady he could boss around.

Dani picked up her cell, then hesitated. Still, she had no desire to be alone with Kipp. He'd been acting crazy and having an armed head of security witness the exchange couldn't hurt. Even kickass female heads of state had bodyguards.

After a quick conversation with Spencer, who assured her that he could be at the mansion by five thirty, Dani messaged Kipp with the time. He demanded an earlier meeting, but she texted, 5:30 or never.

A string of profanity followed, then a single word appeared on her screen: fine.

Her mood slightly dimmed, Dani ventured downstairs to figure out tonight's menu. Once she knew what she was serving Spencer, she'd head out to Meijer. Grocery shopping always cheered her up.

Ivy, Tippi, and Starr had straightened out the downstairs. Everything was back on its shelf or in its drawer. The ripped cushions had been sewn shut and turned over so the damage wasn't visible and anything broken had been thrown away. Dani thanked the girls and gave them each a hug, then made them lunch. They were all going out for the evening, and with a wink and a grin, they assured Dani that they wouldn't be home until well after midnight.

How they had found out she was having dinner with Spencer was a mystery. Did they have the mansion bugged?

While they ate, Dani went through her cookbooks and made a list. She'd been tempted to go with Thai red curry shrimp, but Ivy assured her that Spencer was more of a meat-and-potatoes guy, so she decided on chili-lime steak with roasted veggies and cheesy sliced baked potatoes.

Dani didn't want to spend too much time away from the table, so she went with raspberry fool for dessert. Raspberry-infused whipped cream with the shortbread cookies leftover from the birthday party and fresh fruit could be put together in just a few minutes.

With the simple menu, Dani's trip to the grocery store and prep time was minimal, which left her with a couple of hours to primp. What did one wear for a dinner that wasn't a date but maybe could be?

After trying and discarding most of her clothes, Dani was frustrated. What was it about hanging something in the closet for a while that made it shrink two sizes?

Finally, Dani found a pair of white jeans that cupped her bottom nicely and a sleeve-less tangerine knit shirt that only felt a teeny bit small. At least her wedge sandals still fit. Dani vowed to stop tasting everything she cooked, dig out her Fitbit, and sign up for a Piloxing class — a combo of Pilates, boxing, and dance.

After pulling her hair to the side and loosely braiding it, Dani added simple gold hoop earrings and the floating heart necklace that Kelsey had given her for her birthday. Gazing into the mirror, she was satisfied that she looked casual but pulled together.

She still had a half hour before Kipp and Spencer were due, so she booted up her laptop and typed *Al Aaraaf, Tamerlane, and Minor Poems* into the Google search bar. When she heard chimes twenty minutes later, she was still reading. Tucking her computer under her arm, she flew down the stairs and into the foyer.

Happy it was Spencer standing on the porch, she flung open the front door and said, "You've got to see this."

"Okay." Spencer blinked in surprise. "You look really nice, by the way."

"Thanks." Leading Spencer into the kitchen, Dani put her laptop on the table, flipped up the lid, and pointed as she read, "The last-known copy sold of Edgar Allan Poe's *Al Aaraaf, Tamerlane, and Minor Poems* was purchased for $120,000."

"I take it that's the book your ex is after?" Spencer asked, setting down a six-pack of a local microbrew beside the computer.

"Yes." She handed him a ziplock bag with the book inside. "But this one is in pretty rough shape, and I don't think it's a first edition, so who knows if it's worth anything like that amount."

As Spencer opened his mouth to speak, the doorbell rang and he said, "Might as well get this over with."

"Yep."

"You sure you want to hand over something that might be worth over a hundred grand?"

"It's his." Dani shrugged. "He would have never given it to me if he had any idea it was this valuable. And the giver has to know the price of the gift and still freely give it for it to really be a present."

"I doubt the good doctor has any idea what something is worth until he's already lost it." Spencer ran his knuckle down her cheek.

"You could be right." Dani stepped closer, but as doorbell rang again, she sighed and turned away. "I need to get better at recognizing that myself."

CHAPTER 23

When Dani opened the door for her ex and saw that he wasn't alone, she was relieved that Spencer was with her. The Incredible Hulk standing next to Kipp hadn't been there when she'd looked out the window a second ago. Had the behemoth been in her blind spot or had the guy deliberately kept out of sight?

Dani's ex started to push his way into the foyer but rocked to a standstill when he spotted Spencer. The hulk on his heels evidently didn't get the memo that the Kipp train was stopping because he continued forward, ramming into the good doctor, who face-planted on the marble floor.

Dani put up her hand to hide her grin at the Hulk doing a pirouette to avoid joining Kipp on the ground. He didn't seem the type who would see the humor in his own embarrassment and she didn't want to provoke him.

"What's he doing here?" Speaking at the same time, Kipp pointed at Spencer and Spencer pointed to the Hulk, who had regained his footing and glowered down at Dani's ex.

"Spencer is my guest," Dani said frostily. "And I don't appreciate you bringing a stranger into my house without asking."

"Why is he with you again?" Even from his prone position, Kipp managed to maintain his condescending attitude. "Is he your new boyfriend?"

Before Dani could answer, Spencer moved her behind him and crossed his arms. "You didn't answer my question. Who is your shadow, and why is he here?"

"He's my cousin. The one who was promised the book." Kipp rambled on and on. "He's here for a short visit and has to leave tonight and . . ."

"Interesting." Dani frowned. Providing excessive detail was a sign of lying.

Kipp struggled to his feet and demanded, "Give me the damn thing and we'll get out of your hair."

"You've always referred to your cousin as 'she,' which I assumed meant a woman." Dani glanced appraisingly at the Incredible Hulk. "And unless you're going to tell me this person is female . . ."

"Fine, he's my cousin's husband," Kipp said quickly. "You always were such a suspicious bit —" He cut himself off, appearing to come to the realization that insulting Dani was not in his best interest. Sulking, he said, "Satisfied?"

"Whatever." Dani shrugged. "But I don't think it's worth what you think."

"What do you mean?" Kipp squeaked, his pupils dilating. "I told you, it's just sentimental value."

"Forget it, moron," the Hulk growled. "The chick knows that the book ain't for no cousin." He scowled at Dani. "But she also better know that trying to keep it wouldn't be good for her health."

"Are you threatening her?" Spencer snarled, pushing Dani farther away from the men. He swiftly bent over and unholstered his weapon. "Because if anything happens to her, you'll answer to me."

"Cool your jets, Romeo." The Hulk held out his palm. "Juliet hands over the book, we leave, and neither of you ever has to see us again."

Spencer looked down at Dani and asked, "If you're sure you want to give it to him, go get it and let's get rid of the trash."

"I'm sure." Dani turned and jogged down the hallway, snatched the book from the kitchen, and hurried back to the foyer. "Here."

Kipp reached for the bag, but the Incredible Hulk snatched the Ziploc before he got a grip on the plastic. Tucking the book under his arm, the Hulk took a pair of white cotton gloves from his pocket.

As he stuffed his huge fingers into gloves so big that they had to be a special-order item, Dani bit her lips to stop the giggles that threatened to erupt from her throat. The incongruity of a man who looked like a mutant version of Mickey Mouse delicately turning the pages of a thin volume of poetry that almost disappeared in his gigantic mitts was nearly enough for her to lose it completely.

Attempting to regain her self-control, she examined Kipp. Sweat was pouring from his forehead and he looked as if he wanted to be anywhere else.

"Since we all agree that there's no cousin," Dani said thoughtfully, "what took you so long to ask for the book back from me?"

"I needed some quick cash to, uh . . . to, uh . . . help out a friend." Kipp shot a frightened look at his escort. "So I was going through Mother's things hoping to find something I could sell when I found a letter offering a hundred thousand dollars if the family's copy of Edgar Allan Poe's *Al Aaraaf, Tamerlane, and Minor Poems* proved to be a first edition and in good condition."

"And you recalled giving it to me." Dani rested a hip on the wall.

"Yeah." Kipp shrugged. "I remembered that you were a big fan of Poe, and when I couldn't find the book, I figured it must have been the one you asked for." He narrowed his eyes. "At first, I thought you'd played me. That you knew it was valuable and had sold it to buy this place. But then I heard you inherited the mansion and you sure never lived like you had a hundred grand, so I decided what the hell, maybe you had no idea of its worth."

"And you figured why not ask me to return it," Dani said.

"Well, yeah." Kipp sidled closer and reached out to her. "You were always so sweet and generous. I knew you wouldn't mind."

In a maneuver too fast for Dani really to see and before her ex could touch her, Spencer appeared between her and Kipp and warned, "Stay back."

"I'll deal with this." Dani stepped around Spencer and poked Kipp in the chest with her index finger. "What you mean is that since I was dumb enough not to realize I was the other woman, I'd probably be idiot enough to hand over the book without a fuss."

"You always did choose to think the worst of me," Kipp whined.

"Whatever." Dani crossed her arms. "You're a big-shot doctor. Why would you need to sell your family's antiques to get money?"

"I . . . uh . . . I," Kip stuttered again. "I already told you a friend needed it and I was trying to help him out of a bad situation."

"Liar." Dani lifted her chin. "You never gave anyone anything. *Heck!* Most of the time you didn't even take me out. I cooked dinner and you drank my wine and we watched movies that I paid to stream."

"You said you were fine with our stay-at-home date nights," Kipp protested.

"Like I had a choice." Dani scowled. "Now tell me the truth."

"Fine. I needed the money for me." Kipp pouted. "My investments aren't liquid at this time and rather than taking a loss —"

"He's in hock up to his ears." The Hulk had finished with the book, returned it to the ziplock bag, taken off his gloves, and now put a heavy hand on Kipp's shoulder.

"And you're the debt collector," Spencer

said. "Who's your boss?"

"Probably best for you both if I don't say." The Hulk grinned revealing several gold teeth, one with a ruby-eyed skull on it. "Especially since this book ain't worth no hundred grand."

Kipp gulped. "Maybe you're wrong. To the right collector —"

"Boss man checked with a couple and they told me what to look for." The Hulk pushed Kipp toward the door. "If you're lucky, you'll get half that and only need to come up with fifty Gs more."

As Dani watched Kipp being shoved onto the porch, she shouted, "Did you break into my house last night searching for the book?"

"It wasn't me," Kipp yelled, giving the ogre behind him a significant look.

"Okay." For a second Dani was relieved to know it hadn't been Regina's murderer or Detective Mikeloff. Then she turned to Spencer and asked, "Shouldn't we do something? What if the guy kills Kipp?"

"You can't get money from a dead man." Spencer turned the key in the dead bolt and put the chain in place. "Dr. Dumbass will be fine."

"I suppose you're right. People like him always land on their feet." Dani worried her bottom lip, then shook her head. "Besides, it's not as if I have a bundle of cash lying around to lend him."

"And I hope you wouldn't if you did." Spencer frowned at her.

"I've learned my lesson," Dani said, wrapping her arms around herself. "I won't be taken in by a smooth-talking man again."

"Good." Spencer patted her shoulder. "You need to toughen up a little."

"I guess. But I never want to get as cynical as I was when I worked HR." Resolving to forget her ex and her other worries, Dani smiled and said, "I bet you're starving. I should get cooking." As she led him to the kitchen, she explained. "Everything's prepped, but I'll need about thirty minutes for the potatoes."

"No problem," Spencer assured her as his stomach let out a loud growl.

Dani laughed. "Fortunately for you, I have an artichoke caprese platter to tide you over. You can sit and munch while I get dinner."

Once Spencer was settled at the counter with a beer and the appetizer, Dani set to work on the rest of the food. While the oven preheated, she cut the potatoes into thin slices, drizzled them with melted butter, sprinkled them with chives, then placed them in the microwave. Normally she'd have baked them, but this was faster.

Dani took the steak from the fridge, brushed it with olive oil, and rubbed it with a combination of chili powder, salt, pepper, and lime zest, then after squeezing lime juice on it, set the meat aside to rest for a few minutes.

This completed, Dani asked, "How did it go today?" Spencer had mentioned he'd supervised his staff at the rally against gender-based violence. He'd said he had excellent employees, but a lot were inexperienced.

"Better than I expected." Spencer sipped his beer. "They're a good group."

"Didn't you tell me that the police chief's husband's son was one of them?" Dani asked as she started to toss carrots, onions, and mushrooms in olive oil and sprinkle them with salt and pepper.

"Uh-huh," Spencer mumbled around a mouthful of artichokes and mozzarella.

"Did he have anything interesting to say?" Dani asked, then as the microwave dinged, she pulled out the potatoes and sprinkled them with grated Romano and Parmesan cheeses. When Spencer was silent, she added, "About Vance King's being arrested."

"Well." Spencer took a long swig of beer, then blew out a long breath and said, "I was going to wait until after dinner to tell you."

"Tell me what?" Dani's pulse raced as she returned the potatoes to the microwave, then slid the steak and veggies into the oven.

"Vance was released this morning." Spencer frowned. "His folks got him a fancy defense lawyer and he was able to have him released on bail." He shrugged. "They got him for the breaking and entering, but all the evidence for Regina's murder is circumstantial."

"Which means Mikeloff might come after me again." Dani sighed.

"Maybe," Spencer admitted, his gaze fastened to the countertop.

"What do you think the likelihood of Mikeloff setting his sights on me might be?" Dani turned on the timer and started setting the table.

"Fifty-fifty." Spencer peeled the label from his beer bottle. "If he pursues any other suspects, including you, he weakens the DA's case against King."

"But . . ." Dani took out glasses and filled them from the pitcher of water in the fridge. "You said fifty-fifty, so there's a catch."

"Mikeloff might be so fixated on vengeance for his nephew that he may not care about upsetting the DA."

"Shit!"

"But there's an equal chance he isn't." Spencer got up, rounded the island, and put his arm around her shoulder. "Try to forget about the murder and the idiotic detective and everything else. Tonight, let's pretend that everything is okay."

CHAPTER 24

Monday morning, Dani was still thinking about her nondate with Spencer. Once she had succeeded in putting thoughts of Detective Mikeloff's vendetta out of her mind, she and Spencer had had a wonderful evening. While Spencer was both interesting and funny, unexpectedly, he was also sweet. He enjoyed her food, she enjoyed the nutty flavor of the beer he'd brought, and they'd both seemed to enjoy each other's company.

With the girls out of the mansion, after Dani and Spencer ate, they moved to the family room for dessert. Handing Spencer his dish of raspberry fool, Dani had eyed the spot next to him on the sofa but took a seat on a nearby armchair instead. Although he'd given a few hints that he was attracted to her, he'd always backed away. Which meant she couldn't be the one to move their relationship from the friend zone to something else. It had to be his choice.

When the grandfather clock had chimed twelve times, she was shocked. How had the time flown by so quickly? Spencer had seemed just as surprised but said his good-byes and assured Dani he would call her if he heard anything about Regina's case. She'd promised to do the same and walked him out to the porch.

For a minute, it had looked as if he might kiss her, but she must have been imagining things, because instead, he told her to get inside and lock the door. Once she complied and waved at him through the window, he turned and jogged down the steps.

Now, twenty-four hours later, as Dani sipped a cup of coffee, she finally admitted to herself that she was disappointed at how her Saturday had ended. Didn't Spencer feel any attraction to her at all?

Shaking her head at her foolish heart, Dani opened a new Excel spreadsheet on her laptop. With Starr's help, Dani had finished the lunch-to-go sacks early, leaving her a half hour before the first customers would arrive. And she was determined to figure out who killed Regina Bourne.

After typing the names of the suspects in Regina's murder across the top — Laz, Vance, Bliss, and Gail — Dani considered what she knew about each one. Under Laz, she noted the nude picture of Bliss and his alcoholism. Vance's column contained the memory card showing him in BDSM mode and his break-in. And in Gail's row, Dani put the manuscript theft and the betrayal of the promised sisterhood. Gail had a strong motive, if only it all hadn't happened so long ago.

Bliss's list was the longest. All of the abuses she'd suffered at her supposed BFF's hands, as well as the fact she knew of Regina's bulimia and had a key to the house. Bliss definitely seemed like the most likely murderer, but Dani's instincts said the girl didn't do it.

Dani was staring at the laptop monitor, trying to think of what she was missing, when the doorbell rang. Her heartbeat sped up and she felt unable to move. What if it was Mikeloff coming to arrest her?

Forcing herself to walk toward the foyer, Dani was relieved to hear a familiar voice yell, "Dani, it's me, Frannie. Hurry up. I've got something big to tell you."

Mother Nature had turned up her furnace, and as Dani welcomed the reporter into the mansion, a wave of heat accompanied her.

Once they were settled at the kitchen table, Dani handed Frannie a bottle of water and said, "I already know that Vance is out of jail."

"That's old news." Frannie uncapped the Dasani and guzzled half the contents. Sighing in relief, she reached into her tote bag before plopping a thick sheaf of paper on the table. "I got hold of the manuscript Regina stole from her sorority sister."

"Does it have her full name?" Dani grabbed the top page.

"Unfortunately, no." Frannie made a face. "This is the copy Regina submitted, so it has her as the author. But I think the story is autobiographic, which might help us find the girl. Look at this."

While Dani read the flagged sections, Frannie wandered around the kitchen and helped herself to one of the cinnamon-orange muffins leftover from the girls' breakfast.

The plot was a heartrending story of a girl's struggle with juvenile diabetes. It illustrated how the condition influenced every decision she made, from what she ate, to what she wore, to her reproductive choice. It was a tale of an emotionally fragile young woman who by the end was entering college and beginning to feel like she could have a normal life.

Laying aside the pages, Dani looked at

Frannie and asked, "So you think Gail is diabetic? And who better to have insulin handy *and* know the effect of too much of the medication?"

"Exactly." Frannie nodded enthusiastically.

"Still, my biggest problem is that Regina stole the manuscript so long ago, why would Gail kill her now?" Dani rubbed her chin. "Why not murder Regina when the incident happened?"

"Well" — Frannie's brown eyes sparkled — "I may have some insight into that."

At the sound of a chime, Dani glanced at the sliding window. "Hold that thought."

The lunch rush had started and there were several customers lined up. When there was a break, Dani leaned on the serving counter, focused on Frannie, and said, "Okay, go ahead."

"You didn't ask where I got the manuscript," Frannie teased.

"Fine." Dani rolled her eyes. "Where did you get the manuscript?"

"From Regina's agent."

"You mean her previous agent?" Dani asked. "Surely the woman wasn't still representing her."

"Yes and no." Frannie took a sip of water. "She wasn't until a few months ago."

"What happened a few months ago?" Dani sold a couple more lunches.

"Regina sent her another book."

"Wasn't the agent afraid this one was someone else's writing too?"

"At first." Frannie caressed the manuscript with the tip of her finger. "But she was intrigued by the query letter, so she agreed to read it. And it turned out to be a highly fictionalized story of what Regina went through when she was 'falsely' " — Frannie made air quotes with her fingers — "accused of plagiarization."

"Seriously?" Dani thought she'd heard it all in her years working in human resources, but Regina's actions kept surprising her.

"And" — Frannie paused dramatically — "the agent said it was a really good novel. She sent it out to several publishing houses and there's currently a bidding war for it."

"So, if Gail somehow heard about this new book's potential for success, that could be the thing that pushed her over," Dani mused.

"Oh, she heard about it, all right." Frannie bounced in her seat. "Once the agent realized what a blockbuster Regina's book might be, just to be on the safe side, she emailed Gail to verify that she wasn't the author of the new book."

"So the agent has Gail's last name." Dani held her breath.

"The woman claims she only has an email, but I don't believe her." Frannie pursed her lips. "She hadn't heard about Regina's murder until I contacted her, and I suspect with her original client dead, she might want to make some kind of deal with Gail to write her side of the story."

"Because the two books together could be even bigger bestsellers, and if she represents Gail, the agent will have a live client," Dani guessed. "And she doesn't want anyone to get to the author before she does."

"Bingo." Frannie touched the tip of her nose with her finger. "Now we just have to figure out who Gail is and get her to confess. My boyfriend, Justin, got me the pledge list for the fall that she pledged Alpha Beta Delta, but there is no Gail."

"By 'got you the list,' I assume you mean hacked the sorority's computer?"

"Your sarcasm isn't appreciated." Frannie neither confirmed nor denied Dani's accusation.

"Yeah, well —" Dani interrupted herself. "Wait. Starr mentioned that sororities often use nicknames for pledges. Is Gail a short form of another name?"

"Hmm." Frannie scrunched her face in

thought, then said, "I got nothing."

"Let's put it into a search engine and see." Dani moved from the sliding window to her laptop, saved her spreadsheet, and brought up Google. After a few tries she said, "Except for various spelling of Gail, the only other possibility is Abigail."

"Let me check for Abigails on the pledge list." Frannie tapped her phone and peered at the tiny screen.

Dani heard a chime and walked over to the open serving window. A glance at the customer standing there and in a blinding flash of insight, she put the pieces together. An extreme concern with carbs and sugar could indicate diabetes. Was her customer Abby, Regina's Gail?

Before she could warn Frannie, the reporter yelled, "Eureka! There's a pledge named Abigail Goodman."

Dani glanced at the girl at the window. She stood frozen, guilt and trepidation warred for prominence in her haunted blue eyes.

Continuing to stare at her phone, Frannie said, "I'll bet she's our murderer."

Abby let out a whimper. Her gaze flickering between Dani and Frannie, then she backed away from the window and slid to the ground. Dani rushed out the back door and saw the girl huddled on the sidewalk, clasping her legs to her chest with her head on her knees.

Rocking back and forth, Abby sobbed, "I'm so sorry. So, so sorry."

Dani knelt down beside the young woman and put her arms around her. She smelled of baby powder and strawberries, and the innocent aroma brought a lump to Dani's throat. How had this girl, barely out of her teens, come to this?

Drawing Abby to her feet, Dani guided her inside. After settling her in a chair at the table, Dani grabbed the kettle to make some tea.

The girl sat mute and unblinking. She was clearly retreating further and further into her own world, and if something wasn't done soon, she'd become totally unresponsive.

Returning with a steaming cup of Earl Grey, Dani asked, "Abby, are you diabetic?" The tearful girl nodded and Dani said, "Can I add sugar to help with the shock or will that be bad for you?"

"It's okay," Abby whispered. "When I was younger, I had a lot of trouble keeping my numbers good, but since I got on the pump my senior year in high school, it's a lot better." She slumped. "I'm sorry to be so much trouble."

"No problem." Dani waited until the girl drank some of the tea, then said, "You'll probably feel a lot better if you tell us what happened."

"I don't know if I should." Abby rubbed her eyes. "I probably should talk to a lawyer or something. Right?"

"We're not the police," Dani reassured her, then gestured across the table. "This is my friend Frannie, and she's a writer like you."

"But it's probably dumb to say anything more." Abby's tone was wishful, but she pressed her lips together and remained silent.

Dani searched her mind for a way to get the girl talking, then said, "It seems to me that what you've always wanted was for your story to be told." When Abby gave a little nod, Dani continued. "Frannie is a reporter and her paper is doing a series of articles on Regina."

"Of course they are." Abby clenched her jaw. "Even dead it's all about her."

"Exactly," Dani agreed. "But if you were to tell Frannie your side, it could be about you. Your story would be what people remember."

"I could make sure of it," Frannie agreed.

"What's more memorable? A spoiled, rich girl whose evilness got her killed, or the young woman she wronged taking matters into her own hands to get justice?"

After a few seconds, Abby said, "It's not what it looks like."

"Oh?" Dani shot Frannie a quick glance and mouthed, *Record this.*

"I was just getting over what Regina did to me." Abby sighed. "It took quite a while, but I was finally writing again."

"What happened?" Frannie asked. "Was it the news of Regina's new book?"

"You mean her first book?" Abby looked at Frannie as if the reporter had slapped her. "The other book was mine. It was never hers! Never!"

"Sorry," Dani said quickly. "Of course the book was never Regina's."

"Definitely not!" Frannie shook her head emphatically. "I misspoke and I apologize."

"Right." Abby's tone conveyed her skepticism. "Anyway, I was finally shaking my depression, and then I got the email from Regina's agent." Abby inhaled sharply and snarled, "*She* had an agent that she got because of my work, but all *my* queries have gotten me zilch."

"So you didn't know before that email that Regina was writing a novel about what happened between you two?" Frannie asked.

"No." Abby rubbed her upper arms as if she were cold, then demanded, "Why would she do that? Hadn't she taken enough from me already?"

"I doubt Regina saw it that way," Dani said regretfully. "She was too narcissistic to even consider how you might feel about it."

"Is that when you decided to kill her?" Frannie asked. "When you realized that once again, she was getting the book deal you deserved?"

"I . . ." Abby stuttered, a look of confusion on her face. "I never meant to kill her. It just sort of happened."

"Okay," Dani said thoughtfully. "Let me see if I have the timing straight. Eighteen months ago, Regina steals your book. You find out and stop her from getting it published, but because of the dispute about the rights, no editor will touch it."

"Four years of work down the drain." Pain etched lines around Abby's mouth.

"Regina is kicked out of the sorority, but you still left. Why?" Frannie asked.

"I was afraid the sisters would blame me for losing such a rich, beautiful girl for our chapter." Abby twisted a lock of her hair. "My therapist says that I was wrong not to give them a chance."

"I overheard some alumni talking and I think your therapist was right." Dani tilted her head. "Since the whole debacle, have you had any contact with Regina or her friends?"

"Not until after I got the email from her agent." Abby's nostrils flared. "Once I found out about the book, I confronted her."

"When was that?" Frannie looked up from her notes and Dani noticed the reporter was constructing a timeline.

"Maybe a month ago." Abby's voice rose as she said, "I explained my objections and she told me to go eff myself!"

"Is that when you decided to kill her?" Dani's tone was sympathetic.

"No!" Abby yelled. "I told you. I never meant to kill her."

"So what happened?" Dani said soothingly. "Did you decide to take matters into your own hands? Do something to stop the publication?"

"I . . . I . . ." Abby scrubbed her eyes with her fists. "I started leaving her little . . . presents."

"What kind of presents?" Frannie asked sharply.

"At first, just pictures of people in accidents or in coffins with a note that said *Stop the book or this will be you.*"

"And when that didn't work?" Dani asked.

"I found a dead snake on the road and put it in a fancy gift bag with the same message."

"When was that?" Frannie asked.

"The afternoon right before her luau." Abby lifted her chin. "That got her attention."

"I bet," Dani murmured, afraid to say too much and interrupt the girl's train of thought.

"Regina tracked me down and told me if I didn't stop harassing her, she was going to go to the police." Abby pounded her fist on the tabletop. "She had the nerve to threaten me after what she'd done."

"That must have made you angry." Dani spoke carefully. "What did you do?"

"At first, I didn't know what to do." Abby sniffed. "I called my therapist and she said that I had to stop with the notes and things. That instead of being passive-aggressive, I needed to do something proactive."

Frannie and Dani exchanged a horrified look.

"And you thought your counselor meant that you should kill Regina?" Dani couldn't keep the dismay from her voice.

"No!" Abby shook her head vigorously. "I decided to confront Regina at her luau in front of all those sycophants that she called friends."

"But you didn't." Dani wrinkled her brow. "What changed your mind?"

"When I got there, I saw how drunk everyone was and I knew they'd never take my side against Regina. Not with all her fancy food and booze and power." Abby's shoulders slumped. "I knew they'd never listen to me."

"But you didn't leave." Dani vaguely recalled glimpsing Abby just before Vance set the table on fire. At the time, the girl had just registered as one of Dani's lunch-to-go customers, but now she remembered thinking that she seemed out of place at the party.

"I felt paralyzed." Abby licked her lips. "I couldn't make myself go home, but I couldn't make myself confront Regina either."

"I understand. You wanted to be published so badly and it seemed as if Regina had snatched it out of your hands for a second time. It made you numb." Dani patted Abby's arm. "What happened next?"

"When the party started breaking up, I was going to leave." Abby's voice cracked. "Then I heard Regina lay into her boyfriend and call him a big loser. Laz had always been nice to me, so I hesitated. Then Regina told him that she couldn't stand to, uh . . . eff him one more time. When her book was a big success, she was moving to New York and would never have to see him again."

Regina's cruelty left Dani breathless. She sucked in a lungful of air before she asked, "So he and Vance left?"

"Yes. Regina marched them out to the driveway as if she didn't trust them to go." Abby glared. "And that's when I did it."

"You must have been extremely angry," Dani encouraged.

"I was." Abby made a sweeping gesture with her hands. "I knew that Regina would just go on ruining life after life and never have to experience the consequences of her actions. I remembered hearing her yell at you about the desserts you were supposed to save for her, and I recalled the rumors around the sorority house that she was bulimic, so I grabbed the vials of insulin and a syringe from my purse and I injected all the food you had left her."

"You just happened to have vials of insulin and a syringe with you?" Frannie asked. "I thought you said you use a pump."

"Even with a pump it's vital to have backup," Abby explained. "And I had just bought a new supply of insulin that morning and hadn't taken it out of my purse yet."

"I thought insulin needed to be refrigerated," Frannie said.

"Insulin may be stored at room temperature for up to a month," Abby recited as if she'd explained that fact a hundred times. Then she blinked and said, "Anyway. Once I injected the food, I left. I knew that stomach acid breaks down insulin, but I thought that if Regina binged and ingested such a large amount she'd at least get sick. I never thought she'd die."

"What if someone else ate it?" Frannie challenged.

"Regina's housekeeper was gone and she was alone." Abby screwed up her face. "I hid in the pool house and watched all night and the next morning. No one entered the house. Then Regina came out to the pool a little past noon and began stuffing the food into her mouth so fast, I thought she'd choke on it.

"If Regina hadn't eaten the stuff by the time her housekeeper got back, I would have made some excuse to get into the kitchen and dispose of the tainted food." Abby put her hand over her heart. "I swear."

"You didn't know that Regina was taking a prescription for her ulcer or that the medication would protect the insulin from her stomach acid?" Dani asked.

"I had no idea," Abby said. "If I had, I would never have dosed her food."

The three women were silent, then after several minutes, Abby asked, "Now what?"

With her story told, Dani could see that the girl was fading fast.

"Abby." Dani made her voice soothing and her expression understanding. "You know we're going to have to call the police."

"No!" Abby collapsed against the back of the chair. "You can't. I mean, I thought you were my friends."

"We are," Dani said gently. "But there's no other way."

"What will happen to me?" Abby buried her face in her palms.

"Before you turn yourself in, you need to call an attorney." Dani pushed her cell phone toward the girl. "And maybe your parents and therapist too."

"My parents are in Australia." Abby sobbed. "And I don't know any lawyers."

"You're in luck." Frannie grabbed Dani's cell — her own was still recording the conversation. "I happen to know the best criminal defense attorney in Illinois, and Loretta only lives about an hour away."

While Frannie contacted her friend, Dani

led Abby to the house phone and had the girl call her therapist. The woman agreed to meet them at the mansion ASAP.

After Dani sent a text to Spencer explaining the situation, she insisted that Abby eat lunch while they waited for the lawyer and her therapist to arrive. Being diabetic, the girl couldn't afford to skip a meal and it was unlikely that she'd be fed any time soon at the police station.

As Abby ate, Dani and Frannie stared sadly at each other. The poor girl. She had been doing so well until she'd fallen into Regina's web of deceit. Dani felt sorry for Abby and could only hope that she would get the help she needed rather than a long prison term.

Two hours later, Abby, her attorney, and her therapist left the mansion for the police station. Spencer had contacted the chief and she would be there to process the girl personally. No one wanted to see Abby turned over to Mikeloff.

It was nearly five o'clock when Frannie finally left the mansion and Dani was exhausted. As she collapsed across her bed, her last thoughts before drifting to sleep were that although it seemed as if Abby had been pushed to her limit and Regina had been responsible for her own death, that wasn't true.

Everyone had to be accountable for their own actions and that included Abby. She made the wrong choices and she would have to pay the price. It was a shame that mean girls like Regina always seemed to bring other people down with them.

In the end, everyone suffered because of Regina's narcissism. Dani just hoped that those who had been involved in the whole disgusting mess would learn a lesson and be better people because of it.

EPILOGUE

Dani tugged on the skirt of her black dress. The hem was several inches above her knees and she felt naked. Either the sheath was a lot shorter than she remembered, or her hips were a lot bigger and were hiking it up. When she'd stood in her closet looking for something appropriate to wear, she'd discovered that her go-to navy suit had a huge hole where the breast pocket of the jacket had caught on something and torn off. Which is why she'd been forced to settle for the only other dark piece of clothing she owned, whether it fit well or not.

She hesitated halfway up the steps of the funeral home and stared at herself in the mirrored wall. The length wasn't as bad as she feared. The black tights certainly helped, as did the ballet flats. As long as she didn't bend over, it would be fine.

Slipping the straps of her handbag over her forearm, Dani finished climbing the stairs and walked through the double glass doors. The overpowering smell of flowers hit her full force, and she squeezed her eyes shut trying not to sneeze.

She hated wakes and usually managed to talk herself out of attending them, but due to her involvement in the murder investigation, she'd considered herself duty-bound to come to Regina's. Dani felt torn between her abhorrence of someone taking another's life and her sympathy for Abby.

Although a week had passed since Abby had confessed, and her attorney was working on a plea bargain, they wouldn't know for months what would happen to her. And Dani feared that the best the girl could hope for was an offer of involuntary manslaughter, which in Illinois carried a two- to five-year prison sentence and up to twenty-five thousand dollars in fines. Her parents had stated that they would pay any fines, but Abby would definitely have to spend time behind bars.

Pushing thoughts of Abby aside, Dani took her place at the end of the line of people waiting to pay their respects and studied the Bournes. Although she shouldn't have been, she was surprised to see Honoria looking her usual sleek, patrician self. Any evidence of grief or regret was well hidden by makeup and there were no telltale mascara tracks on her cheeks.

Anson stood next to his wife, sober in a charcoal-gray Brooks Brothers suit. His countenance was stoic, but Dani noticed an occasional tic near his left eye and he constantly clenched and unclenched his fists.

Dani was trying to interpret the tycoon's expression when she noticed she was next in line.

"Mr. and Mrs. Bourne, you have my deepest sympathy."

Regina's mother nodded regally, but her father asked, "How did you know my daughter?"

Dani thought fast. Now that Abby had confessed, was it okay to acknowledge that she'd catered the luau? Maybe, but it was probably best to avoid it. "She and the girls who live with me were friends."

Before Anson could respond, Honoria said, "Thank you for coming." She took Dani's arm and firmly propelled her down the line.

Spotting Mrs. Carnet chatting with a group of people, Dani waved and the housekeeper walked over to her.

Mrs. Carnet held out her hand and said, "I just wanted to express my gratitude to you for helping me when I had that flat tire. I should have sent you a note long ago, but I started a new job and have been so busy."

"No need. You already thanked me that night." Dani clasped the older woman's fingers. "It's wonderful that you found work so quickly. What are you doing?"

"I'm the new housemother for Alpha Beta Delta and I love it. Better pay, hours, and the girls are so polite." Mrs. Carnet beamed. "Bliss recommended me when she heard that I was out of a job."

"That was really sweet of her." Dani looked around. "Is she here?"

"Yes." Mrs. Carnet nodded toward a trio of young women. "She's over there with some of her sorority sisters."

Patting the older woman's shoulder, Dani said, "I'm going to go say hi to Bliss. See you later."

When Dani reached the girl, she hugged her and introduced herself to her friends. They all seemed genuinely concerned for Bliss, and Dani was relieved to see that she had such a good support system.

After a few minutes of chitchat, the two other young women excused themselves to use the bathroom and once they were out of earshot, Bliss took Dani's hand. "I never did stop by to thank you for listening to me the night of the football dinner. I've been thinking about what you said."

"Oh?"

"I forced myself to take a good long look at Vance and I . . . I realized that I didn't love him." Bliss's lips twisted. "Heck. I didn't even like him."

"So you called it quits?" Dani asked. "What about your plan to marry some guy to support you?"

"I still have a year." Bliss shrugged. "There are other fish in the sea and I have pretty tempting bait." She ran her hands over her hips. "But this time, I'm going to really make sure he's a good guy before I reel him in."

"How about love?" Dani asked, amused at the young woman's determination.

"That too."

Bliss's friends returned and Dani said goodbye. She made her way out of the main room and into a small parlor. Slouched on one of the two chairs was Vance King.

Wondering what her reception would be, Dani perched on the love seat and said, "Hi. I don't know if you remember me or not. I catered Regina's luau."

"Yeah." Vance sat up straighter. "Your food was great. Sorry about knocking over the torch."

"Thanks. Glad I was able to put out the fire so fast." Dani studied the young man. He was pale and seemed to have aged ten years. "Are you okay?"

"What do you think?" Lance pulled at his necktie. "I'm off the team, my girlfriend broke up with me, and my parents are so disgusted with me they can't stand to have me around."

"That's tough." Dani scooted closer so she could lower her voice. "Will you have to go to trial for breaking into Regina's house?"

"Nah." Vance's fair skin reddened. "My folks got the Bournes to say that I had permission to be in their home."

"Why would Regina's parents do that?"

"Since Regina and I had dated, they didn't want the contents of the video to get out any more than my parents did." The young man squirmed. "Although people have heard about it, seeing it is a different matter. If there was a trial, it would be played in the courtroom. Then it would doubtlessly get on the internet and live forever."

"Well." Dani patted Vance's clenched fists. "At least you won't have to worry about having a criminal record."

Vance shrugged and didn't respond.

"I'm sorry you lost your spot on the football team, but it's probably for the best that Bliss broke up with you."

Dani was surprised when Vance sighed, "Yeah. We weren't right for each other." His lips quirked at the corners. "One of the cops took me aside and talked to me about my . . . ah . . . unusual tastes." He glanced at Dani and when she nodded her understanding, he stared at his hands. "He has similar preferences and steered me toward a club of like-minded men and women. He's going to mentor me in the lifestyle."

"That's good." Dani was thankful for her experience in HR. This was far from the first time that she'd heard about BDSM. "I believe the rule is safe, sane, and consensual. As you follow that tenet and find a woman who likes what you like, I bet you'll end up a lot happier than trying to change or hide who you are."

He grunted his agreement and Dani said goodbye, then wandered into the other room. Holding back a giggle, she wondered if anyone else had ever dispensed advice about BDSM at a funeral.

A commotion at the funeral-home door drew Dani's attention away from her speculation. Standing just inside the room, arguing in whispers, were Chelsea and Trent Karnes.

Dani moved toward them in time to hear Trent say to Chelsea, "I feel like a hypocrite being here."

Chelsea tightened her grip on her husband's arm and hissed, "Just say you're sorry for their loss. You are sorry Regina is dead, right?"

A mutinous look on his handsome face, Trent muttered, "Of course I'm sorry. But those people didn't even come home when they found out their daughter was murdered. They're no more in mourning than my computer is."

"You're probably right," Chelsea said, guiding her husband toward the front of the visitation room, "but since when does sincerity matter in our crowd?"

As the Karneses moved off, Dani rolled her eyes. She was glad she only had to cook for the upper class, not socialize with them. Speaking of which, what was Ivy doing here with Laz? She hadn't said anything when Dani had told her she was going to the wake.

Dani spotted them seated on a small settee situated off to the side of the row of folding chairs. Curiosity drove Dani over to them and as soon as Laz spotted her, he dropped Ivy's hand and shot to his feet.

His ears red, he said, "Ivy didn't mention you were coming to the wake."

"Oh?" Dani raised a brow. "Maybe she didn't remember me telling her."

"You were already gone when Laz texted to see if I'd go with him," Ivy explained.

"How are you doing, Laz?" Dani asked.

"Okay." The young man shrugged. "Today's hard. I keep trying to reconcile the Regina I knew all my life with the one she'd turned into at the end."

"It seems that there's often a distance between our visions of someone we think we love and who they really are. A lot of us never make that crucial leap because the price can be too high. We're afraid that if we see the real person, we won't be able to handle it."

"I suppose that's true." Laz slumped. "I knew my folks expected us to get married and I didn't want to see who she really was because then I'd have to disappoint my parents one more time."

"And now?" Dani asked, glancing at Ivy. She hoped the girl wasn't letting herself in for a world of hurt.

"Now, I'm going to keep working my program and make them proud of me." He touched Ivy's cheek. "And not just because

407

I do what they want me to do."

"That's good. Because life may not always be tied in a bow, but it's still a gift."

Seeing Laz and Ivy looking at each other with such affection, Dani thought of Spencer. She'd only seen him once since Abby confessed, and that had been to check on the girls. He hadn't said anything to Dani about them getting together again. Evidently, they were back to being just Ivy's landlord and uncle. It was probably for the best, but it certainly didn't feel that way.

Pushing down her regret, Dani said goodbye to Ivy and Laz and headed for the exit. The scents of flowers, perfume, and sweat were closing up her sinuses and she needed a breath of fresh air.

ABOUT THE AUTHOR

Denise Swanson is the *New York Times* bestselling author of the Scumble River mysteries and the Devereaux's Dime Store mysteries, as well as many contemporary romances. She worked as a school psychologist for twenty-two years before quitting to write full-time. She lives in rural Illinois with her husband. Visit her online on Facebook, Twitter, and Pinterest.

The employees of Thorndike Press hope
you have enjoyed this Large Print book. All
our Thorndike, Wheeler, and Kennebec
Large Print titles are designed for easy reading, and all our books are made to last.
Other Thorndike Press Large Print books
are available at your library, through selected bookstores, or directly from us.

For information about titles, please call:
(800) 223-1244

or visit our website at:
gale.com/thorndike

To share your comments, please write:

Publisher
Thorndike Press
10 Water St., Suite 310
Waterville, ME 04901